TIME IT RIGHT

Siera Maley

CHAPTER ONE

Valerie Marsh sat down at her usual lunch table to find it already occupied by two girls she'd known for most of her seventeen years of life. Disgusted by the sweat stains still evident on her own shirt, she crinkled her nose and pulled her long, brunette hair up into a ponytail and tied it off with the piece of elastic she'd been keeping around her wrist. Two of her best friends, Amber Hunt and Kathryn Frost, looked on with mild discomfort.

"This school seriously needs to get a showering policy," Amber voiced, tossing her dirty-blonde hair over her shoulder with her nose upturned in mock-snobbery. "They should give you time before class ends."

Valerie nodded and exhaled wordlessly, still feeling drained from her Gym class, and then began to dig into the food on her tray. Mac n' cheese and chicken nuggets, the school cafeteria's delicacy. It wasn't much, but it was more than Amber was eating. Amber had developed a microscopic gut in the past year, and no matter how often any of her friends told her she wasn't fat, she'd just launch into a dramatic monologue about how girls with guts never stayed on the cheerleading squad for long and how her waitressing job at Mackie's was entirely dependent on getting tips, and guys gave the hot, skinny girls the biggest tips.

Funnily enough, drama in any and every form was usually Kat's thing. With her dyed dark-red pixie cut and icy blue eyes that made her stand out in any crowd, Kat was an avid and self-proclaimed theater geek. While Amber went to cheerleading practice or to work after school, Kat was busy being

1

the lead in every school play to grace the stages of Riverbank High, or else she was spending time with her boyfriend, Nick. She was the only girl of their group that had ever managed to keep a steady boyfriend, in fact. Amber was all about playing the field, and Valerie herself had only ever dated one boy, if it could even be called "dating". She'd held hands with Daniel Owens in the hallway for a few days, until he'd kissed her on the cheek and she'd dumped him. It was pretty tumultuous as sixth-grade relationships go.

Their fourth friend was much too engrossed in her schoolwork to find time for love –or anything *other* than schoolwork, really- and so it was no surprise when Tara Davis was ten minutes late to their lunch period, and greeted them by abruptly dumping fifteen pounds of textbooks onto their table. Kat jumped at least a couple of inches into the air and Amber snorted into her cup of applesauce, then looked down in horror at what she'd done. Kat and Valerie roared with laughter, but Tara was busy eyeing Valerie's shirt.

"Val. Seriously. You need to talk to someone about letting you guys shower after Gym. We have to eat with you every day like this."

"You don't *have* to," Valerie pointed out, quirking an eyebrow at Tara with the smallest sign of a smirk on her lips. Tara just rolled her eyes and sat down with a sigh.

"Of course we do. We love you in spite of your pit stains."

"Gross." Amber pulled a face while Kat chuckled.

Tara grinned at Valerie before changing the subject. "Anyway, Kara's gone."

She said it so conversationally that it took the other girls a moment to register her words. When they did, three heads swiveled to stare at her.

"Seriously?" Amber questioned.

"I thought she wasn't supposed to leave until next week," Kat interjected.

"Yeah, I don't know. I guess she found some cheaper plane tickets for this week or something. I didn't ask, but Mom mentioned saving money by sending her early."

"Do you miss her already?" Kat asked knowingly, and then bit off the end of a carrot and chewed. With her mouth full, she added, "I know I would."

"It's not like we're inseparable," Tara replied, shrugging her shoulders. "I'm okay. She'll have fun. And as long as the new girl isn't terrible, it should be a lot quieter around the house, at least."

"When's she coming?" Valerie asked.

"The day Kara was supposed to leave. So in a week."

The other three girls nodded their understanding, and then settled back in their seats. Valerie zoned out when the subject was changed, wondering how different things around school would be for them, if at all, in the months to come.

Tara was a twin, and Kara was her twin sister. They'd both been blessed with the same gorgeous, identical looks. Sleek brunette hair that stopped halfway down their backs, and the kind of brown eyes that boys could get lost in, if Tara would ever allow it. Instead, Tara, from a young age, had covered her eyes with a pair of thin-rimmed brown glasses and assumed the role of the nerdy twin. Valerie knew Kara had a monopoly on male attention between the two of them, but that was understandable. She was two minutes older, and for some reason seniority had made her more approachable and more outgoing. Tara kept to herself and let Kara have the spotlight, and she'd done it ever since Valerie had known her. They'd been best friends since Kindergarten, and each other's only truly close friend until they'd met Kat in 3rd grade and then Amber in 6th.

Valerie had known Kara for just as long, but they'd never clicked quite as well. Kara was intimidating, and everything Tara was not. And while Tara loved Kara, she was still a willing participant in many conversations held about some of Kara's abrasive, borderline-obnoxious tendencies. Kara wasn't a part of their "group", so to speak. She was more of a fringe acquaintance, and occasionally spoke to Amber if they ran into each other outside of school. And now she was gone completely.

In a move that had shocked Kat, Amber, and Valerie equally, Kara had done something that seemed far more in character for Tara: She'd signed up for an exchange student program. As they spoke, Kara was probably taking London by storm, and in a week, a British girl they'd all never met was coming to live with Tara for the next six months. Which also meant that Tara was going to go six months without seeing her twin sister. She didn't seem to be affected yet, but Valerie had a strong suspicion it would sink in soon enough.

After lunch, which took up their 5th period hour, Valerie headed to Calculus with Tara for 6th. It was the hardest class on Valerie's schedule, but Tara made it bearable. Valerie liked her schedule. She got to start off the day with a bullshit 1st period: Drama class with Kat, who'd convinced her to join and do tech work. And since senior year was notoriously meant to be a year of bullshit classes anyway, she'd agreed. Following Drama, she and Kat both headed off together to meet up with Amber for 2nd period Lit. Then she was alone for Chem and Gym, before meeting up with all 3 girls for lunch. After that there was Calculus with Tara, and another class by herself: Cooking. Overall, her day wasn't too difficult. Valerie was not a math and science person, but she had Tara to help her in one class, and her neighbor Lucas was her lab partner in Chemistry, and that made things a lot easier.

Valerie noticed Tara was even quieter than usual in Calculus that day, and after several minutes of turning toward Tara in an attempt to catch her eye, she gave up and grew more subtle in her looks, glancing over at one point to see her friend immersed in the series of numbers and symbols on the board while she nibbled on the end of her pencil. Valerie knew the eraser didn't stand a chance. It was a bad habit Tara had tried many times to break. Valerie liked it, though. It was part of what made Tara who she was.

Gripping the pencil Tara nibbled on were her pointer finger and thumb, both sporting bitten-down unpainted nails. Another bad habit of Tara's. Normally Valerie didn't take kindly to hearing Kara criticize her younger twin, but she was definitely spot-on about the nail thing. Tara needed fakes, and badly, if only just to function as a buffer between her mouth and her fingertips.

Tara caught her looking at last and shot her a quizzical look. Valerie felt embarrassed for some reason, and shook her head, hastily mouthing, "Sorry. Zoned," before turning away and searing her gaze to the notebook on her desk. She heard Tara chuckle quietly beside her, and felt a little better.

Calculus dragged on, and when it finally ended, Valerie spent an hour failing at making cupcakes from scratch, and then headed out to the parking lot, car keys in her hands. Lucas caught up with her before she reached her car, huffing in a way that told her he'd probably ducked out of his last class early to get a smoke break in before the final bell.

"Hey," he huffed out, shoving his hands into his pockets and falling into step beside her. Yep; she could smell it on his breath.

"That's really gross, you know," she told him, finally making the decision to speak up about it.

"You think so?

"Of course. Doesn't everyone?"

"No idea. But that's the thing about being an addict. It's hard to stop."

"Don't you worry about lung cancer? Bad breath and teeth? Like over half of all women being completely unwilling to date you because smoking's a deal-breaker?"

"Well, I *do* only need to date one girl," he countered with a grin.

She rolled her eyes and brushed him off as they reached her car. She walked around to the driver's side to unlock it, leaving him standing alone on the other side. "I get why people *keep* smoking," she called out to him, "I just don't get why they *start.*"

"Because it's what the cool kids are doing. Haven't you heard?" he teased, hopping into the passenger's seat the instant her car was unlocked. He smirked at the look of frustration on her face, and she started the car wordlessly and pulled out of the school parking lot. He cranked up the radio and head-banged overdramatically beside her to get a smile out of her. It worked.

Most days, Lucas rode home with her. He didn't have a car and she had a spare seat, and every now and then he'd slip her five or ten bucks. It was an easy arrangement. Sure, there was about a ninety percent chance the money he was giving her was obtained through the sale of certain illegal paraphernalia, but she didn't ask questions, and he didn't offer answers, and she liked Lucas, so that was all there was to it.

But he didn't look like a smoker, or like a drug dealer, if there was even a way to look like either of those things. He looked more like he belonged in one of those stock photos they stick into picture frames for sale at Walmart. Wholesome. He was thin but not lanky, and he had blonde hair just long enough to style. Once, they'd taken advantage of the latter fact in an afternoon where a Chemistry study session had morphed into a 2-hour attempt to turn his hair into a perfect impression of a Bieber cut using only a comb and a bottle of hairspray. It had worked, and Valerie hadn't laughed so hard since.

They reached Valerie's house and she moved to park on the street out in front so as not to block either of her parent's cars, which would typically pull into the garage at some point later in the night. Lucas unbuckled his seatbelt before she'd even stopped the car, dug into his pocket and pulled out a ten-dollar-bill, which he left on the console between their seats, and then opened the passenger's side door just as Valerie was putting the car into park.

"See you tomorrow," he called as he hopped out.

"Stay in school!" Valerie managed to retort a second before the door slammed shut. She heard a muffled chuckle from Lucas as she shut off her car and moved to grab her backpack from the back seat.

Her house was devoid of life when she entered, which was normal for the time of day. Her little sister, Abby, was in the 8th grade and didn't get home until an hour after Valerie did. Her parents showed up at any point after that, basically.

Her dad was a manager for the local newspaper, which meant that he worked six to seven days a week. There had to be a new paper every day but Sunday, after all. Her mom worked five days a week as a nurse. Between the two of them, they made a lot of money. Valerie was the most well-off of her friends, and she took great measures to ensure that they didn't feel awkward about it. Most sleepovers were funded by her when necessary and were held at her house, and if they made plans that involved bringing snacks, like going to the movies, she offered to buy them. To be fair, though, Tara also wasn't exactly poor, and Amber didn't really have much to complain about money-wise either. It was only Kat who was relying on scholarships to go to college in a year. But none of Valerie's friends had a mother who was on her way to becoming a surgeon, so to speak.

Still, there was a price to pay for financial comfort. Her parents loved her and her sister, but both girls certainly had a lot of time to themselves. And Valerie dedicated more time than she would've liked to making sure that her sister didn't get into any trouble without her parents around to monitor her. In particular, she took great measures to ensure that when Lucas was around, Abby wasn't, and vice-versa.

She climbed the stairs to her room and dropped her backpack on the floor, then crossed to where she'd left her laptop on her bed. She opened it and checked her Facebook, scrolling down through a newsfeed laden with passive-aggressive statuses about betrayal and pictures of people she'd shared one class with five years ago. A chat window popped up in the bottom right-hand corner of her screen. Someone was messaging her. It was Nick, Kat's boyfriend. That was weird.

"Hey."

She blinked, and then furrowed her eyebrows in confusion. She hung out with Nick when he hung out with Kat, and he too was in their drama class, but that was the extent of their relationship. He was a nice guy, sure, but they didn't talk without Kat around.

Still, she knew it'd be rude to ignore him. *"Hey, Nick…"*

It took a moment for him to respond. *"Sorry, I know this is weird. I wanted to ask u if u knew Kat's favorite color."*

She chuckled to herself when she read what he'd typed. Nick really was an airhead, to put it kindly, but he also seemed majorly in love with Kat. Last year he'd even played a small role in one of the drama club's plays, despite a fear of public speaking, all because Kat had asked him to after a last-minute dropout. He'd turned out to be a natural, and now had the same passion for theater that Kat did. The two of them were honestly perfect for each other.

"Blue, Nick," she reminded him, and his response was quick this time.

"Thx!!!"

And then he was gone. Valerie surfed around Facebook for a few more minutes, until the idea struck her to see what Kara was up to. Sure enough, there were already pictures up of her in front of Big Ben and several other British landmarks. She'd also put up a picture of her drinking tea, and another of her sporting massively horrific fake teeth, which Valerie frankly thought was a little offensive. Sometimes it was strange seeing Tara's face doing things that Tara would actually never do. This was one of those times.

She abandoned Facebook after just a few more minutes and lay back on her bed, staring up at the ceiling blankly. Amber would be finishing cheerleading practice in another hour, but it was a Monday, so she'd be working for most of the evening after that. Auditions for the Winter musical were starting soon, and Kat would no doubt be at home throwing herself into practicing lines. And Tara... well, Tara was always studying, and this week it was also highly possible she was preparing for her upcoming British invasion... but she was still Valerie's best bet for company.

Reaching for where she'd left her cell phone on her nightstand, she picked it up and went straight to her "favorites" list, where the names of her parents, sister, and three best friends could be accessed with ease. She pressed her finger to Tara's name and then lifted the phone to her ear. Two rings in, Tara answered.

"Hey, Val! What's up?"

"Just really, really bored. You're not studying, are you?"

"Nope! I'm test-free all week. Wanna come over?"

Valerie grinned. "Definitely."

"Awesome!" There was some noise in the background, and Tara called out, "Val!" Valerie heard more noise and then Tara's attention was back on their conversation. "Just give me like ten minutes to clean my room, okay?"

"Yep."

They hung up and Valerie hopped out of bed and went into her bathroom to fix her hair and makeup. There was always something intimidating about going over to Tara's house, even though they'd known each other for over ten years. Tara's parents were like a second family to Valerie, but they were also the reason for Tara's constant studying. Kara had the social connections and extracurriculars to get into a good college, while Tara had her intelligence. So while Kara was pushed to maintain club memberships and stay friends with girls who had older sisters in sororities at some of the better universities nearby, Tara had it hammered into her that her life would be over if she ever failed a test. There was something undoubtedly uncomfortable about being close with a friend's parents while simultaneously realizing that they were pretty damn crazy sometimes, and as a result, Tara came to Valerie's house much more often than the reverse.

Her own parents preferred a more hands-off parenting style, which meant that they basically just crossed their fingers and hoped that their kids didn't screw things up for themselves. It wasn't her parents' fault they were gone all day, of course. They were just trying to be the best parents they could be in the only way they knew how. Tara's parents were all about pushing their kids hard to make sure they could get themselves into college, while Valerie's opted for the "we're just gonna make a ton of money so you can buy your way in if all else fails" approach. Both had their pitfalls, obviously, but when she wasn't bored out of her mind, Valerie did enjoy the free time she was allowed to have.

She used her ten minutes to write a note to Abby so that her sister wouldn't wonder why she was coming home to an empty house. Then she made Abby a sandwich and stuck it into the fridge. By the time she was done, she was on track to get to Tara's with just a minute to spare.

She pulled into the driveway just a short while later, then walked up the stone walkway to the front door, where she rang the bell. Tara's parents always insisted that she not bother announcing her presence, but she'd never really felt comfortable with just walking into their house, even despite knowing them for as long as she did.

Tara answered the door seconds later, beaming out at her before hastily tugging her inside. "I'm *so* glad you called. I have to show you something."

Before Valerie could ask what, Tara was practically dragging her upstairs to her room. She didn't even get a chance to see Tara's parents before Tara was hurrying over to grab her purse from her bed. From within it, she withdrew her cell phone and began to press a few buttons on it.

"Did your sister send you something?" Valerie asked, wondering if this would explain Tara's unusual quietness earlier.

"No. I got this near the end of lunch. What do you think it means?"

Tara twisted the phone around and shoved it in her direction. Valerie had to lean back a little to get her vision to adjust to the words on the screen.

What was visible was the end of what seemed to be a long string of text messages. Only a few were on the screen, starting with one from Tara.

"I think you'll do great."

Following it was a response. Rather than reading it, Valerie glanced to the top of the phone, and felt a strange pang from within her chest upon seeing the name at the top. "Oliver Fields? Isn't he that guy in your Physics class?"

Tara nodded excitedly and moved to take the phone back, but Valerie stopped her. "Wait, I didn't even read it yet." Her eyes went back to the texts.

"I think you'll do great."

"Not as great as you. You're definitely smarter than I am."

"I am not! I just study a lot."

"Well, maybe we should study together sometime?"

Valerie's eyes flickered up to meet Tara's, who waited with baited breath. "It sounds like he's flirting with you...?" she tried. She wasn't exactly the expert on this sort of thing; this was all Amber's territory. She wondered why Tara was showing her this first, and got her answer a moment later.

"Do you really think so? I want to ask Amber and Kat but I don't want them to laugh at me."

"Why would they laugh at you?" Valerie sighed out, finding it hard to interject some emotion into her words for some reason. She felt a little drained suddenly, like she should've maybe stayed home and just taken a nap.

"Because it's *Oliver.* I mean, I know he isn't the most popular guy in school, but... I don't know, I've kind of always thought he was cute. And intelligence is totally a turn-on in my book." She bit her lip when Valerie just looked at her. "So what should I say?"

As the reality of the situation hit her, Valerie let out a dry laugh. "Wait. You haven't replied since lunch? He's probably headed to go throw himself off of a cliff as we speak."

"But what should I tell him?"

"I don't know; stop being stupid," Valerie sighed out, rolling her eyes and missing the way Tara's smile faded just slightly. "Tell him whatever you want. He's just a boy."

There was a brief silence, and then Tara shook her head, looking disappointed in herself. "I'm sorry. I should've asked Amber."

Valerie looked to her sharply, surprised. "What? Why?"

"Because…" Tara almost looked like she didn't want to finish her sentence, but she pressed on, "…it's probably a sensitive topic for you. You've never had a boyfriend."

"So? Is there some invisible line I didn't know about that divides every girl into two all-consuming categories now? 'Had a boyfriend' or 'never had a boyfriend'?"

"Why are you being so snippy about this, then?"

"I'm not!"

Her shout sent Tara's eyebrows upward, and she immediately felt herself color with embarrassment. "Sorry," she amended. "I just didn't think I was coming over here to discuss some dumb guy. We were supposed to hang out."

"We *are* hanging out. And he's not dumb. He's actually really smart." Tara let out a sigh and ran a hand through her hair. "God, Val. I just wanted some advice from my best friend." She hesitated, and then added, "And… I was thinking, *hoping*… maybe it doesn't have to be so awkward for Oliver and me if… if maybe you and I take the guy-plunge together."

Valerie immediately looked confused. "Excuse me?"

"Well, there's you and Lucas… You guys seem pretty close."

"I don't like Lucas like that."

"Are you *sure*?" Tara looked at her like she knew something Valerie didn't, and in that instant, Valerie almost turned and left. She hated everything about this conversation, and she didn't know why. But she didn't leave, and Tara continued, "Because I think he likes you. And if you wanted, I bet we could set up a double-date with him and Oliver."

Valerie didn't even consider it. "I don't think that's a good idea." She felt a little sick to her stomach, and she forced herself to glance at Tara long enough to tell her, "I think you should ask Amber for advice. Or maybe Kat."

Tara sighed, a sympathetic frown spreading across her lips. "Are you sure,

Val?"

"Positive. I need to go home now. Homework and stuff."

"Val..." Tara tried again, but she was already on her way out of the bedroom. She raced down the stairs and out to her car, glad to not encounter anyone on the way out, and then she was speeding back to her house with her heart pounding wildly in her chest.

She didn't know why it bothered her that Tara was talking to some guy from her Physics class. All she knew was that just thinking about it was enough to make her want to throw up.

She and Tara didn't date guys. That was the way things were. They spent sleepovers exchanging weird looks and smiles while Amber ranted about her newest boy toy or Kat described the most recent time Nick had done something stupid to piss her off. It was like they were both above it all; too good to let immature high school boys waste their time and cause the drama Amber and Kat were forced to deal with on a daily basis. She felt like Tara had betrayed her. Like she'd just been faking being not interested in dating because she didn't want Valerie to feel alone.

Well, she certainly felt alone now. Not only for being the only girl to not have some boy after her, but for being the only girl to not *want* some boy after her. Without Tara matching her every reaction at their next sleepover while Amber or Kat shared boy stories, it would just be Valerie lying there alone, not understanding or relating. She'd no longer be in on a private joke between two people, but on the outside of a three-person one.

The implication that that held made her eyes tear up, and she drove the rest of the way home struggling to see through blurry vision.

CHAPTER TWO

For a while, Valerie sat alone on her bed, buried in Chemistry formulas and Calculus theorems in an effort to take her mind off of her conversation with Tara. When her initial reaction finally faded, she regretted getting so upset, and hoped that it didn't mean she and Tara were fighting. They very rarely fought, and though Kat was good at staying impartial, Amber almost always took Tara's side, as they were closer than Amber and Valerie were. A fight with Tara meant Amber would be colder to her too, and that left Kat to talk to her out of sympathy.

She sighed down at a line of text explaining how to find derivatives, and looked up at her closed bedroom door as audible footsteps padded past it. Abby liked to shut herself up in her room, too. Valerie assumed she spent most of her time doing homework, although honestly it probably didn't take her very long. Abby was gifted with intelligence.

Everyone seemed to have a gift but Valerie. Kara and Amber were pretty and popular. Kat and Nick had great acting potential. Tara and Abby were geniuses. Even Lucas was good at *something*, even if that something wasn't exactly condoned by society. Valerie got by in her classes, flicked light switches on and off when she was told to in Drama class, and was a terrible cook. Most of the time she was inept at whatever she was doing, and she couldn't even pull off making it endearing. Hell, she didn't even have a *hobby*.

And now she was the only one without male attention. Not that male attention was supposed to be used to measure her value, of course, but it was one more thing to add to the long list of things Valerie didn't have or couldn't do.

She spent two depressing hours wallowing in self-deprecation before her parents finally got home. First her father, and then her mother, the latter of which knocked on her door at ten o'clock to ask her if she wanted dinner.

"Not hungry," she mumbled in response, and then rolled over and tried to go to sleep.

As it turned out, Tara wasn't upset with her the next morning. Valerie got a text on the way to Drama class from her, asking her if she'd known how to take the derivative in question two of their Calculus homework. Valerie proudly informed her that she did in fact know how. She decided to leave out the part about only knowing the answer due to spending several hours studying in a depression.

Because none of the roles had been cast for the upcoming play yet, Drama class entailed Valerie sitting with Kat and Nick while everyone else spread out and read lines and their teacher, Ms. Merriweather, wandered around, often giving overly-cheerful words of encouragement. She was a very eccentric older woman, like how Valerie imagined Kat would look and act in thirty years or so.

Their upcoming musical, titled "A Winter Wonderland", was about a boy and a girl who, alone on Christmas Eve for varying reasons, elect to spend it together helping the less fortunate out when they discover there are others who will have it worse than them on Christmas Day. Valerie had a sneaking suspicion their drama teacher had written it herself.

Kat and Nick, of course, were practically shoe-ins for the leading roles, and they were the only ones who didn't act like it. Were they to leave their seats and wander around the room as Valerie did sometimes when she got bored, they'd realize that they were the only ones reciting lines from the leading roles. It also helped them that their real-life chemistry tended to come through onstage, because the leads in the play were meant to fall in love. It was clear to everyone that the roles were meant for Kat and Nick.

Valerie spent most of drama class texting Tara about Calculus, until finally Kat and Nick took a break and Kat glanced over her shoulder just in time to see her send Tara another message.

"Are you talking to Tara?"

"Yeah," Valerie confirmed. "Why?"

"She was upset last night. She thought you were mad at her, and she told me about Oliver," Kat explained. "I tried to tell her you weren't. It's weird for me too that she might be getting a boyfriend."

Nick guffawed on Kat's other side, leaning in closer to join their conversation. "Wait. *Tara's* getting a boyfriend? About time." He glanced to Valerie and colored. "No offense."

Kat ignored his last comment. "Possibly. She's been talking to Oliver Fields. "

"No way." Nick said. Valerie almost opened her mouth to suggest to Kat that they shouldn't go around telling other people, but then she remembered that Nick didn't really count. Boyfriends worked that way. Nick probably knew stuff about *her* that she'd rather he not know. The thought made her very uncomfortable all of a sudden. She began to wonder how many of Amber's flings knew her secrets. Would Oliver know them soon, too?

"Anyway," Kat continued, turning back around to face Valerie. "I'm glad you guys aren't fighting. You're best friends; I'm sure you're happy for her." She laughed suddenly. "I can't even imagine how Amber reacted, though. She's probably *still* squealing."

"I don't know. Tara was worried you guys would judge her," Valerie said without thinking, and immediately wished she hadn't. Kat didn't seem affected, though.

"Why, because he's…well, *Oliver*?" Valerie nodded. "So he's a dork. Tara is too. They can be super dorky together. Just like Nick and I are total drama geeks together."

"Are not!" Nick cut in, clearly offended.

"Honey, you *rocked* the role of Romeo last Spring. You can't deny it." She ignored Nick's protests, then, and added, "And when *you* get a boyfriend, Val, I'm sure he'll be just as sweaty as you."

"Very funny," Valerie parried, but she couldn't keep herself from feeling uncomfortable again.

Class ended a few minutes later and the three of them left together. But they'd hardly made it ten feet from the auditorium before a loud bang caught their attention. It sounded like someone had slammed their locker shut too hard, but before Valerie could locate the source of the noise, Kat was gasping angrily beside her and grabbing at Nick's arm to get his attention. She pointed, and Valerie finally saw it.

Tony was a short, dark-haired, and mildly effeminate kid from their drama class, and he was currently struggling to get to his feet as three beefy boys from the football team stood around him, laughing and pushing him back down over and over again. One glance around the hallway told Valerie that there were no teachers around, and no one was bothering to help Tony, either. Most students that passed the scene looked obviously uncomfortable, but none of them were getting involved.

"Look!" Kat demanded, watching as Nick caught sight of what was going on. "That's terrible!"

"Yeah, but..." Nick trailed off, looking around uncomfortably. Valerie watched them, wishing nothing more than to be anywhere else. "Maybe we should go," Nick voiced, much to her relief, but Kat wasn't having any of it.

"You don't think we should help him?"

"It's none of our business, babe."

"They're bullying him just because he's gay!"

"It's still none of our business."

"Wouldn't you want someone to help you if *you* were getting picked on?"

Nick sighed, and then lowered his voice. "Yeah, but what if they think *I'm* gay for helping?"

Kat rolled her eyes so hard Valerie worried they might pop out of her skull. "Go!"

"Alright, alright!" Nick countered defensively, grudgingly heading over to Tony with Kat hot on his heels. Reluctantly, Valerie followed. "Alright, guys," Nick began, clapping one of the football players on the shoulder to get their attention. Tony finally managed to get to his feet while their eyes were on Nick. "That's enough. Let the kid get to class."

"Why, what's it to you?" one of them retorted, sneering. "You a faggot, too?"

Valerie watched Tony's eyes lower at the word, and she felt like his emotions were suddenly radiating off of him in waves, filling her with the same sadness. Her stomach twisted into a knot and she looked away from him.

Meanwhile, Nick sighed, then glanced to Kat as if to say, "I told you so."

Kat cut in from there. "So what if he is? Maybe I am too! Are you gonna beat up both of us as well?"

"She's kidding," Nick interjected hastily. "We're not gay."

"What if I'm *not* kidding?" Kat countered, shooting him a glare. "Maybe we're only dating each other to cover it up, huh?" She pointed at Valerie suddenly, and Valerie immediately felt like a deer in headlights. "And Val could be gay, too! So now it's four against three. I wonder how many other people walking past us right now are gay too, and just aren't saying it. I bet *they're* not too happy about how you're treating Tony, are they? Or else they're wondering about you three, giving a boy this much attention and all..."

"Alright, we get it. You can shut the hell up now," the boy replied, body-checking Nick hard enough to send him off-balance and then turning away from Kat. "Stupid bitch," he murmured under his breath, and then left, his friends following behind him.

"Thanks, guys," Tony told them quietly, and then walked away without saying else, his head bent low like he wished he could turn himself invisible.

"I'm not gay," Valerie felt the urge to clarify the instant he was out of earshot. "And I didn't want to be brought into that."

"Well, more people need to stand up to guys like those," Kat explained to her two upset counterparts. "The only reason this stuff still goes on is because no one lets the assholes know they're in the minority."

"It was still none of our business," Nick mumbled, but luckily for him, it was only loud enough for Valerie to hear.

The encounter with Tony was something Valerie would've liked to forget about the instant it was over, but Kat kept it going in their Lit class with

Amber, relaying the whole story to her when they were supposed to be having group discussions about the latest chapters of the book they were reading for class. Amber's reaction wasn't the one Kat was hoping for, and it was evident that this was the case the instant the first sentence was out of her mouth.

"But don't you think he kind of brought it on himself?"

Valerie had a feeling she was watching the beginnings of a verbal tennis match.

"What's that supposed to mean?"

"I mean, it's pretty obvious he's gay. He wears skinny jeans and talks like a girl. If you're gonna be that open about it, you should expect that there might be some repercussions."

"*Or* maybe there's nothing wrong with being who you are, and people shouldn't have to worry about getting beaten up for it."

Amber laughed at Kat's response and lowered her voice, looking around like she wanted to make sure she wouldn't be overheard. "Except, I mean…it's wrong to be gay. He shouldn't get beaten up for it, but you have it admit it's kind of weird."

Kat looked incredulous. "Um, no it's not. There are plenty of gay people in our drama class. Aren't there, Val?"

Valerie, put on the spot once again, wordlessly opened and closed her mouth for a moment, not sure what to say. Amber cut in before she could speak.

"Val's not like you, Kat. You've just been desensitized to it because you're around it so much. I go to church every Sunday and I know it's a sin. Right, Val?"

"Um…"

"Bigotry is *really* not cute, Amber," Kat told her in a thin voice that made it clear things were about to get ugly if the topic of conversation didn't change. Their teacher walked by, listening to the discussions being held in the area.

"So I thought it was interesting how the curtain could also symbolize a disconnect from the outside world," Valerie said quickly, attracting the attention of both girls. "It's like they almost function as the bars of a jail cell. She's imprisoned inside her own home."

"Excellent analysis, Valerie!"

Their teacher left and Kat tensed her jaw, refusing to look at Amber now. Amber, in turn, just rolled her eyes and focused her attention on Valerie. "So I heard about you and Tara. Personally I think it's adorable that she likes Oliver, so I don't really see what *your* problem is."

"I don't have one," Valerie replied quietly, and then willingly buried herself in their book after that.

Lunch was almost as tense as Lit class, with Tara spending nearly the whole hour recapping her texts with Oliver from that morning, getting date ideas, and then finally switching gears to the girl who would be coming to stay with her in four days. Amber and Kat didn't say a word to each other the entire time.

By the end of lunch, Valerie had been informed that Oliver did indeed have a crush on Tara, who had in turn confirmed with him that it was mutual, and that per Amber's advice they would be going out to dinner at the restaurant where she worked. Amber also promised to pull some strings and make sure she'd be their waitress that night. It wasn't until after lunch that the tension was diffused, as Amber went one way and Kat another to their next respective classes, leaving Tara and Valerie to walk to Calculus together.

"I'm sorry about last night," Valerie apologized the instant she had the chance. "I guess I really was just jealous or something. I don't know."

"It's okay," Tara confirmed, smiling over at her. "I googled it. I think you were being normal. We don't get to be single and lonely together anymore."

"Yeah, now I'm just single and lonely by myself now," Valerie pointed out, hoping she didn't sound as though it bothered her as much as it actually did.

Apparently, her tone didn't give her away, because Tara just nudged her playfully and replied, "Seriously, the offer still stands. If you want to make it a double date Friday night, I'm all for it."

Valerie didn't reply for a moment. "…Yeah. Maybe."

"Well, just let me know. Because if you don't come with me I'm thinking about asking Kat."

The rest of her day went uneventfully until she got a text from Amber in the middle of her Cooking class. She looked to the top of the screen and saw that it was a group text, sent to both her and Tara. It said: *"Val, didnt u think Kat was so weird this morning about defending that gay guy? Tara we need to fill u in on this."*

Tara replied before Valerie could. *"Wait, what?"*

Valerie put her phone back in her purse with a sigh, temporarily removing herself from the conversation. She was sick of hearing about gay people all day. She didn't know how she felt about them and she didn't want to think about how she felt about them.

It wasn't until class was over and she was headed out to her car that she checked her phone again. There were more messages.

"Ok, so basically this kid she barely knew was getting teased for being gay so she forced Nick to go defend him and then told off like half the football team."

"Did she say y?"

"I mean, I guess she felt bad for him but who does that? U think she and Nick r faking it?"

"What do u mean?"

"Like, she could b gay or bi…??? Ew."

"Idk? I don't think so, she loves Nick."

Valerie put the phone in her purse again just as Lucas caught up with her by her car. "Hey," he greeted her, looking proud of himself. She raised an eyebrow at him in response to his strange attitude and he spread his arms out to the sides, like they were wings. "Smell me."

"Ew, no."

"I promise it's not bad," he insisted.

"I'm not smelling you," she maintained, sliding into the driver's seat and starting the car's engine. He got in beside her with an expression of mock-

20

indignance on his face.

"Fine. But I'll have you know that I do not smell like smoke." She looked over at him just in time to see him pull up his shirt sleeve. A small patch rested on his bicep. "I'm gonna try to quit with nicotine patches."

Valerie raised an eyebrow. "You're kidding."

"Nope. It causes cancer and shit. Don't wanna get that." He laid back in the seat and relaxed as Valerie began to drive them home.

"That's…logical. Why didn't you tell me this in Chem?"

"Because I just decided. I know this kid who's on 'em in my last class. He let me try one."

"Well, good for you."

"Thanks."

They settled into a comfortable silence, until Valerie remembered her phone. She leaned over to try and fish it out of her purse, which was sitting on the console between the seats, but Lucas stopped her. "Whoa, hey. No texting and driving. I won't have you killing me. Let me get it."

"And let you read my texts?" she replied incredulously, but let him have it anyway.

"New text from Amber, Oh-Em-Gee," he announced in his best impression of a teenage girl. "Girl, I am *so* freaking excited for the new Johnny Depp movie. He's 50 but I bet he'd still have sex with me!"

"It does not say that," Valerie deadpanned, but she was unable to keep from smiling just a little bit.

"Might as well. Let's see…" He paused for a moment. "Amber says: '*Well good. I can't be friends with a lez.*'" He roared with laughter beside her while her own smile turned downward and her eyebrows furrowed. "Is this chick serious right now? God, no offense, but you have some bitchy friends. What the hell is she talking about?"

Valerie glanced over to see him scrolling upwards and immediately reached over to snatch the phone away. "None of your business."

He raised both eyebrows at her, as though it was just dawning on him. "Whoa, wait. *You?*"

"No!" she retorted immediately, glaring at him. He raised his hands defensively.

"Okay, okay. Sorry. Didn't know you were homophobic too."

"I'm not!" She hesitated. "I mean, I don't think I am... No. Of course I'm not."

"Alright," he replied in a tone that made it seem like he wasn't entirely convinced. "Cool." They fell into silence for a moment and he added, "So now that I know your stance on gay people..."

She forced a laugh and the car went quiet again as they turned onto their street and approached their usual parking spot on the road in front of Valerie's house. She stopped the car and Lucas unbuckled his seatbelt.

"Well, it's been a ball. Same time tomorrow?"

He moved to get out, and without thinking, she reached over and grabbed his arm. "Wait."

He paused, glancing over his shoulder. "What's up?"

She hesitated, inwardly berating herself for stopping him in the first place. But it was too late to back out now without looking awkward. "Uh, what are you doing Friday night?"

He blinked. "Um. Probably the usual."

"Which is...?"

Now he grinned. "Do you really want me to answer that?"

"Okay, never mind," she sighed out. "Just, um... Oliver and Tara are going on this date, and Tara thought maybe it would make it less awkward if two more people tagged along..."

"Are you asking me out on a double date?" he caught on, quirking an eyebrow upward. His expression was serious now.

Valerie shot him a pained look. "That depends. Would you say yes if I did?"

He tilted his head to the side as though to consider it, his usual aloof demeanor back now. "Huh. That depends. Can we bang after?"

She smacked him on the arm and he laughed at her as she retorted, "You are such a jerk! And who says 'bang' anymore, seriously?"

"Alright, alright!" he gave in, pulling away when she didn't stop hitting him. "Ow! I'll go out with you, okay? But you're taking the brunt of the work on our next Chem lab."

She gaped at him. "What? Why?"

"Because. I did you a favor. I could've made this more awkward for you."

"I doubt it."

He moved to close the car door before she could get another word in. "Titration's all yours!" he called, and then the door was shut and she had no time left to argue.

Sighing to herself, she took a moment to collect her thoughts, wondering what her friends would say when she told them there would be a group of four on Friday night, after all.

CHAPTER THREE

"Oh my god. This is great!"

Valerie wasn't sure how to respond to Tara as she stood with her three friends in the hallway, awaiting the bell to signal they needed to part ways and head to their first class of the day.

"You really are serious?" Amber questioned. "But Lucas is so hot!"

Valerie pressed her lips together. "Thanks, Amber."

"I mean, not that you aren't cute, but God, the things I would do to that boy if he'd let me…"

Something told Valerie he wouldn't.

"And he knows it's a date and everything?" Kat questioned, all traces of animosity between her and Amber gone now that two of their friends were going on a date the upcoming Friday. Clearly, there were preparations to be made that Valerie was unaware of, because as soon as Valerie nodded her response, both of them immediately launched into discussions of color coordination and starting making shopping plans, as well as trying to figure out if Kat would be available to help both Tara and Valerie get ready on Friday.

It was true that the term "date" had been used when she'd asked Lucas to join her for dinner, but Valerie honestly wasn't sure if he considered it to be one. Dating meant romance and implied that more dates were to come if things went well, and she didn't want to date Lucas. She'd only asked him because… well, because Tara needed a friend and she'd rather be that friend than have Kat fill the role instead. She hoped instead that Lucas understood it was just a hangout for them, even if it would be a date for their company.

But even if it wasn't a real date, there was no need to tell her friends that. Not when they were already so amped about it.

So she let Kat talk her ear off about it in Drama, and then she let Amber join in in Lit, and then came Chemistry, where she would spend an hour with Lucas after hearing about him for two hours straight already.

He smiled at her when she walked in, already at their designated table. "Hey," she greeted, taking a seat beside him and setting her things down. He put his elbow on the table and his hand on his cheek, facing her with an eyebrow raised.

"So did I have a really weird dream last night or do we have a date Friday night?"

Valerie noticed a few people glance their way and tried her best to ignore them, although she had to admit it felt good to know that people thought Lucas was interested in her. He was blonde and cute, and he could probably get a lot more girls than he was aware of. And people thought a cute guy like him would be willing to date *her*.

"You weren't dreaming," she confirmed, and he immediately let out a sigh of relief.

"Awesome, because that would've been super embarrassing if I was."

She laughed, and with that, they got to work on their lab assignment.

When they finished an hour later, they left class together, but Lucas walked alongside her down the hallway instead of parting ways with her outside the classroom door, as he usually did.

"So where do you go next, again?" he questioned. Valerie shifted uncomfortably, a little confused, and finally answered.

"Gym."

"Oh. Sucks."

"Yeah."

They fell into silence. It was awkward, and Valerie could practically feel tension permeating the air around them.

"So, uh, I'm on my next patch now." Lucas attempted to create conversation, lifting his shirt sleeve up and revealing a fresh new nicotine patch on his skin.

"You're really committing to this," Valerie observed.

"Yeah, well… I thought about what you said."

"You quit because of *me*?"

To her surprise, Lucas colored slightly. "Well, that's… I wouldn't say *that*, but you said some things and I listened. That's all."

"Right…" She glanced over her shoulder. "Isn't your class in the opposite direction, Lucas? You always go that way after Chem."

"Oh." He mimicked her, glancing over his shoulder as well. "Yeah. You're right. I should go."

"Probably."

Awkwardly, he waved at her and then moved to leave. "Bye. See you this afternoon."

"Bye."

The hours ticked by and school eventually ended for the day. She made plans to go shopping that afternoon with Amber, Tara, and Kat, as Amber didn't typically work Wednesdays. But before that, she had to drive home with Lucas in the passenger's seat, which wasn't pleasant. There was more tension between them than there had ever been before, and Valerie began to question if she'd made the right decision in asking him out. What if he did treat Friday night like a real date? Lucas was a good friend of hers, and she didn't want to lose that. But she also couldn't disappoint her friends. Not when they were so excited for her.

They spent hours at the mall that afternoon, trying on different outfits. Tara settled on a nice shirt and a jacket and skinny jeans to go with it, while, with Amber's coercion, Valerie opted for a black skirt and a low-cut V-neck shirt, with a necklace to match it.

"You two look so hot," Kat complimented when they'd come out of the dressing rooms in their chosen outfits, which earned her a judgmental look from Amber. Tara didn't seem fazed, though, and grinned and did a little twirl while Valerie shot Kat a smile. "If I were into girls I'd do either of you."

"Don't make jokes like that," Amber immediately countered, motioning for Valerie and Tara to head back into their dressing rooms. "No one likes it."

"Are you serious? You need to take a chill pill."

They bickered for the rest of the trip home, and Valerie was happy to drop them off at their houses first. Amber lived with her parents and her older sister Hannah, who was currently attending a local college, and Kat lived with just her dad. Every now and then the four girls would hang out at Amber's house together, but ever since Kat's parents had divorced one year prior, Kat had subtly made it clear that her house was off-limits. Valerie didn't necessarily understand why, but respected Kat's wishes, just as Amber and Tara did.

"So do you think they'll ever give the gay thing a rest?" Tara sighed out as they neared her neighborhood. "They're driving me insane and it's only been going on for a little over a day."

"Hopefully," Valerie agreed quickly, eager to change the subject. "So are you excited for Friday?"

"Oh, so much Val, you have no idea," Tara immediately replied. "This is so great. We're both gonna do this together. I can't believe we're both this lucky. Oliver's amazing; I *knew* Lucas liked you and he's so cute… we're gonna have the best time Friday night."

"I'm surprised your parents are letting you go, though," Valerie pointed out. "Since your new British sister is moving in Saturday."

Tara laughed as they pulled into her driveway. "Yeah. But they're way too excited to make me cancel. You all should come over Saturday to meet her, though. I don't know her name yet but Kara's met her. She texted me a picture of them together."

"Really?"

"Yeah. Here." Tara pressed a few buttons on her phone and Valerie's cell phone beeped from within her purse. "Now you have the picture. I'll see you tomorrow. This week is gonna be so much fun!"

After dropping Tara off, Valerie drove back to her own home and parked out front. To her surprise, both of her parents' cars appeared to be in the garage, and when she went inside, there they were, sitting in the living room and watching TV with Abby.

"Hey," she said, not bothering to hide her surprise. "You're home early."

"And you have stuff," her father observed with interest, eyeing the bags in her hands.

"Oh, yeah. We all went to the mall."

"You bought new clothes?" her mother asked, getting up and crossing to her with Abby on her tail. "Let me see!"

She let her mother have the bags, and out came the skirt, the shirt, and the necklace. She realized she'd have to explain her situation to them.

"I have a date Friday night, BUT..." she said quickly, heading off her parents' surprised looks by hastily adding, "It's only with Lucas. And we're only going as friends. Tara has a real date and she really wanted to make it a double."

Her father and mother exchanged awestruck looks, matching smiles on their faces. "Oh my God, our daughter's going on her first date!" her mother exclaimed, and Valerie suddenly found herself smothered in a hug. "We'll have to take pictures!"

"Mom, it's not a real date!"

"And Lucas is such a nice boy, too. You chose well," her mother continued. "Even if you aren't really interested in him yet. I'll take what I can get."

"*Mom...*"

"Hey," Valerie heard Abby interject somewhere nearby. Her mother finally un-smothered her in time for her to watch her sister argue, "If Lucas is such a nice guy, how come Valerie won't let me hang out with him?"

"Because, honey," her father explained, luckily before Valerie had to try to come up with an excuse, "older kids have older friends, and they don't want their little sisters showing up and stealing them away."

"So basically you're saying I'm lame," Abby deadpanned. "I'm not six years old, Dad, *God*. Stop talking to me like I'm stupid." She immediately stormed off, and they heard footsteps stomping up the stairs a moment later. Their father blinked, clueless.

"What did I say?"

"No idea," Valerie replied quickly, eager to get to her room. "Anyway, I have homework."

"Oh, okay," her mother said. "We could have a family dinner tonight later if you'd like."

"Sure," Valerie agreed noncommittally, and then gathered her things and headed upstairs, missing the disappointed look her mother and father shared behind her.

Once in her room, she clipped the tags off of her new clothes and hung them in her closet. Next she took her phone from her purse and sat down on her bed, curious to view the picture Tara had sent her. She had two new texts: one from Tara and the other from Lucas, to her surprise. She opened Lucas' first.

"Uh, what am I wearing Friday night?"

"Go casual," she responded, and almost immediately received a response.

"K thx."

Next was Tara's text, which she opened to see a miniature version of the picture of Kara with Tara's upcoming new visitor. She pressed her finger to the screen to make it larger, and then examined it for a moment. Kara looked right at home in front of the camera, a practiced smile on her face while sunglasses rested on the top of her head, leaving her eyes exposed. It was the lack of glasses and the smile that made Kara immediately discernible from her twin sister; Tara couldn't perfect her camera smile even if she took classes from Kara.

Kara's arm was slung around the back of another girl who was just about her height. She was blonde and looked athletic, but most of her face was hidden by sunglasses, so it was hard to judge much of her appearance.

So this was the girl who'd be coming to live in Tara's house and go to Tara's school. Valerie predicted their small town would be a downgrade from England. They were lucky they even had a mall to go to.

She was about to minimize the picture when her phone abruptly rang, catching her off-guard. It was Kat. She answered it and raised it to her ear.

"Hi, Kat."

"Hey." Kat sounded upset, and a little angry. "I just had to talk to someone."

"Did something happen with Nick?" Valerie guessed.

"No, of course not. It's Amber! Can you believe the things she said today?"

Valerie wanted to say "yes", but she wasn't sure that'd be the right answer. She waited, and Kat predictably continued.

"I'm so sick of her ignorance. How has this never come up with her before? How could I have no idea I'm best friends with someone this bigoted?"

"Um... well, we always knew she was religious. There were probably hints growing up, but why would we ever talk about gay people? It's not like there are many at our school," she pointed out. "Pretty much all of them are in our drama class."

"But not all religious people are the way Amber is. I don't know; it just really bugs me."

"Uh huh," Valerie said just to let Kat know she was listening. In truth, she was reaching for her homework and already wondering how she'd word an excuse to get off the phone.

"I mean, you don't think Tara agrees with her, right?"

"Definitely not. I know she doesn't."

"But they're super close. Sometimes I feel like it's me and you against them, you know? Which is weird because it's you and Tara that have been friends for the longest, but Amber's just such a dominant person..."

"Kat, can I ask you something?" Valerie finally questioned, her Lit book now open in front of her. Kat's passion about the subject of homosexuality *was* beginning to get suspicious, and as much as she didn't want to stoop to Amber's level, she couldn't help but think that maybe Amber had a point.

"What is it?"

"Don't get offended, but... you don't like girls, do you?"

There was silence on the other end for a moment. "…Would it make a difference if I did, Val?" Kat's tone sounded a little tense, and Valerie hesitated.

"I mean… probably not, but-"

"Why 'probably not'?"

Valerie didn't know what to say to that.

"Alright," Kat sighed out. Valerie could almost see her shaking her head. "Fine. I get it. It's not me and you against them, it's everyone against me."

"Kat, that's not-"

"And for the record, I *don't* like girls. Not that it should matter."

The line went dead with a click, and Valerie pulled her phone away from her ear and stared at it. "Great," she murmured, and then leaned forward and put her head in her hands, groaning quietly to herself..

CHAPTER FOUR

It rained the next day, which seemed strangely fitting given the current status of Valerie's social life. First she'd fought with Tara, then Kat and Amber had fought with each other, things were awkward with Lucas, and now Kat was fighting with all of them, and Valerie wasn't even sure what she'd done wrong. Kat had abruptly taken a stand for gay people in a town where the average citizen didn't particularly care one way or another at best, and was severely homophobic at worst. And she'd offered no explanation for this stance beyond a personal belief that it was the right thing to do. That kind of view had to come from somewhere, didn't it? Was it really such an offensive jump for Valerie to assume that maybe Kat did actually like girls?

But in any case, Kat apparently was in fact straight, and now she was not only mad at Amber for being homophobic and at Tara for not standing up to Amber, but at Valerie too. Frankly, Valerie was just sick of all the fighting.

She sat alone in Drama class, which was absolutely miserable given that the class was basically just an hour-long excuse to socialize until auditions for the school play began, and so with Kat and a confused Nick placing themselves across the room from her, she was left with nothing to do but text.

She scrolled through the names in her cell phone, immediately passing by Amber's without hesitation. She liked Amber, sure, as it was impossible to be friends with someone for six years if she didn't *like* the person, but in truth she and Amber had never been that close compared to how close Valerie was with Kat and Tara. They rarely hung out together outside of their group of four, and when they did, Valerie felt a little suffocated by Amber's dominant personality. Amber usually wasn't one of her go-to friends when she needed someone to text her for a class period, and now was no exception.

She reached Lucas on her contact list and paused, debating for just seconds before she pressed a button and then began texting him. *"So my drama class is hell right now."*

Her phone beeped less than a minute later, and she knew she'd chosen the right person. *"Is she making u do singing exercises again? Open ur mouth wider, Val, remember!"*

"No! Kat's pissed at me so I'm sitting alone."

"Y is she pissed? More girl drama?"

"Yeah I asked her if she was gay."

"LOL!"

His response made her smile, at least, and she was thinking of something to say in response when suddenly she wasn't alone anymore.

Tony plopped down in the seat beside her, to her surprise, and greeted her, "Hey, Val. Do you mind reading lines with me? I'm going for the part of Austin, the homeless kid who wants to meet his parents for Christmas."

"Um... sure," she replied with a shrug, opening her backpack and rummaging around for the script she never used. She finally found it, and when she straightened up, Tony smiled at her.

"Thanks. I wouldn't have bothered you but I usually read lines with Nathan and he's not here today."

"Oh, okay." She thought of what he'd said and tried to conjure up a mental image of Nathan. It took a second, but then she remembered him. Tony did practice with him most days, and from what Val could tell, Nathan was gay too. Before she could rethink asking her question, she blurted, "So are you dating him?"

Tony raised his eyebrows in surprise, then immediately looked embarrassed. "No. It's bad enough just being gay here; I don't need an even larger boyfriend-sized target on my back."

"You don't think people would just leave you alone if you stuck together?" Valerie questioned. It seemed logical to her. Two guys would get picked on less than one guy, right?

"No," Tony replied shortly, and then gestured to his script. "Can we read lines now, please?"

His tone had an edge to it, and Valerie immediately felt guilty. "I'm sorry."

"It's okay. I'm glad you guys helped me out the other day and everything, but I don't want to talk about it anymore, alright? I just want this part."

She cringed inwardly at herself and nodded to Tony, and they spent the rest of class reading lines.

If Drama class was bad, Lit was horrible. Kat sat across the room in a seat that was normally empty, which left Valerie alone with an extremely curious and gossipy Amber, who obviously wanted to know why Kat was avoiding them. After Valerie had explained the whole story, Amber of course demanded they rehash it with Tara at lunch.

Chemistry with Lucas was a nice break in the meantime, and thankfully this time there was no awkwardness. Even more thankfully, when Lucas brought up Kat and got a glare from Valerie, he immediately knew to shut up and change the subject.

It was at lunch, while Amber ranted about Kat and Kat sat alone at a different lunch table, that Valerie decided she'd had enough. She immediately texted Lucas to inform him that he'd need to find another ride today, and when school was over, she stalled for long enough to make sure she wouldn't beat Kat to Kat's house, and then headed there instead of to her own.

She knew Kat had been determined to keep her house off-limits to her friends ever since around the time of her parents' divorce, but she'd always assumed Kat had just become suddenly self-conscious about its size and decided that she felt too uncomfortably poor. Frankly, it was ridiculous; Kat wasn't poor, and her house was comfortably sized. Valerie didn't know why Kat felt the need to ban everyone from it with the exception of Nick. If she knew Nick wouldn't judge her, couldn't she trust her friends not to?

She pulled into Kat's driveway minutes later, and at last, hesitated. If Kat was already angry at her, breaking her rule was probably not the best way to fix it. But on the other hand, showing up at her house to make up was a pretty obvious way to show that she really did regret what she'd said. Maybe Kat would disregard the small rule breach if it was for a good cause.

Making up her mind, she shut off her car and got out, then strode up the walkway that led to Kat's front door. Without further ado, she rang the doorbell.

It took a moment, but then the door swung open and she was staring at a man she didn't recognize. "Hi, how can I help you?" he asked. His speech patterns reminded her of Tony.

Wondering how on Earth she'd ended up at the house of a random probably-gay guy when she'd meant to go to Kat's, she glanced over her own shoulder, confused, and then said, "I'm sorry; I think I might have the wrong house."

The man laughed, then opened the door a little wider. "Don't be silly; you're one of Kat's little friends, aren't you? She talks about all of you constantly. Are you…" He paused, examining her while she stared back at him in surprise. "Valerie?"

She nodded, and he looked proud of himself. "Come on in; I'll get her."

Valerie stared at where he held the door open expectantly, then glanced inside the house. She could see the living room in the distance, with all of the same furniture as she remembered being in Kat's living room. This was definitely Kat's house. She felt like she'd entered the Twilight Zone. What was this guy doing at Kat's house? Where was her dad?

She stepped inside and the man shut the door behind her, then made a startled sound and said, "I'm so sorry. Where are my manners?" He held out his hand and she shook it. "I'm Kenny."

Valerie opened her mouth to reply, but it was Kat who spoke next as her footsteps sounded from the hallway that led to her room. "Hey Kenny, who was that at the-?" She came into view and her voice died as she stared at Valerie. Valerie stared back, certain she looked like a deer in headlights at the moment. There was a long silence. Kenny cleared his throat uncomfortably. Whatever was going on, he'd understood it before Valerie could.

"Hey, Kat," she said meekly, waving to her friend. She had a feeling she'd strongly misjudged how pissed Kat would be at her for showing up at her house. So it wasn't the size of the house. She was upset because Valerie had met Kenny? Because Valerie knew that she lived with a gay man? She lived with her dad and a gay man...

Her eyes widened to the size of saucers and she was pretty sure Kat witnessed the light bulb going off in her head, because a second later she was being yanked down the hallway to Kat's room, and then the door was being slammed shut behind them. Kat immediately rounded on her with a furious glare.

"If you tell *anyone*-"

"Wait," Valerie insisted, putting her hands up defensively. "I was just here to apologize, I swear. I didn't know-"

"Yeah, you didn't know. And now you do."

"I promise I won't say anything. But why didn't you tell us?"

"Because," Kat explained, exhaling sharply, "Amber's a stupid gossip. The whole school would've known within a day."

"But why does that matter?"

"Did you not see what happened to Tony?" she replied incredulously. "He gets picked on for being gay. I'll get picked on for having a gay dad. That's how it works around here."

Valerie watched Kat run a hand through her hair and then collapse on her bed. She felt like she was looking at a whole new person, though not in a bad way. The way Kat had acted recently suddenly had an explanation behind it that made sense to her. Sure, there had always been a chance that Kat had just decided to defend gay people on principle, but now that she knew Kat's dad was gay, it was no wonder Kat felt the way she did.

She sat down next to Kat on the bed, her mind still reeling. "But I thought you didn't care if people said stuff like that about you. The things you said to those guys on the football team..."

"That was different. That's me. If anyone's dumb enough to pick on me because I don't hate gay people, I don't care. But if they're bullying me because of my dad, that's different... And can you imagine how he'd feel?"

Valerie mulled that over for a moment. She supposed it made sense, although she was pretty sure if everyone thought *she* was gay and picked on her for it she'd be pretty upset.

She and Kat sat in silence for a minute or so, until Valerie finally told her, "I came over to apologize. I feel, um..." She took a deep breath. "It's weird not hanging out with you. I'm sick of all the fighting. I'm so stressed out."

Kat sat up and looked at her, her expression a little warmer now. "Thanks, Val. You're a good person and I know you mean well. I'm just... so sick of this small town, I guess. I assume everyone's out to get me and in reality they're mostly just ignorant."

"Can you make up with Amber and Tara, too? I know Tara's not upset with you, and Amber's just being stupid."

"Val, Amber's a bitch," Kat sighed out. "I don't think she and I would be friends at this point if we didn't both like you and Tara. But I definitely don't want to eat lunch alone again, so..." She forced a smile and nodded.

"Thanks."

Kat nodded again, then got up and walked to her bedroom door, opening it for a moment and then peering out. Then she shut it again and moved back to the bed. In response to Valerie's confused look, she explained, "I was making sure Kenny wasn't listening. He's a little nosy. I just figured I should explain everything to you, now that you know. It's not a long story, I promise."

"Okay."

"So about two years ago, my dad tells my mom he's gay, and that he'd known since he was a kid but was hoping it'd just go away eventually. She's not homophobic, but as you can imagine, she was a little shocked and had a hard time with it. They both talked about divorce, but ultimately decided to try and put it off until I graduated, since I only had about three years to go. They didn't tell me what was going on. Then my dad actually met someone... Kenny. And that was that."

"So your mom moved out because of Kenny?" Valerie interrupted.

"Yeah. And my mom didn't really work, you know, so my parents figured it was best for me to stay here with my dad while she moved somewhere cheaper and looked for a job. And Kenny moved in. So I told my dad I didn't want my friends to find out, banned you guys from my house, and until now only Nick knew. And that's just because he basically did what you just did, only about seven months ago instead. I guess Kenny must've thought I'd decided to tell you, otherwise he wouldn't have let you in."

She finished her story with a sigh, and Valerie tried her best to take it all in. Finally, she observed, "You hid all of this from us."

"Yeah. It wasn't easy. But everyone had their secrets, don't they? I bet Amber's full of them. As much as we like to say we tell each other everything, we really don't."

Valerie chewed on her bottom lip for a moment. She knew Kat was right, but there was something unsettling about having it said out loud. She herself had kept something from her friends too. But Kat was trustworthy, and she'd just shared something big. Maybe it was fair to do the same.

"I'm not actually going on a date with Lucas," she admitted abruptly. "Not a real one, anyway. We agreed to go as friends, and then when everyone was so happy for me..." She trailed off and Kat cracked a smile, to her surprise.

"Aw, Val... That's still really sweet. You really don't have to date until you're ready. You know that, right?"

"But what if I *am* ready? I feel ready," she insisted. "Or... I think I'm ready. I'm seventeen! I'm just not ready with Lucas."

"Are you nervous because you like him?" Kat questioned with genuine curiosity.

"I'm not nervous, and I don't like him. I mean, he's a nice guy... I like hanging out with him..."

"And do you think he's cute?"

"Everyone says he is, don't they?"

"But do *you* think he is?"

Valerie considered it. Every girl she knew thought Lucas was attractive. She didn't find him repulsive or anything. And he was funny, and a sense of humor was supposedly appealing in a guy.

"Sure?"

Kat let out a little laugh and reached out to put her hands on Valerie's shoulders. "Val, listen to what you just said. He's nice, you like spending time with him, and you think he's cute. This is adorable. You have a crush. You're just so used to *not* having one that you don't know what it's like!"

Valerie instinctively opened her mouth to disagree, but then she considered Kat's words. *Would* she know a crush if she had one? She certainly liked Lucas a lot more than she'd liked Daniel Owens in the 6th grade, and she and Daniel had participated in some scandalous hand-holding back in those days.

"I think he's funny, too," she offered, and Kat's grin only grew wider.

"Val, seriously. This is so adorable. Does he think you're just going out as friends?"

"I think so…" Her eyebrows furrowed. She was so sure she hadn't liked Lucas like that. Could she have been wrong? Kat seemed to know what she was talking about. "He's been a little weird since I asked him, though."

Kat looked absolutely giddy. "Weird like awkward around you? Strange changes in behavior?"

"Yeah. Both."

"Okay, seriously. This date is tomorrow night and you need to get it together, girl. This poor guy likes you and you're taking him out on a date as friends!"

Valerie blinked at her. "But Lucas is… *Lucas*."

"No, he's a cute guy who likes you! And if you like him, what's to stop it from being a real date? You need to make a move, or give him a signal that *he* needs to make a move."

The thought of doing anything remotely similar to what Kat was suggesting caused an uncomfortable knot to make a cameo in her stomach. "I don't know…"

"At least think about it. If you like him, don't hold back, Val," Kat told her gently. "Everyone on this planet who has ever had a first date was nervous about it. Tara will probably be sweating bullets all day tomorrow. Just follow your instincts and you'll be fine. You and Lucas would make an adorable couple."

Valerie tried to envision it. She wasn't sure how she felt about the idea. But being the girl with the cute boyfriend was an appealing thought, and if she had to date someone, she supposed Lucas was the best option at the moment. But she couldn't shake the feeling that something was off. Maybe she was just inexperienced, like Kat thought, but if what she felt for Lucas was a crush, then having a crush was nothing like what she'd expected.

She left Kat's house as it was getting dark and headed home with a lot on her mind. Her date was in twenty-four hours, and she had no idea how she felt about the guy she was going with. Lucas knew they were going as friends, but what if Kat was right, and he did like her? What if he put his arm around her? Held her hand? *Kissed* her?

She startled herself with the last thought and immediately put it out of her mind, forcing herself to focus on her driving, and later, her homework. Lucas wasn't the kind of guy to force himself on a girl who clearly didn't want it. So she could just act normal, and if he made a move, it would be because he thought that she wanted him to. Kat had said something about signals. So if Lucas tried to take things in a more romantic direction, it was because she had somehow signaled that she wanted him to. Maybe it was possible to give signals unconsciously. She trusted Lucas, and so if he tried anything, it was probably because she'd unconsciously let him know that she wanted that, right? That was all there was to it.

It was totally simple.

CHAPTER FIVE

Kat made up with Amber and Tara the next day. Tara hadn't had a problem with Kat in the first place, so that half of things was mostly just Kat letting Tara know she wasn't upset with her. Amber and Kat, on the other hand, made a big show of forgiving each other and hugging and apologizing, but Valerie was pretty sure they both hated each other's guts at this point. Considering they were teenage girls, though, they both were plenty good at faking it, and would most likely continue to fake it until graduation in six months. But as long as they kept it mostly convincing, both Tara and Valerie were content to ignore the truth.

At lunch, they all discussed date plans. Valerie was picking up Tara and Kat in the evening and bringing them back to her house, where Kat would help Tara and Valerie get ready for their dates. When they were done, Oliver would come and pick up Tara, and Lucas and Valerie would take Valerie's car to drop off Kat on the way to the restaurant: Mackie's. Once there, they'd join Oliver and Tara, who would make sure to be seated in Amber's section for the night. At the end of the night, Oliver would drive Tara home and Valerie would drive herself and Lucas back. Then, on Saturday, they'd all reconvene at Tara's for updates on the night and for the British invasion. It was guaranteed to be a chaotic weekend.

And so it began, first with Valerie's drive home with Lucas, who seemed antsier than ever. "You're nervous," she observed, a little amused at the fact. He stuck his middle finger up at her without even a glance her way, and she laughed at him as she drove.

Her parents were home when she got there, much to her horror, and she noticed a camera resting on the kitchen counter as they bombarded her with questions about her upcoming date. She had to give them credit. When they *were* around, they were such enthusiastic parents that it almost balanced out all the times they weren't around.

And too soon, it was nearing dark and she was picking up Kat and then Tara, who double-checked that she'd brought all of the clothes and make-up she needed. "I can't believe you're leaving me alone with him," Tara complained as Valerie drove them back to her house. "It's too much pressure!"

"Relax," Kat insisted. "This isn't a Calculus test; it's just a guy. Unless Val wants me breathing down her neck the second she gets back from her date, *and* unless I'm willing to spend the evening hanging out with her parents and Abby, she needs to take me home. Which means separate cars."

"I know," Tara whined, sighing. "I'm just really nervous."

"It's normal. Valerie, how are you?"

"I don't know. I think Lucas is more nervous than I am."

Tara took a break from hyperventilating to comment, "Are you serious? That's adorable. I wonder if Oliver's nervous…"

"Something tells me your dork is breaking out into hives as we speak," Kat responded, which made Valerie laugh.

They headed straight to Valerie's room when they got to her house, and Kat did Tara's make-up for her while talking Valerie through hers. They both straightened their hair, and then Valerie changed into her outfit and moved to examine herself in the mirror by her dresser while Tara changed in the bathroom. She raised both eyebrows at herself while Kat grinned excitedly behind her.

"Lucas is gonna pass out when he sees you."

The bathroom door swung open, and both girls turned as Tara emerged, fully dressed and ready to go. Valerie swallowed hard, a lump suddenly in her throat. Tara looked *really* pretty. Too pretty for Oliver.

"Wow," Tara said simply when she got her turn in the mirror. "I look… like Kara with glasses." Then she laughed. "It's so weird."

"This is one time where you definitely do not look like Kara," Kat argued. "Kara could never be this classy."

Tara sighed, but she was smiling. "True. I think she'd have more cleavage showing."

They gathered their purses, then, and descended back down into the living room, where Valerie's parents awaited them. This time, Abby was there too, and even she seemed a little excited to watch the proceedings as Mr. and Mrs. Marsh took pictures of both their daughter and Tara. Then they insisted upon having some pictures of Valerie and Lucas together, and so Valerie grudgingly texted Lucas and asked him if he was ready. He told her he was, and she lied and said he wasn't.

Thankfully, the one thing her parents did right was that they were so excited for her date that they gave off the impression that it was a real one, which left Tara in the dark about Valerie's white lie.

When they finally managed to get away from the Marshes, Valerie went over to Lucas's and knocked on his front door. She knew his parents were rarely home, and so it wasn't surprising when he was the one that answered it. His eyes widened when he saw her.

"Wow. I thought you said casual! Not that you don't look... I mean, of course-" He cut himself off and shook his head, then glanced down at his own outfit: a passable shirt and cargo pants. "I feel like a douche."

"You're fine," she insisted, rolling her eyes and yanking him out of his own house. "And always a douche. You look like yourself."

"You sure know how to flatter a guy," he replied even as she tugged him across his yard and over to her driveway. Right on time, Oliver pulled up to her house and parked in the street, and as Tara went to greet him, Kat met Valerie and Lucas by Valerie's car. Lucas asked, "What, am I not even meeting the parents I've already met five-hundred times?"

"No, you're suddenly very shy," Valerie informed him, motioning for him to get into the passenger's seat. "And you have a fear of cameras."

"This is going well," he replied simply, then let her shut the door on him.

Valerie turned to Kat in time to see her grin and whisper, "He's flirting." She barely stopped herself from rolling her eyes, and moved to get into her car. Kat hopped into the back seat, and over at Oliver's car, Tara clambered into the passenger's seat. And just like that, they were off.

"So I get two dates tonight, then," Lucas observed, glancing back at Kat as Valerie drove. "If only I'd known this ahead of time."

"I think my boyfriend would have something to say about that," was Kat's response. Lucas winced and faced forward.

"Right. Nick from the wrestling team. Got it."

Valerie changed the subject as they headed for Kat's house. "So let's just make sure we're less awkward than Tara and Oliver tonight, and our job is done."

"Something tells me they've already lost that competition," Lucas guessed. Kat laughed from the back seat.

"Those dorks are perfect for each other," she said affectionately. Valerie felt Kat poke her shoulder. "Now if only this one would stop being so shy."

"Val could get it," Lucas agreed, stretching his hands back over his head to grab the top of his seat. Valerie felt embarrassed, and was relieved when they finally reached Kat's house. The instant Kat was done wishing them luck and had shut the car door behind herself, Lucas asked, "So she's trying to set us up, then?"

"Basically," Valerie sighed out.

"Not too subtle, that one. You'd think those acting lessons would've come in handy."

"I have a feeling she wanted to be obvious."

Lucas clucked his tongue in disapproval, and she saw him glance at her out of the corner of her eye. "So this is totally friendly."

She hesitated in answering. She'd wanted to put the ball in Lucas's court tonight. Now it was in hers.

She stalled. "You wanna know if I'm friend-zoning you?"

He made an affronted noise. "Excuse you. The friend-zone is a sexist myth appropriated by quote unquote 'nice guys' who are pissed off their female friends won't have sex with them. Please do not use that offensive term in my presence."

"I didn't peg you for a social justice warrior."

"I'm awesome; I know."

"That's debatable."

"Asking me out and then insulting me on our date... I'll tell you one thing; you certainly are not getting into my pants tonight."

"Oh, however will I survive?"

They shared a grin and Lucas leaned forward and turned up the radio, then played drums on everything in sight, including Valerie's newly-straightened hair while she struggled to bat his hands away as she drove. "Ass!"

"Mine or yours?"

They arrived at the restaurant only five or so minutes after Oliver and Tara had, and joined them at a booth, with Valerie seated across from Tara while Lucas sat across from Oliver. Oliver was the kind of guy girls that liked Calculus found attractive, which basically made him perfect for Tara. He, like her, sported glasses and brown hair, which he'd done his best to style for the night. He wasn't as obviously good-looking as Lucas, but Valerie had a feeling that within the clique of AP students at their school, he was probably considered a hot commodity. In a way, he was the male Tara: Not very confident in an appearance that was actually quite appealing.

His speech, however, was another issue entirely. The first thing he said as she reached across the table and shook Lucas's hand and then Valerie's, was, "Hello there; it's really a pleasure to meet the two of you. Tara's told me so much about you, Valerie."

She gave a nervous laugh and smiled at him, but didn't respond. He hadn't used the word "salutations", at least, but he did remind Valerie's vaguely of every parent she'd ever met.

For Tara's sake, she elbowed Lucas under the table to get him to speak, and the two of them chatted with Oliver about schoolwork and grades until Amber finally showed up, looking thrilled to see that her plan had worked and she'd get to peek in on the date every now and then. She took their drink orders and then hurried away with an unsubtle squeal, and Valerie was still cringing as Oliver asked her and Lucas, "So how exactly did you two meet?"

Valerie froze. She hadn't told Lucas that Oliver and Tara thought they were on an actual romantic date, because why would she? She'd have to explain why she'd let them think that, and that would be beyond embarrassing to share. Now Oliver was asking them a question that made it sound like he thought they were a couple.

Lucas answered for the both of them. "We're neighbors. We've known each other for a while now."

"Oh, that must've been interesting," Oliver replied. Valerie wanted to sink into her seat and disappear. "Taking that next st-"

"Drinks!" Amber chimed in, arriving just in time to interrupt Oliver and serve them what they'd ordered. Valerie had never been happier to see Amber in her life. "Do you guys know what you want to eat?"

Valerie scanned the menu for the cheapest thing she could find. She only had ten dollars on her, and she needed money for tipping, too. She eventually settled on an order of chicken fingers, and Amber took their menus and asked, "Should I put that on two checks, then?"

"Sounds great," Lucas replied, pulling his drink toward himself and taking a sip. Amber left and Valerie shot him a look of surprise. He was paying for her. He caught her gaze and shrugged, then put his drink down and looked back to Oliver. "So what about you guys, then?"

Oliver smiled, moving to put his arm around Tara. Valerie couldn't stop herself from letting her nose begin to wrinkle in disgust, but luckily she caught it before it became obvious. Oliver may have been mildly attractive, but she still didn't see what everyone else seemed to see in him. "Physics class."

"Sounds romantic," Lucas replied, totally convincingly, and Valerie was suddenly overwhelmingly thankful for his presence. Regardless of what he thought or felt about her, he wasn't taking this date seriously at all, and she loved him for it. "Val inspired me to quit smoking."

"Aw, that's so sweet," Tara chimed in, directing her attention to Valerie. "Why didn't you tell me about that?"

She shrugged. "Must've slipped my mind."

"My sacrifice slipped your mind?" Lucas gasped. "I thought you cared!"

Oliver and Tara looked on in horror, but Valerie chuckled. "Relax, guys. He does this."

Oliver looked thoughtful. "I guess that's the mark of a good match. Understanding each other like that." He looked to Tara as Valerie grew uncomfortable for what felt like the 20th time that night. She reached for her drink to distract herself. "I'd really like to have something like that one day."

"Me too," Tara breathed out. Lucas went to take a sip of his drink and accidentally stuck the straw too far back in his throat, gagging on it. Reacting to Lucas, Valerie nearly spat out a mouthful of Sprite, and at least half of it ended up dribbling down her chin and into her lap. Lucas took one look at her and snorted, reaching for his napkin.

"Jesus, Val."

She forced herself to swallow the rest and then immediately started laughing again as he tried to dab the Sprite off her chin. She snatched the napkin away and did it herself, then tossed it back onto his lap with a flourish. Oliver and Tara watched the display with wide eyes from across the table.

Amber interrupted them yet again, this time with their food, doling the plates out one by one. "Alright, guys. If you want anything else, feel free to ask. In fact, please do. *Please.*" She grinned at them and then shot Tara and Valerie not-so-subtle winks, then hurried away to go serve her other customers.

"What a piece of work," Valerie heard Lucas mumble under his breath.

The rest of the dinner went smoothly. As much as Valerie couldn't help but disapprove of Oliver, he and Tara got along as though they'd been dating for months, and she and Lucas managed to help each other through the meal by exchanging looks of disgust at the couple's mushier moments, elbowing each other hard under the table to test their poker faces, and throwing fries into each other's mouths, much to Oliver and Tara's horror. It didn't feel like a date; it just felt like she and Lucas had went out and had fun together.

So it was a surprise to her when she pulled up to her driveway and he didn't immediately hop out and tell her he'd see her Monday, much like he would've after a ride home from school on a Friday. Instead he unbuckled his seatbelt as she unbuckled hers, and then he glanced over at her and gave her a small, sincere smile. "That was a lot of fun, actually."

She nodded, then smiled back. "The gag was particularly well-timed."

"Hey, that wasn't on purpose!" he insisted. "But yeah, it was pretty awesome."

She chuckled, and then they lapsed into silence. Finally, Valerie opted to break it. "Well, goodn-"

"Can I walk you to your door?" he interrupted, his eyebrows furrowed.

She hesitated, a little confused. "Okay?"

"Cool." Without further ado, he hopped out and walked around to her side of the car, then opened her door for her. She laughed as she got out, and he smiled and asked, "What?"

"Such a gentleman."

"Such a lady, laughing at the gentleman," he countered, motioning overdramatically for her to lead the way to the door. "Last time I do something nice for you."

"I highly doubt that," she retorted as they settled by her front door. "But thank you, really. I had a blast."

"Did you?" he quirked an eyebrow upward, smirking. She punched him lightly in the arm.

"Shut up; of course I did. Seeing you stick a fry up your nose was seriously the highlight of my life."

"You need better highlights," he observed. Silence fell over them and she saw Lucas lick his lips. It dawned on her that maybe he hadn't walked her to her door just to be funny. Maybe he wanted to kiss her. Had she done something to make him think she wanted to kiss him, too?

She looked at his face. His blue eyes, rounded nose, strong jaw... He *was*, objectively, handsome. If he liked her, and she liked hanging out with him, and Kat thought they were into each other... maybe kissing him was the right thing to do.

"What kind of highlights?" she heard herself ask.

Lucas looked nervous. He licked his lips again and ran a hand through his hair, then kind of half-laughed, like he had to force it out. "Shit, Val," he murmured quietly, and then he was stepping closer, his hand was on her cheek, and he was leaning in toward her.

She swallowed hard and felt her heart thud in her chest. She'd never kissed anyone before, and she suddenly couldn't remember how it was supposed to be done. For that matter, she didn't know if Lucas had ever kissed anyone, although she'd assumed he had. What if she was a bad kisser? Or he was?

His lips made contact with hers and they kissed. Lucas didn't taste like smoke, thankfully, but he didn't really taste like anything. He didn't really feel like anything, either. Valerie's eyes were shut tight as she kissed him back, and she could feel his lips moving against hers, but they were just... there. It wasn't what she'd thought it would be, and it wasn't like the movies made it seem, either. It was just a kiss.

He pulled away and she almost opened her eyes, but then, to her surprise, he learned forward and kissed her again. Her eyebrows furrowed. Okay, they were going for round two. She wasn't sure exactly why that was necessary after the first one, but maybe Lucas thought the second time would be better. Or maybe the angle had been wrong the first time around.

She reached for him and put a hand on his shoulder, trying to get him down closer to her height. Her neck was hurting from tilting her head up and she felt overwhelmed with his face over top of hers. His lips were chapped and although he was gentle, she could feel the microscopic hairs on his chin scraping against her skin. It hurt.

Finally, he pulled away and it was over. She did her best to mentally prepare herself for the humiliation that no doubt came with having a bad first kiss. She only hoped he wouldn't blame her for it.

"Wow," he breathed out, reaching out to brush her hair out of her face. He was looking at her like she was a whole new person to him, and not at all like she'd just given him the worst kiss of his life. "That was... wow..."

"Mhmm," she replied, more confused than ever now, and eager to get the hell out of there. "I think I better go. I'll see you Monday?"

He nodded, dazedly, and she immediately went inside and then shut the door behind herself. Through the glass window panes next to the door, she saw Lucas slowly make his way across her lawn to his house. He was clearly overwhelmed and even stumbled once.

Her house was quiet as she climbed the stairs to her room and moved to remove her make-up. She had utterly no clue what had just happened. Was she interpreting something wrongly? Maybe their kiss had actually been great, and she just hadn't known it, with nothing to compare it to. But if that was as good as kissing got…

She made a face in the mirror and sighed aloud, wiping the last of her make-up off and then getting changed into her pajamas. She checked her phone as she climbed into bed and saw several texts from Amber and one from Kat. Her phone beeped as a new one came in from Lucas: *"Nite, Sprite fountain."*

She smiled softly. Lucas really was a great guy. He was also, it seemed, a terrible kisser. But a great guy. *"Nite, fry mucus."*

With that, she set her phone aside and went to bed, vowing to answer the other texts in the morning.

CHAPTER SIX

The next morning, Valerie awoke to an empty house. She'd expected it: Abby had gymnastics on Saturdays, which her mother always took her to, and her father, as always, had work.

She dressed herself quickly and was nearing the last bite of a bagel she'd chosen for breakfast when it fully hit her that last night wasn't a dream. It had actually happened.

Having slept on the kiss with Lucas, she immediately began to wonder if it had actually been as bad as she now remembered it to be. Weren't all first kisses bad? Then again, *he* had liked it. So either he was a bad kisser or there was something wrong with her. She didn't want to blame things on Lucas, but if he had enjoyed the kiss and she hadn't, clearly he was the one lacking in that particular department. Maybe it really had been his first kiss.

The blonde girl from England was due in at ten o'clock, and the drive to the airport was about an hour long, so Tara had asked them all to come by at around noon. Valerie wasn't sure how Amber or Kat were getting there, so she decided to text them to see if they needed a ride. That, unfortunately, meant scrolling through texts from both of them about how her night went. When she checked her phone, she now also had an additional text from Tara asking how things had gone with Lucas after they'd left Mackie's. Valerie ignored every text with the knowledge that they'd surely end up talking about it at Tara's house anyway.

She wound up arranging to pick up Kat and Amber, all while avoiding several more texted questions about Lucas, and then at fifteen til' noon she set out to go get them. They were a blur of questions and observations the second they were each in the car, and she could hardly keep up with it as she drove.

"You guys were so cute!"

"How did it go?"

"Did he make a move?"

"I can't believe you went out with someone so hot!"

"Did you kiss?"

"What's he like in bed?"

"Okay, seriously, what kind of girl do you think I am?" she could help but respond to Amber eventually. "Of course I didn't sleep with him."

"But you kissed?" Amber pressed, as Kat waited patiently for an answer in the passenger's seat.

"I'll talk about it later, when we're with Tara. Shouldn't we be focused on the fact that there's a stranger living in her home for the next six months? This could change a lot of things, you know."

"Not as much as a kiss from Lucas McConnell would!" Amber countered.

"I never said I kissed him!"

"You never said you *didn't*, either."

Valerie groaned and then clammed up for the rest of the drive, much to Kat's and Amber's frustration. They got to Tara's house in time to see her duck into the back seat of her mom's car in the driveway and emerge with a box full of stuff, presumably belonging to her new pseudo-sister. Valerie parked the car and they approached as Tara struggled to try and get it into the house.

"So," Amber immediately said, tapping Tara on the shoulder and startling her. "How'd your date go?"

Tara, recovering, set down the box with a grin, looking as though she'd like to explain everything as soon as possible, but then she glanced over her shoulder as Mrs. Davis exited through the front door and joined them.

"Hey girls, glad to see you came to help. Everything in here is going up to the guest bedroom, just across the hall from Kara's room."

She moved to grab another box from the car, and Tara shrugged at her friends.

"Sorry, we're just getting the last of it inside. We can talk later; you guys have to meet Lindsay. She seems pretty cool so far. We talked the whole ride back from the airport."

A new set of footsteps came from the front door now: Mr. Davis, heading out for another box. But just behind him was a girl their age, and Valerie immediately recognized her as the blonde girl from the picture with Kara. She was without sunglasses now, though, and it was immediately clear that the girl was cute. Her long, blonde hair was swept back into a ponytail, and she had bright blue eyes that widened excitedly when she caught site of them. She made eye contact with Valerie first, grinned, and then looked around to Amber and Kat, approaching them without a falter in her smile.

"Hiya," she greeted them, her accent clear but understandable. Kat immediately lit up upon hearing it and Valerie knew exactly what she was thinking: If she could spend enough time with this girl, she could perfect a fake British accent. "I'm Lindsay Walker. Tara told me a bit about all of you already."

"Nice to meet you," Kat replied happily, immediately reaching out to shake Lindsay's hand. "I'm-"

"Wait, no, don't tell me. I want to see if I can figure it out," Lindsay interrupted. "Okay, you're definitely Kat, the actress."

"You called me an actress?" Kat asked Tara, flattered. Tara grinned at her.

Lindsay looked Valerie up and down for a moment, thinking hard, and then finally guessed, "Amber, the cheerleader?"

Valerie laughed and Amber looked affronted. "No, I'm Valerie. It's nice to meet you."

"Oh, I'm sorry!" Lindsay corrected. "Okay. Valerie, and you're Amber. I've got it. You guys don't have to carry my stuff up or anything; don't listen to them."

"Awesome. Tara," Amber responded, pulling Tara away to no doubt discuss her and Oliver. That left Kat and Valerie to stand with an amused Lindsay, who watched the other two girls for a moment, before returning her attention to Kat and Valerie.

"Sorry about that," Valerie explained for them. "We kind of had an interesting night last night."

"How so?"

"Those two had a double-date," Kat explained, gesturing first to Valerie and then to Tara. "And I still can't get this one to tell me whether or not *her* date kissed her or not."

Lindsay looked to Valerie knowingly. "Oh, he definitely kissed her."

Valerie laughed. "How do you know?"

"I have eyes. Just look at you," Lindsay countered, and then just like that, she was heading back to the car to get another box. Kat shot Valerie an impressed look, then licked her finger and pressed it to Valerie's shoulder, making a sizzling noise as her finger made contact. Valerie, only half paying attention to Kat, brushed her off playfully and moved to go grab a box.

"I'm gonna go make sure Amber doesn't start torturing Tara for information," Kat announced, which left Valerie alone at the car with Lindsay.

"You really don't have to do this," Lindsay insisted when she spotted Valerie lifting out a particularly large box. "I can make a few extra trips."

"It's no big deal."

Lindsay didn't respond to that, and neither of them spoke until they were up in Lindsay's new room and the boxes were on the floor.

"So Tara tells me the four of you have been friends for ages."

"Yeah. Tara and I since Kindergarten. Then we met Kat in 3rd grade and Amber in 6th."

"They're very… um. Boy-centric."

"You caught them at a bad time."

Lindsay laughed, then moved to sit down on her bed. She looked around the room and sighed. "It'll be an interesting six months. I have to pick out my class schedule Monday morning."

"Oh, we can definitely help out with that," Valerie told her. "You're a senior, too, right? If you want, we can make sure you get a lot of classes with us. I know I could use some help in my cooking class; I'm terrible at it."

Lindsay laughed again, this time louder. "Wait, you're rubbish at cooking? How is that possible?"

"I don't know; yeah. Totally... rubbish." She shrugged and the other girl grinned at her.

Footsteps on the stairs alerted them to a new arrival, and seconds later, Kat burst in and announced, "Oliver and Tara made out last night." Then she was gone, no doubt expecting Valerie to hastily follow. Instead, Valerie couldn't cover up an instinctual reaction of disgust, and she could tell from the way Lindsay raised an eyebrow at her that she'd caught it. Embarrassed, she quickly left the room, following Kat's hurried footsteps into the living room, where Tara and Amber were seated as Tara's parents obliviously continued to move boxes in through the front door.

"Tell us every little slimy detail," Amber demanded, and Valerie held back another disgusted look as Tara folded her hands in her lap shyly. Valerie took a seat at her side as Kat sat down next to Amber.

"I don't know...it was nice," Tara offered simply, clearly hesitant to go into any more detail.

"But what happened? Did he kiss you at your door... in his car...?" Amber pressed.

"In his car. He drove me home and it just...happened."

Kat leaned forward, her chin in her hands. "Was he any good?"

Tara looked embarrassed as she nodded. Beside her, Valerie stood uncomfortably, having half a mind to go out and grab another box. Mr. Davis showed up before she could.

"Hey, girls. The wife and I are gonna go grab some takeout; any requests?"

"Thanks, Mr. Davis," Kat replied genuinely, while Amber shook her head beside her. "I'll have whatever you guys want."

"Alright. We'll be back in half an hour," he informed them. "Tara, make Lindsay feel comfortable, okay?"

"Sure, Dad." Tara looked around as her father nodded and left the room. "Where'd she go, anyway?"

"Her new room," Valerie informed them, taking a step toward the stairs that led up to the room in question. "I can go get her…"

"Oh, no you don't," Amber corrected, standing up and moving behind Valerie, before promptly guiding her back to the living room by her shoulders. "Don't think we've forgotten about you. You're up next after Tara." She looked to Tara. "Okay, spill."

"What are we talking about?" Lindsay asked, coming down the stairs just as Amber pushed Valerie back down onto the couch. The other three girls looked to Tara for permission.

Tara sighed. "Um… well, Valerie and I had a double date last night. I guess we're hopefully gonna be good friends, right? So if it's okay with Val, we'd love your input."

She looked to Valerie, who shrugged, refusing to make eye contact with anyone. Lindsay laughed. "Okay. Thanks." A second later, she was sitting down on a large chair, just across from Valerie.

"Anyway, Tara was just saying that Oliver did *what?*" Amber questioned, giving Tara a pointed look. She groaned in response.

"I don't know; there's nothing to tell! We kissed and it was really really nice and now he's my boyfriend. Are you happy?"

Kat wolf-whistled and Amber grinned. Valerie didn't really react, but then she noticed Lindsay watching her and forced a smile in Tara's direction.

"Okay, Val, your turn. Please tell me you took advantage of an opportunity to kiss Lucas." Amber turned to Lindsay and continued, "Valerie got to go out with one of the hottest guys in school. He's her neighbor *and* her lab partner in her Chem class and I always see him flirting with her."

"Oh, he was *so* flirty last night," Kat confirmed. "You two totally hooked up, didn't you?"

Valerie reddened as they all watched her expectantly. What was she supposed to tell them? Just about the kiss? Or the whole truth? Tara had had her first kiss last night from dorky Oliver and *she'd* enjoyed it. Maybe something was wrong with Valerie after all.

She hesitated, and then gave the smallest of nods. "I mean... we kissed."

"I knew it!" Amber cried. "He made the move?"

Valerie nodded.

"Why don't you look happier?" Kat noticed. "Didn't you like it?"

"Umm..." She hesitated for what felt like hours, wondering what to say. But she'd already lied once about the nature of her date with Lucas. It was probably best to be honest now. "Not really."

Her three friends blinked at her. "Why not?" Amber finally asked. "What's not to like?"

"I don't know. It was only the first kiss, so..."

"It does usually get better," Kat confirmed, which made her feel a little less embarrassed. "Was he bad or something?"

"I don't know," Valerie repeated, shrugging.

Even Tara looked confused now. "How do you not know?"

"I mean... it just... *was*. I didn't... I mean, he kissed me, and then we were done and I went to bed. It was really... mechanical, I guess? Yeah. And he had chin stubble which hurt pretty badly."

"So tell him to shave," Amber suggested. "If that's your biggest complaint..."

"I'm not complaining," Valerie insisted. "It wasn't terrible. It just wasn't what I expected. Everyone freaks out about it and it's like nothing. I just did it because he wanted to and I thought maybe I wanted to."

"And now you don't wanna kiss him," Amber deadpanned, looking appalled.

"I don't know. Do you think it really was just because it was the first time?"

"Of course. It definitely gets better," Kat explained, and Tara and Amber nodded on either side of her.

"I disagree, actually." That was Lindsay, speaking up for the first time in minutes. Every girl's attention went straight to her, including Valerie's. Lindsay stared back at her. "If you didn't feel anything, maybe you just don't like him."

Amber scoffed. "You haven't seen this guy. Any girl with eyes would like him."

"Well, that may be the case, but if you're describing kissing him as mechanical, that's not a good sign. What made you think you liked him?"

Valerie stared back at her, opening and closing her mouth for a few moments when she realized her first instinct had been to say because Kat told her she did. "I... Well, I told myself that he's a good guy who wouldn't take advantage of me, and so if he kissed me, maybe it was because he could tell some part of me wanted him to." It felt stupid to say aloud now, and Lindsay quirked an eyebrow upward, amused. "I know it sounds dumb; I just..." she trailed off, unsure of what more she could say.

Lindsay crossed her arms and stared for a moment, like she was looking straight through Valerie. The intensity made Valerie uncomfortable, and she shifted slightly and cleared her throat. She saw her other friends briefly exchange looks of discomfort as well.

Finally, Lindsay asked her, "It felt like kissing a wall, didn't it?"

Valerie immediately opened her mouth to protest, but the words died in her throat. Amber, Kat, and Tara all watched her with surprised anticipation now, and Valerie took a moment to collect herself, then laughed a little and shook her head. "Okay, c'mon, guys. This is dumb. Why are we putting so much weight on one kiss and one date? Why do we have to rehash everything?"

"So you *do* want a second date and a second kiss?" Amber questioned uncertainly.

Valerie groaned. "I don't know what I want. And I'm perfectly fine with that. No more grilling me about Lucas, okay?"

"Alright, alright; fine. Chill out."

To her relief, her friends backed off after that, and soon, Tara's parents showed up with takeout and they all went out into Tara's expansive backyard to relax and just hang out for a while.

Although initially instilling some apprehension in the other girls, Lindsay turned out to actually be quite nice. She was witty and talkative, and not afraid to speak her mind, the latter quality one of which Amber was noticeably drawn to, although Valerie had a feeling it would lead to some problems between the two girls at some point in the next six months.

The girls all helped her plan out her new schedule, with Kat strongly recommending their drama class and the entire group agreeing that Valerie needed some serious help in her cooking class. Between those classes and lunch, Valerie would end up having just as many classes with Lindsay as she had with Kat. Lindsay's other classes were to be taken without the other girls, as the different curriculum in her country left her with different gaps in her graduation requirements than the typical American student would have. They all realized pretty quickly that she'd be sharing a few classes with freshman and sophomores – something Lindsay was not at all happy to hear.

It wasn't until Valerie took a trip back inside to go the bathroom and Lindsay followed her to throw away her takeout box that they were alone again. Lindsay caught her attention and told her, "Hey, I'm sorry about earlier, if I offended you or anything. It's all a bit of a culture shock and I guess I'm a bit…" She made a fast motion with her hands about her head. "You know. And possibly a little jet-lagged."

Valerie nodded. "It's okay."

"I'm sorry if things don't work out with your guy. I'm sure he's nice."

"He is. Really nice."

Lindsay gave her a sympathetic look, but there was something else Valerie saw in her expression, too. It was that knowing, see-through look again. Lindsay cleared her throat suddenly, and then laughed a little. "Oh, sorry. You can go. I didn't mean to keep you."

"You're fine," Valerie told her simply, and then left for the bathroom.

She spent most of the day thinking about Lucas after that. She couldn't believe she'd called her kiss with him mechanical. The poor guy probably thought the world of her now, and here she was telling her friends she hadn't felt anything when she'd kissed him.

But there was one thing Lindsay had been right about: 'kissing a wall' was the perfect analogy. So perfect that Valerie had to wonder if Lindsay herself had had the same experience with a guy at some point. At any rate, Lindsay seemed happy now, so if that was indeed the case, at least that meant the kiss with Lucas didn't spell doom for Valerie's love life, as she had no doubt that Lindsay had droves of boys aching to date her.

And then there was the advice her friends had given her: try again. Kiss Lucas a second time and see how that goes. It was certainly a viable option.

There was a third option, as well, and one that she didn't consider until around dinnertime, when Kat, Amber, and herself were bidding Lindsay and the Davises goodbye and then were on their way home in her car. She could kiss a different guy. If the problem was Lucas, she'd know, then. The biggest roadblock was finding another guy to kiss. But that option was a complete longshot, and she kept it in the back of her mind for all of five minutes before she started to feel guilty on Lucas's behalf.

"So what'd you guys think of Lindsay?" Amber piped up from the back seat as Valerie drove.

"I think she seems cool," Kat admitted. "I want to pick up her accent."

"I like her, but she's definitely gonna be competition," was Amber's response.

Valerie was confused. "Competition? For what?"

"Boys, of course. A hot blonde British exchange student; are you kidding me? She's gonna be the talk of the whole school."

"Well, I guess she'll have a good time here, at least," Kat said with a shrug.

Valerie stayed silent for a minute. She didn't know what she could really say about Lindsay without coming across as strange. She was pretty, yes, but to Valerie, her most noticeable characteristic was the intensity of her eyes. She was both intrigued and shaken by the way Lindsay had stared right through her earlier and then labeled her feelings on her kiss with Lucas to a "T". And then later, she'd brushed the whole thing off and apologized, like it wasn't a big deal.

"She's interesting," Valerie finally said, and that was the last word on Lindsay before Kat and Amber were dropped off at their houses and

Valerie was on her way back home alone.

Her mom and Abby were home when she got there, and her mother tried to ask her about how her date had gone the night before, but she was long past sick of talking about Lucas at that point. Not long after getting home, she retired to her room for the night, and then drifted off to sleep to thoughts of Lucas's kiss and Lindsay's stare.

CHAPTER SEVEN

By noon on Sunday, Valerie had received a friend request from Lindsay on Facebook. Accepting the request led her down a wormhole of pictures, recent Facebook statuses, and favorite movies and bands lists. Lindsay was into a lot of punk rock but listed Taylor Swift and Marilyn Manson as her top two favorite artists, which Valerie thought was pretty much the most amazing combination of anything ever. She liked chick flicks and the color green, and she'd been to America once before, but only to New York and only for a few days, for a wedding.

Lindsay seemed to have a lot of friends back home judging from her pictures, both equally male and female, and it was around the time that Valerie was beginning to be able to match the faces from the pictures to the names Lindsay had tagged at various points in time in her Facebook statuses –particularly a girl named Molly, who was all over Lindsay's page up until about four months prior – that she began to wonder if she was going a little overboard with the stalking.

With that realization, she logged out of Facebook quickly and looked for other ways to kill her Sunday. She knew Lucas would probably be home alone, but she didn't quite feel comfortable talking with him yet. Abby and her mother were home, and she eventually headed downstairs to spend some time with them when it became apparent that there weren't enough sources of entertainment to keep her occupied in her room for the rest of the day. They watched two movies and Mrs. Marsh talked her daughters into a game of charades, and then it was evening and Mr. Marsh was home for dinner. For the first time in weeks, Valerie joined her family at the dinner table.

They talked first about Lindsay's arrival, and then her parents brought up Lucas again, only to have Valerie immediately shut down the conversation for the second time. Dinner was a little awkward after that.

The next day, Valerie and Kat met up with Tara outside of the school's front office. Inside, Lindsay met with a counselor and had her schedule ready in all of five minutes, and then Kat and Valerie guided her to the auditorium for drama class.

"We're doing a play in December called 'A Winter Wonderland'," Kat explained. "But if you're not into acting you can always do tech stuff like Valerie. She does the lights almost every play."

"I actually think I'd like to act," Lindsay replied. "I've done theater before. Only a couple of times, but it was fun."

Once inside the auditorium, Kat went straight to greet Nick, leaving Valerie and Lindsay to trail behind. Lindsay watched Kat and Nick with raised eyebrows.

"That's Nick, her boyfriend," Valerie recapped quickly. "Totally airheaded at times, but totally in love with her. He wrestles and he's almost as good onstage as Kat. The two of them get the leads for every play."

"That doesn't seem fair," Lindsay observed.

"Well, they're the best for the job and everyone knows it, so there's not much of a movement to overthrow them, exactly. I mean, they're not assholes about it or anything."

"No, I didn't think so. Kat seems nice. But maybe it should be someone else's turn, anyway."

Ms. Merriweather caught sight of Lindsay and joined the four of them as they moved to sit down at the edge of the auditorium. "Well hello there. What brings a new student to my domain?"

"Lindsay's an exchange student from London," Kat explained. "Val and I talked her into taking this class."

"Well, isn't that convenient?" Ms. Merriweather replied, immediately perking up excitedly. "You know; I'd thought about having the play take place in Britain, to give it a more old-timey feel. Perhaps I'll change it after all, now that we have an expert on the accent." She winked and handed Lindsay a script, then moved away to greet Tony and Nathan as they walked in.

Lindsay flipped through the pages, amused. "She's eccentric. And did she write this herself?"

Valerie laughed, and Lindsay made eye contact with her and smiled. Kat, meanwhile, just shrugged, took a seat, and began mouthing lines to herself quietly. Valerie saw her try them with a British accent at one point, too.

After a few minutes of Kat line-reading and Nick quizzing Lindsay about the same kind of stuff Valerie had already read on her Facebook page, Lindsay finally turned and looked at the light booth at the back of the auditorium and asked, "So that's where you'll be during the play, Valerie?"

Valerie nodded. "There's an entire board with switches and knobs on it. I use them to control certain lights at certain parts of the stage."

"You should show me," Lindsay suggested. Valerie wanted to protest, but Lindsay was already getting to her feet and moving past Kat and Nick to get out of their aisle. Valerie hesitated, looking around for Ms. Merriweather. No one normally went anywhere near the light booth unless they were actually rehearsing the play.

But Lindsay was not to be deterred, and it wasn't long before she had already ducked into the booth and Valerie could see her through the glass window at the front of it, looking down at the light board. Only out of fear that Lindsay would touch something and Ms. Merriweather would blame Valerie for it, Valerie hastily hurried up to the booth and joined Lindsay inside.

"Don't touch anything," she warned, moving to stand by Lindsay as she examined the light board.

"There are so many switches. None of them are even labeled," Lindsay observed. "How do you keep track of them all?"

"Memorization."

"You took the time to remember what they all do?"

"Not all of them. Just the ones I need to know. And everyone else memorizes lines. I memorize these switches instead. My job's probably a little bit easier, to tell you the truth." As she finished speaking, Lindsay reached out toward the board. Instinctively, Valerie caught her by the wrist with a quick, "Hey."

Lindsay turned, raising an eyebrow first at where Valerie's fingers were wrapped around her wrist, and then at Valerie herself. Embarrassed, Valerie released her. Lindsay took a moment to examine their surroundings.

"So Tara's really into schoolwork, based on the amount of time she spent studying yesterday," Lindsay said, abruptly changing the subject. Valerie wasn't sure where she was going with this line of conversation until she continued, "Amber cheerleads, and Kat acts. And *you*... cook badly and memorize the functions of light switches?"

"You're very observant," Valerie told her. That just made Lindsay grin.

"What do you do for fun, then? Got any other hobbies?"

"Not any that trump my passion for flicking switches."

"I'm sure."

Lindsay crossed the booth, and, to Valerie's relief, looked to be planning to leave it entirely. Before she went, though, she paused by the exit and peered at Valerie for a moment. "Well, when you figure out what you're interested in, let me know. Maybe we have something in common." And then she was gone.

Valerie stared at the doorway for a moment, eyebrows furrowed, and then shook her head and laughed a little, moving to exit the booth herself.

After class was over and it was clear Lindsay would be able to find her way around for the day, Valerie's thoughts shifted to her upcoming Chem class with Lucas. They'd had no contact since their texts Friday night, and she was dreading seeing him. She didn't even know how she wanted Lucas to react to her at this point. If, for whatever reason, he elected to act like nothing had happened between them, things would be beyond awkward. The other option was that he'd ask to talk about it. Valerie wasn't convinced the former option was necessarily worse in comparison.

Although Kat and Amber were both in her Lit class, it was Tara she trusted most, and so it was Tara who she asked for a final word of advice.

"Hey. Idk what to say to Lucas today in Chem."

She sent the text off and waited. Tara often chose not to text in class, but hopefully she understood that Valerie was panicking and this was an emergency.

Valerie sighed with relief when her phone vibrated in her lap just a minute later.

"Don't let him brush it off! U 2 need 2 talk. I think u should give him a chance. Ppl have awkward 1st kisses all the time. Don't stress."

Valerie stared down at the message. She swallowed hard, and considered Tara's words. They echoed the same message Amber and Kat would've given her anyway. She'd gone over what they'd said at Tara's house at least a dozen times in her head by now: Her kiss with Lucas was a fluke, and another one would fix the problem. It was that simple to them. Valerie wasn't so sure she agreed.

And then there was Lindsay's input: "If you didn't feel anything, maybe you just don't like him." She was more inclined to believe this was the case. A part of her wanted very much to like Lucas the way he appeared to like her, but she wasn't confident that she did.

But at the same time, what were the odds that a girl she'd just met knew better than her closest friends did? And she trusted Tara more than all of her other friends combined. If her best friend said a second try with Lucas was her best plan of action, who was she to argue? And if that didn't work out, then she could cross that bridge when she came to it. There was no use obsessing about other options at this point when another kiss could easily be the answer to her problems.

Her mind made up, she waited anxiously for the end of Lit, and then headed straight to Chemistry when it was finally time to begin 3rd period. Lucas was already seated at their usual desk. She noticed his leg was bouncing nervously and his hands were folded in his lap. He avoided her eyes as she approached, which killed a little of her confidence. What she'd planned to be a bright "Hi!" came out as a quiet, "Hey," instead.

"Hey, Val," Lucas replied just as quietly, and then cleared his throat. "How was the rest of your weekend?"

"Good," she said shortly, and then remembered Lindsay. Lindsay was a good conversation-starter. "Kara's replacement got here on Saturday. Today's her first day in her new classes."

Lucas relaxed a little upon hearing that, and looked to Valerie with interest. "Really? What's she like?"

Several adjectives immediately came to mind, but the one that Valerie finally settled on was, "Outspoken."

Lucas smiled. "So not much different than Kara, then?"

"Actually, way different. She talks to me, for one."

"Well, I guess that's a good thing."

Their teacher demanded the class's attention before they could say anything else, doling out directions for a particularly complicated experiment that they were given only the class period to complete. Unfortunately, that left little time to discuss Friday with Lucas, and so against her better judgment, Valerie parted ways with Lucas at the end of class without having talked with him about their date or their kiss.

The majority of the day after that went by in a blur. Lindsay had some trouble finding their lunch table two periods later, but once they were all seated, things went as they usually did, only this time with the addition of a fifth person. Her friends made her promise to talk to Lucas after school that day, and Valerie noticed that Lindsay stayed completely quiet during this particular topic of conversation.

Lindsay was mostly silent during Cooking as well, even though their teacher let her take the normally empty seat next to Valerie. For the first time since her arrival, it seemed the girl was temporarily out of things to say.

And then school was over, and Valerie was guiding Lindsay in the direction of the buses, already familiar with the bus Tara typically rode home. Once she was sure Lindsay could find her own way, she headed across the parking lot to her car, where Lucas was waiting for her, his back resting against the passenger door and his head tilted up to face the sky.

"Don't stare at the sun," she warned him as she arrived, digging her car keys out of her purse.

"I wasn't," he protested. "I was thinking."

"About what?" She got into the car and he hopped in beside her, watching her as she started the engine.

"How I should bring up the fact that we kissed Friday night and now it's weird." There was a pause. "Hey, mission accomplished."

She sighed, and focused on the road as they pulled out of the parking lot. "You go first."

"Why do I have to go first?"

"Because you brought it up."

"So you wouldn't have if I hadn't?"

"I didn't say that."

He groaned, giving in. "Alright. Fine. I... I'm about to sound really stupid. Here goes my pride." He hesitated, and then told her, "I guess I always thought you were cute. Hot. Or whatever. But I didn't think too much about it because we were friends. And I knew Friday was friendly, but we were having fun and you looked nice and... next thing I know I'm asking to walk you to your door like an asswipe."

His admittance was followed by more silence, and it didn't take long for it to grow uncomfortable.

"Okay, this is the part where you tell me to fuck off, or if we're in a rom-com, you confess your undying love for me. So... hurry it up." He cleared his throat awkwardly while Valerie determinedly didn't look away from the street ahead of her. They were nearing their neighborhood now.

She knew what she wanted to say, and what she felt deep down. Hearing Lucas's side of the story only made her surer about her own side. The problem was gathering the courage to say it. Lucas was such a nice guy, and she didn't want to hurt him.

"Lucas..." she finally began. She could tell from the way he tensed beside her that her tone had already given her away. "I like you. A lot. I just... I'm not so sure that it isn't just friendly. Friday was fun, like you said. It was fun for me until... until we kissed."

"Ouch," he murmured, wincing. He was still trying for humor, but she knew she'd hurt his feelings.

"I thought about it all weekend," she explained, trying her best to make him understand. They reached her house and she parked her car, then unbuckled her seatbelt and turned to face him. Grudgingly, he mirrored her actions. "I kept wondering… and I guess I'm *still* wondering… if maybe things were just weird for me because it was my first kiss, or your first kiss. If maybe it'd be better a second time. But I don't know if it would be. I just know that the first one wasn't what I thought it would be."

"If I did something wrong, you can tell me," he told her. "First kisses are always awkward. Maybe a second one isn't a bad idea, you know?"

She sighed, looking up at him. She considered it. It was what she'd wanted, but it didn't seem like the right thing to do now. "But I don't want to take advantage of you."

He looked around the both of them, mocking surprise. "I see no one taking advantage of anyone here. I get a second chance to impress you; you get to answer your question. If anything, *I'm* goading you into giving me a second kiss." When she didn't reply at first, he turned serious. "Look, Val. You're my friend. Rejection sucks but chances are I'll get over it, and I trust your judgment. If you don't like me, you don't like me. What do you want to do?"

He waited while she mulled it over. Tara's advice had been to kiss Lucas again. Lucas was offering to kiss her again. Was there any harm in trying one more time?

She bit her lip, gathered her courage, and then nodded at him. "If you don't mind, maybe a second kiss-?"

"Absolutely," he replied before she could even finish, a genuine smile on his face. "And for the record, my first kiss wasn't with you. I know that different girls have different preferences. If I'm doing something you don't like, it's okay to let me know."

"Got it," she told him shortly, still trying to mentally prepare. Lucas made the first move, leaning forward and shifting awkwardly in his seat, trying to make the angle easier. Then he leaned across the center console and reached out to steady her face with a hand on her cheek. Valerie already felt distinctly uncomfortable, and there was an awful pit forming in her stomach. And then Lucas was kissing her.

It was no different than the first time. The painful scruff, the lack of passion, the unpleasant angle… it was all still there. Only this time she wasn't so sure that Lucas knew it was bad.

She forced herself to kiss him back until he finally pulled away. He sounded slightly out of breath and a little dazed as he asked, "How was that?"

He was met with an awkward silence, and he leaned further away until he could get a good look at her embarrassed expression.

"What? It was bad?" he asked, confused. Shyly, Valerie nodded. "How? What'd I do?"

She shook her head and made no move to answer his question. "I'm so sorry, Lucas. I should go."

She began to gather her things while he watched, his jaw hanging open. "Wait, but what did I do wrong? Seriously?"

"Nothing, I don't-" She sighed, cutting herself off, and then finished, "Maybe it's me. I'll see you tomorrow, okay?"

"But-"

She closed the car door before he could argue and headed up the walkway to her front porch, her footsteps heavy. That was that. Lucas was a dud. Her friends had been wrong and Lindsay had been right. A girl who'd known her for minutes had been able to pinpoint not only how she'd felt while kissing Lucas, but the reason she'd felt it, as well. Meanwhile, the friends she'd known for years had been clueless.

Maybe getting to know Lindsay would be in her best interest, after all.

CHAPTER EIGHT

It took shorter than expected for things to return to "normal". Or as normal as they could be, given the circumstances. Lucas fell back into being Valerie's friend, and with a few weeks of time, he finally stopped asking what had gone wrong, and accepted, albeit grudgingly, that Valerie just wasn't interested. Valerie, meanwhile, focused on college applications, mostly to avoid thinking about the fact that she'd been unable think of a viable answer to any of the questions raised by Lucas.

She came to realize that she had very few extracurricular activities to put on her applications, and her grades were only slightly above average. She ended up only sending out four applications: three to local colleges, and one to Cloverdale University, a decent school about two hours away that accepted applications on a regular basis until February, which meant that applying earlier gave her an advantage. Tara was going for Ivy League, with Cloverdale as a backup, from what Valerie understood, while Amber was shooting for her sister's school and Kat applied to a few liberal arts colleges. Chances were that they'd all end up at different schools in another year, but Valerie did her best to put that from her mind.

Lindsay, too, most likely had college plans, but Valerie didn't know what they were. In less than a month, she'd managed to make herself a natural part of their group, and even a natural part of their school. It was alien for Valerie to watch. She was sure everyone felt uncomfortable in their own skin to some degree, but if Lindsay felt it, she never showed it. She got along with everyone, and everyone wanted to know all about her. Valerie could tell Lindsay's popularity made Amber jealous, but Amber wouldn't dare speak a word against Lindsay for fear of the social retribution for it. In three weeks, Lindsay had become untouchable, and Valerie openly marveled at that fact.

Even more interestingly was that despite having the pick of anyone at Riverbank High, Valerie seemed to be Lindsay's companion of choice. They spent an hour daily learning to cook together and another hour talking in drama class while Kat and Nick ran over lines, and sometimes Lindsay even hitched a ride home with Valerie and Lucas to hang out at Valerie's house, something Valerie appreciated even more when Lucas seemed to be slowly shifting his affections to Lindsay instead.

Lindsay, however, did not share those affections, and she said as much the instant Valerie pointed out that Lucas seemed interested in her. Her reasoning was that he'd liked Valerie first anyway and was only looking for someone to replace her, but Valerie noticed that Lindsay didn't seem to talk about boys, much like Tara hadn't used to before Oliver. And considering Kat had Nick, Tara had Oliver now, and Amber always had someone new every week, it was nice spending time with Lindsay, when boys weren't always thrown into the mix. It was like she and Lindsay understood each other, in a way Valerie had thought Tara understood her.

Things were going well. They weren't perfect, but they were nice.

Valerie got the first inkling that that was about to change when Lindsay pulled her into the light booth in drama class, clutching a script in her hand while her eyebrows turned up in nervous concern. "I need your opinion on something," she stated, bluntly.

Valerie blinked at her. "Okay...?"

Lindsay sighed, gesturing towards the script. "Please don't saying anything to Kat yet, but... I've been memorizing lines for auditions."

Valerie was confused. There was nothing out of the ordinary about what Lindsay had just said; auditions for the Winter play were in a week and so it was expected that she'd have a part to audition for.

Her lips parted in surprise as it hit her. "You're really going for it," she realized. Lindsay wanted Kat's part. The female lead.

Lindsay confirmed with a nod of her head, then bit her lip. "I just think it could be fun. Do you think she'll be mad?"

"I don't know. I don't think Kat and Nick realize that no one else ever goes for the leads because they expect Kat and Nick to get them anyway. They just think no one else *wants* the lead. Kat won't admit it but I know she expects to get it because she thinks no one else wants it. So it's hard to say how she'll take the competition."

"I just don't want her upset with me. This is your school, not mine," Lindsay insisted.

"I'd talk to her. See what she says. And before the auditions next week."

Lindsay nodded, then reached forward and pulled Valerie into a hug. "Thank you." Lindsay liked hugs and gave them often, Valerie had noticed. She kind of liked them too, when certain people gave them. Lindsay was one of those people.

As she was pulling up in front of her house with Lucas in the passenger's seat after school that day, her phone buzzed in her purse. As always, Lucas immediately reached for her phone, despite her protests.

"AmBAH," he announced, miming a hair flip, "wants to know if you'd come to a college party her sister's throwing at her house this Saturday night." He looked to her, impressed. "Can I come too?"

She scoffed. "You'd really want to go to Amber's house?"

"For alcohol? Totally. Do you think Lindsay will be there?"

"You're so obvious," Valerie told him, rolling her eyes.

"I'm doing what any man would do," he assured her. "I'm bouncing back after a terrible, heart-breaking, crushing rejection. If you're not gonna pick up the pieces, someone has to."

He smirked at her, clearly amused with himself, but she didn't match his amusement this time. "Why don't you just leave her alone?"

"Jeez, no need to be so harsh about it," he retorted, backing off. "Look, *you* turned *me* down. I'm allowed to try and move on, or do you expect for me to be depressed forever?"

She rolled her eyes again, not wanting to get into another argument about their not-even-a-breakup again. "Bye, Lucas."

He took the hint and left the car, but not before mumbling something angrily under his breath. The car door slammed behind him and her phone buzzed again. She picked it up. It was Amber again. *"And invite Lucas! The more hotties, the better!"* She scowled at the text and then chucked her phone back into her purse.

At lunch the next day, Amber brought up the party again while they were all sitting together. "I really *really* need all of you guys to come, okay? And look nice when you do. Some of Hannah's sorority sisters will be there and I need to show them I hang out with girls just like them. Which means, Tara, no glasses."

Lindsay laughed at Valerie's side. "What? Tara looks nice with glasses."

"It doesn't matter; they'll think they're dorky," Amber dismissed. "And Val, please tell me you'll make sure Lucas comes."

"I will," she said stiffly, and if Amber caught her tone, she ignored it.

"Okay, so the party's Saturday because that's when my parents will be gone, but I was hoping we could all get together Friday night and that way you guys could help my sister and I prep for the party, and then we can repay you by doing your clothes, hair, and makeup before the party. Does a sleepover Friday night sound good?" The way she said it left no room for argument, and so no one argued. Not even Tara, who Valerie was almost certain wanted to get a jump on studying for their Calculus test the following Wednesday.

And so, the party preparations began. Valerie was assigned to do about half of the shopping, which involved Hannah giving Amber one-hundred dollars to give to Valerie, who then went to the store to buy just about everything that she could, while Hannah took care of the alcohol. Kat's biggest role involved decorations and convincing Nick to come, while Tara was left to her own devices, which gave her time to do her studying during the week that she would've been doing on Friday and Saturday night.

Lindsay joined Valerie on her shopping trip, and it was when they'd returned to Valerie's house and were relaxing alone on her living room couch as a *Full House* rerun ran on the television that Lindsay asked something Valerie herself had wondered for a while: "So why exactly don't you do anything for fun? You seem to have so much free time."

Valerie immediately shrugged. She'd asked the question of herself many times, and never had an answer.

"You really don't have anything you're interested in? What do you want to do when you get to uni- erm, college?"

"I haven't chosen a major yet," Valerie admitted. "I don't know. I guess I'm good with technology."

"There must be something you're interested in. We should run an experiment." Lindsay grinned at her. "There're loads of stuff I bet you'd be into if you tried them. Like a sport. Swimming, maybe. Or football."

"Getting tackled by two-hundred pound guys isn't really my thing."

Lindsay laughed at that. "Sorry, soccer. I'll bet there's a pitch around here we can play at."

"Are all Europeans good at soccer?" Valerie guessed, arching an eyebrow.

"No, I'm terrible actually. But you could be good! Or, um... what do you call that, with the guns... and you wear vests."

Valerie watched Lindsay struggle for a moment.

"You know what I mean, right? And it's electronic; they make noise..."

"Laser tag?"

"Yes!" Lindsay threw her hands up like she'd just won the lottery. "That one! Aren't you lot into that?"

"If laser tag is my best talent, I have a very very sad future in store for me."

Lindsay huffed as Valerie grinned at her. "You're taking the piss. Anyway-"

"What?" Valerie interrupted, laughing. "Is that another British thing I don't understand?"

"You're making fun of me!" Lindsay corrected, looking embarrassed as Valerie chuckled. "*Anyway*, my point is that we're gonna find something you like. How about computers?"

Valerie shrugged. "I mean, I guess. Social media's fun."

"Telecommunications, then," Lindsay announced with a snap of her fingers. "Or Mass Media Arts. Or Journalism. Or even Computer Science."

"I'm sorry; what?"

"College majors," Lindsay clarified, smiling at her.

Valerie shifted uncomfortably. "I don't know. It's too weird to think about it right now." She looked over at the bags they'd left on the kitchen counter. "Do you think maybe we should put those somewhere where my parents won't find them until I can get them to Amber? They're bound to wonder why I have, like, four bags of red solo cups."

"Okay," Lindsay agreed, and neither one of them spoke about the topic of hobbies or college majors for the rest of Lindsay's visit.

The second indication that all was not well in regards to Lindsay's presence was that Valerie got a text from Tara on Thursday night, asking her, "*If I tell you something will you promise not to share it with anyone? Even Kat and Amber.*"

She called Tara right away. Tara answered it with another, "Promise?"

"Of course. Is it Oliver?" Valerie immediately guessed. She knew Tara and Oliver wouldn't last long. After about a month of dating seemed like the appropriate time for Tara to come to her senses.

"No, it's Lindsay," Tara told her, catching her off-guard.

"Lindsay? What's wrong with Lindsay?" Practically nothing was wrong with her in Valerie's book. Sure, she was smart and pretty and funny and popular, which explained why guys would like her a little more than girls would, but she didn't flaunt any of those things. So what kind of issue could Tara have?

"I don't like living with her and it's driving me crazy," Tara admitted. "I hate it so much, Val. I don't think I can take it for another five months."

"Why? Does she not clean up or something?" Valerie tried to envision Lindsay having a messy room, but she'd been inside it multiple times and it was always relatively clean. Not spotless, but not a pig sty either.

"No, she's fine. It's just…well, it's the opposite. I don't know if it's gonna wear off once she gets more used to it here, but she's so polite to my parents, and she cleans up without asking, and her grades are almost as good as mine but she gets them without as much studying." Valerie could hear the tears coming in Tara's voice. "You know what my mom told me today? She said I should offer to help wash the dishes more after dinner, like *Lindsay* does. I wanted to tell her that I needed to go study so I could get the grades she *forces* me to strive for, but no, I couldn't, because that would be disrespectful, and then it'd be: Why can't I be more *respectful*, like *Lindsay*?" On the other end of the line, Tara sniffed, and Valerie let out a sympathetic sigh. "Not to mention Oliver stares at her sometimes; I see him do it."

"Tara, Oliver likes you a lot," Valerie reassured her. "Boys will stare at anything with boobs. Do you think maybe the problem is with your parents and not with Lindsay?"

"Of course you'd say that; she's like your new best friend or whatever," Tara bit out. "I should've known not to talk to you about her."

"That's not fair," Valerie insisted. "You know you're my best friend. You're busy with Oliver now."

"I tried to include you with that! Remember? I could've asked Kat to double with me but I asked *you*. And then you decided you didn't want to go out with Lucas again."

"Well, I can't help that I didn't like him," Valerie replied, suddenly feeling small. "I just want things to be like how they were before."

Tara exhaled on the other end of the phone, and they were silent for a moment. "Before Oliver?" she finally asked.

"Yeah," Valerie sighed out. "Remember? We'd stay over at my house and Amber would just complain for *hours-*"

Tara giggled on the other end and interrupted, "Yeah, I remember that. And all of her nasty sex stories. I still think they're gross, you know. Getting a boyfriend isn't like getting a brain transplant. But you've been different since then too, you know?" There was a pause. "You miss me before Oliver, but I miss you before Oliver, too. Are you hanging out with Lindsay so much because she doesn't have a boyfriend?"

Valerie considered it. "Maybe. Maybe that's part of it. But I like her, too. She's nice."

"So nice that my parents wish they'd had her instead of me."

"Don't say that. You know that's not true."

"It is. But she'll be gone in six months anyway. Amber'll be happy, too, you know. She doesn't like Lindsay at all."

"She's jealous," Valerie immediately replied.

"Maybe. Maybe not. But I'll bet Kat's patience for her is running out, as well. She told me Lindsay told her today that she's going for the lead in that play they're doing."

"Was Kat upset?"

"It didn't seem like it. She's probably excited about the competition right now. But she might be upset if she loses, especially if Nick gets the other lead." Tara paused to say something aside to someone who seemed to be one of her parents, and then told Valerie, "Alright, I've gotta go eat dinner. I'll see you tomorrow?"

"Yes. Your parents love you, Tara."

"I guess so," Tara replied distantly, and the line went dead with a click.

After school on Friday, Valerie gave Lucas Amber's address, and then proceeded to pack up her things and drive herself there, picking up Tara, Lindsay, and Kat on the way.

Amber and Hannah were there with both of Amber's parents, and the instant she got the chance, Hannah made it blatantly clear that the girls needed to keep their mouths shut about the party or else risk giving it away. She also promised them alcohol for their sleepover if they succeeded in keeping quiet until her parents went to bed.

It was Lindsay's first time meeting Amber's family, so their eight-person dinner had an awkwardly polite tone to it, and when it was over, Amber directed the other four girls up to her room, where they sat on Amber's massive bed and chatted about the plans for the next night.

Valerie zoned in and out during the conversation. She wasn't sure if she was imagining the tension now, or if had been there all along and she hadn't been aware of it. Kat and Lindsay were competing for a lead in a play, Lindsay had upstaged Amber in popularity over the course of the past month, and Tara felt like her parents preferred Lindsay to her. All three of those girls had a reason to have a problem with Lindsay, no matter how flimsy the reason actually was.

But not Valerie. Valerie had nothing but nice things to say about the girl.

But she didn't want her friends to think she was abandoning them or siding against them, either. She was officially caught in the middle, and she didn't know how to get out without choosing a side.

Hannah popped in at one point after Amber's parents went to bed, bringing them cups, juice, and a half a handle of vodka, and warning them to save themselves for the following night. Tara looked at the concoction Amber poured her like it was toxic, but ended up sipping it anyway. Kat, Lindsay, and Amber drank like they'd done it several times before, and Valerie knew either from experience or through conversation that they all had. Valerie herself followed Tara's lead to avoid a hangover, but sipped slightly faster.

"Okay," Amber announced once they'd all been drinking and talking for about half an hour, "We need to spice things up a little. Who wants 'I Never' and who wants 'Truth or Dare'?"

"Tara'll just win 'I Never'," Kat giggled out, shaking her head. "Or lose, depending on how you look at it. We should definitely go for 'Truth or 'Dare'."

"But 'I Never' might get some interesting stuff about her and Oliver out of her," Lindsay pointed out, reaching over and patting Tara's knee playfully. Valerie saw Tara blush a little, and wished she hadn't.

"We can still get that with 'Truth of Dare'," Amber surmised, making the decision herself. "Tara, you're going first. Truth or dare?"

"Dare," Tara replied hastily, her thoughts almost definitely still on the questions she could be asked about Oliver.

"Awesome. I dare you to tell us about the last time you fooled around with Oliver. I want every detail."

"That's cheating!" Tara complained. "It's practically a truth."

"Yeah, c'mon. Give her a real dare," Valerie chimed in, nudging Amber. "She can do something gross or something."

"How eloquent," came Kat's voice, and she grinned at Valerie as Valerie stuck her tongue out in response.

"Fine. I dare you, Tara, to finish the rest of that drink in one minute."

The rest of the girls laughed as Tara sighed, then tipped the drink back and grudgingly got the rest of it down. Amber got up to pour her another one as Tara declared, "Alright. Um, Val. Truth or dare?"

"Truth," she replied, and got boos from the other girls. She ignored them, watching Tara.

"Is it true that… you have a crush on a guy right now and you're just not telling us about it?"

Valerie got booed again by Kat and Amber as she shook her head. "No, seriously, I don't! I would tell you."

"Lucas is so hooooot, though!" Amber complained. "You wasted your chance!"

"Whatever, he couldn't kiss," Valerie dismissed, only feeling badly about the statement after the other girls laughed. "Um, anyway… Lindsay, truth or dare?"

"Definitely… truth," Lindsay answered, ignoring another round of boos.

"Okay. Speaking of Lucas, do you like him?" Valerie questioned. It was something she'd been wondering in the back of her mind. There was a chance Lindsay was just being respectful and didn't want to risk upsetting Valerie. "Because if you do, you don't need to feel like you can't date him just because we kissed a couple of times."

Lindsay swirled her drink around in her cup for a moment, then looked Valerie dead in the eyes. She smiled. "I don't like Lucas. Kat, truth or dare?"

The game went on for a while as the alcohol continued to take effect. By the time thirty more minutes had passed, Valerie was having trouble seeing straight, and she knew Amber at the very least had to be nearly out of it, because when Tara dared her to simply walk in a straight line, she nearly fell over twice, and then sloshed her drink all over her carpet. She was too drunk to clean it up, so she simply collapsed back on her bed with the nearly empty cup and declared, "Lindsay's turn! Gonna be lame and pick truth again, like always!"

"Yep," Lindsay declared, nodding and then giggling a little. Valerie stared at her, grinning widely.

"Fine, I'll make it really bad, then," Amber decided, and then said the last thing any of them expected to hear: "Someone puts a gun to your head and demands you make out with someone in this room. Who do you choose?"

Kat immediately burst into laughter at the question and then nearly dropped her drink. One glance at Tara told Valerie she was silent, but amused, and so Valerie wasn't sure why she seemed to be the only one uncomfortable with the question. Heck, even Amber had asked it, so surely it wasn't something she should feel awkward about?

"Um..." Lindsay gave a nervous laugh, and her cheeks flushed brightly now. Whether that was due to the alcohol or embarrassment, it was impossible to tell. She glanced around, and her eyes found Valerie's. Valerie felt the uncomfortable feeling expand, stretching into both her chest and her stomach. She knew the answer before Lindsay said it. "Val, I guess."

Tara bit her lip to hide a smile and Amber and Kat found that answer really funny, for whatever reason. Valerie suspected they would've found any answer humorous at this point. Lindsay shrugged, and then took another long gulp of her drink, avoiding Valerie's eyes for a moment as Valerie felt her own face heat up.

Finally, the commotion died down, and Lindsay let out a deep breath. "Okay, Val, truth or dare?"

"Dare her to actually do it!" Kat suggested, and Valerie's heart rate skyrocketed for a millisecond until Amber cut in, making a disgusted noise and waving her hand.

"No, no! That's so gross; don't!"

"Relax. I wasn't going to," Lindsay defended, giving Amber a particularly scathing look for some reason. "Besides, she has to pick first."

"Truth," Valerie chose, just to be safe.

"Okay." Lindsay didn't hesitate. "Same question."

Valerie's heart sank and she swallowed hard, finding it more difficult than usual. Her mind pulled her in ten different directions and she tried to work out her choices. She could lie and say Kat, who would take in stride and find it hilarious. Amber wasn't an option. If she said Lindsay, there would probably be more teasing, but she'd save her pride by picking someone who'd already picked her back. But there was always the option of just telling the truth.

She looked at Lindsay and saw her quirk an eyebrow upward, waiting. The look was back. The look that made her feel like Lindsay knew what she was thinking. That look told her she wasn't about to get away with a lie.

"Tara," she replied, and as the other girls began giggling again, Lindsay nodded and smiled, almost as if to congratulate her on a job well done.

CHAPTER NINE

All five girls woke up with hangovers the next morning. Hannah called them all "dumb bitches", but made them some kind of drink that was supposed to get rid of it once the house was free of parents.

The party wasn't due to start until that night, so they spent a lot of the day setting up decorations, putting the finishing touches on mix CDs, and perfecting the ideal combination of booze and punch in the punch bowl. Even though Hannah claimed to know all of the guys that'd be at the party, she warned against having any punch, as there was always a chance it could be drugged. On that topic, Hannah talked for at least fifteen minutes, until she was confident they'd all learned the nuances of keeping themselves safe. Valerie, admittedly, was impressed with the talk; most of the time Hannah seemed really shallow.

She and Lindsay were put in charge of testing CDs to make sure they all worked with the stereo system, and so they eventually ended up alone in the living room while Hannah and Amber mixed drinks and Kat and Tara finished cleaning and decorating. Valerie felt a little tense around Lindsay now, and she could tell Lindsay noticed, because they didn't talk much while they worked.

After a long, drawn-out four hours of prep, Hannah finally let them relax for a few hours while she ran some last-minute errands, claiming they needed more snacks than they had, and Kat and Tara texted Nick and Oliver over on two different chairs in the dining room while Amber,

Lindsay, and Valerie caught the tail end of a movie on the couch. Lindsay sat in the middle, and Valerie scooted away from her a little when their legs brushed. Lindsay didn't seem to notice the action, but if she did, Valerie didn't feel badly about it. It was Lindsay's own fault for making her uncomfortable. Why hadn't she just lied? Why hadn't she just let *Valerie* lie?

It wasn't even that she wanted to kiss Tara. Tara was her best friend. She just thought the girl was pretty. She'd always thought Tara was pretty, and had always loved Tara's personality, as well. That was normal of best friends. Lindsay, she knew now, was trying to turn it into something it wasn't. Lindsay had it wrong. She had it very, very wrong, and Valerie wanted no part of that kind of twisting of words and actions and thoughts and feelings. That knowing, smug look made her sick to even think about, now.

The hours ticked by and at last it was time for them to do hair and make-up. None of them required much fixing up, and it didn't take long. The most difficult part was getting Tara to finally try the contacts her parents had bought her months ago. Amber had to put them in for her, but they eventually were in and functioning, and then they were all dressed in Amber's or Hannah's clothes and, as Hannah put it, "Ready to mingle with college boys."

Valerie hadn't considered that yet. Nick and Oliver would be showing up, and they would keep Kat and Tara occupied. But Amber and Hannah, no doubt, were going to be playing the field for the night, and she had no idea what Lindsay would be up to. Possibly dodging Lucas, if he wasn't busy trying to make up with Valerie during the night.

The first guests arrived at ten o'clock: a few of Hannah's sorority friends, a couple of which brought boyfriends. They helped get the music going, and after that, more people began to flood into the house. Oliver turned up pretty early on, and Nick joined Kat soon after. Not long after eleven, the drinks were being poured, the punch bowl was being refilled, and the music was blasting loudly enough that Valerie had no doubt the neighbors could hear it.

As the crowd began to fill the house, she lost touch with her friends. Kat disappeared with Nick, and Tara and Oliver sat at a table in the corner together, holding hands and simply watching everyone dance as they sipped their drinks. They were awkward, but looked happy together.

With Amber, Hannah, and Lindsay all missing, Valerie polished off one drink and then moved to get another, mixing it herself as per Hannah's instructions. It wasn't long before she felt a tap on her shoulder.

The boy was a couple of feet taller than her and was definitely older; he had to at least be in college. He held his hand out to her and shouted over the music, "Hey! Do you wanna dance?"

She wasn't sure what to say at first. She was intimidated by him, and she didn't want to dance with him. But Kat was with Nick and Tara was with Oliver, and she was absolutely certain that Hannah and Amber were off dancing with guys, too. Lindsay probably was, as well. At this point, it was out of the ordinary not to at least socialize.

She nodded and took his hand, and he led her closer to the crowd, then turned her around and wrapped one arm around her, keeping one arm and hand free to hold his drink. They swayed together to the beat of a song she only recognized because she'd tested the CDs with Lindsay earlier. She felt nervous throughout the duration of it, and not in an anxious, anticipatory kind of way. It was an unpleasant nervousness.

But she stayed put for four more songs while he leaned in, pressed closer, and moved his face so close to her head that she could feel his heavy, alcohol-scented breath tickling her ear as they danced. At some point during the fifth song Kat walked by with Nick, noticed Valerie, and grinned at her, giving her a thumbs-up. So she stayed for two more songs. And then another.

And it wasn't until after that eighth song that they stopped, and, while the next song was just starting and it was quiet enough to hear, the boy too old for her leaned into her ear and asked, "Hey, where are the bedrooms around here?"

She immediately pulled away from him and pushed out through the crowd, fast-walking toward the emptier dining room and then toward the back door. She needed air.

She pushed open the door and stepped outside, sucking in deep breaths as she stood on the patio and ran her hands through her hair, trying to make sense of what had just happened. She knew she'd just screwed up. Amber would've told the guy what he wanted to know, had she been in her position. Kat probably would've as well, if she'd thought he was cute enough. Even Tara would've been smart enough to think up a better way to reject him while still coming across as interested. Instead, Valerie had literally just fled the scene.

Her heart thundered in her chest and she sank down into a crouch, the heels on her feet keeping her perched precariously as she stuck her head between her knees and took a couple deep breaths. She jumped and nearly fell over when she felt a hand on her back.

"Hey, Val. What's wrong?"

She smelled smoke before she saw Lucas. Then she saw the cigarette in his hand as he kneeled down next to her.

She sniffed quickly, trying to hide that she'd been about to start crying. "Lucas, what are you doing out here?"

He shrugged, then gestured to the cigarette. "Smoking. I know it's bad, but it beats coming out here to have a mental breakdown."

She sniffed again, openly this time. "You're such an asshole."

"Yeah, yeah." He offered her a hand and helped her to her feet, and together they walked further out into the yard, where the fence at the edge of the yard was just the perfect height for Lucas to rest his arms on top while Valerie leaned against it. She guessed this was probably where he'd been before he'd seen her.

"So you're not enjoying the party either?" Valerie guessed.

"Not really," he admitted. "I mean, I followed all the protocols, you know… started pounding shots, found a cute girl to dance with, found a cuter girl to dance with, tried to talk Lindsay into dancing with me and failed at that… She was too busy hanging all over some other girl to get all the frat guys' attention. It was sad, really." He sighed, then scraped the cigarette against the fence and let it fall to the ground. "And the whole time there's only one girl I'm thinking about dancing with and she's with some creepy douchebag."

She stayed silent. Lucas scuffed his foot across the grass as she watched him.

"I thought about saving you but I thought, you know, maybe you were enjoying it. I couldn't tell. I'm sorry that I... that I didn't." To her surprise, his voice cracked on the last word and he ran a hand through his hair, turning away from her abruptly and then letting out a deep breath. "Fuck, I *hate* caring about people, you know? You can spend your whole life not caring, and then one person comes along..."

"I'm nothing special, Lucas," she told him gently. "I'm not even normal."

"So? Fuck normal! I don't even know what that means. You're not normal how? Because you don't want to grind on some drunk creep in your skanky friend's house? Give me a break."

She felt her jaw tense as the nervous discomfort crept back into her body. "No, I'm not normal because..." She bit her lip and took a deep breath. "Because I really like you Lucas, and I really want to like you the way you like me, and I can't. Anyone else could just like who they want to, so why can't I?"

"Are you kidding me? No one can do that," he countered, shaking his head. "You either feel or you don't. Why else would hearts get broken? If some asshole fucks up and cheats on his girlfriend and she goes back to him, why is that? It's because she wants to hate him but she can't do that because she loves him. She can't help it. Why are we in this situation right now? Because I like you and I want to stop and you don't like me and you want to start. One of us changes and suddenly we're both great. But neither of us has changed, so here we are. You're no less normal than I am."

He exhaled, and she stared at him, eyes tracing the sharp angles of his jawline and the masculine way it tensed up as he reached down for another cigarette. His fingers, rough and calloused, fumbled for his pack, and the cigarette went between two thin lips surrounded by dark shadows that promised the beginnings of facial hair. And she felt nothing, looking at all of it. Lucas had features her friends would kill to have on a guy, and he was right here, telling her he'd fallen hard and fast and she'd really hurt him, despite his best efforts to play if off before. But she felt nothing. Nothing but empathy.

She looked at him, and watched him lift a hand to light the cigarette. "I thought you were quitting," she told him.

"I only need to date one girl," he echoed, and lit it.

They stood in silence for a few minutes, Lucas smoking while Valerie did her best to stay upwind from him, but then the back door opened and they turned to see Lindsay making her way toward them, sweaty and panting, but happy.

"Hey, there you are!" she greeted them, but her eyes were on Valerie. "Why are you out here?"

"It was better than getting harassed by some guy while you were performing for ten others," Lucas bit out, and then sucked hard on his cigarette as Lindsay's smile fell and she looked questioningly to Valerie.

"Are you okay?" she asked, and Valerie noticed her swaying a little. At the very least, she was tipsy.

"I'm fine." She sighed, and looked to Lucas. "Alright, I'm gonna go take care of her. Will you be okay out here?"

Lucas nodded. "I'm gonna head out soon anyway. I'll see you Monday."

Valerie nodded back, then reached out to take Lindsay's hand and led her back toward the house.

"What was he talking about?" Lindsay questioned. "Somebody said something to you? You should've come and gotten me!"

"I didn't know where you were," Valerie explained. They entered the house through the back door and wound through the crowd again, a clear destination in Valerie's mind. She guided Lindsay past the central party area and toward the side of the house, where the bedrooms were. Lindsay giggled when Valerie opened a random one, found it empty, and pulled Lindsay inside.

"Ooh, taking me to bed, are you?"

"Stop," Valerie demanded immediately, and watched Lindsay's smile die again. She let go of her hand and stepped away from her, crossing her arms. "Stop whatever you're doing here, okay? Whatever that was last night."

Lindsay looked confused, and then a little angry. Finally, she scoffed and replied, "I don't know what you're talking about."

"Really? Telling my friends you'd make out with me-?"

"It was a question I was asked! We were playing a game! What did you want me to do; lie?"

Valerie shifted uncomfortably. She'd known Lindsay had been telling the truth, but having her admit it was different. "Not said me. So… yes. Lied."

"What does that change?"

"You made it sound like you wanted to kiss me, and then you asked me who I'd kiss! How do you think that looks?"

"I don't *care* how it looks," Lindsay retorted, laughing a little. "Why do you?"

"Because!" She paused, breathing hard, and then finally spat out her answer, "I don't want people to think I like girls!"

"Why?" Lindsay pressed. Valerie's nostrils flared as Lindsay stared at her. She was giving her that look again.

"Stop looking at me like that!"

"Like what?"

"Like you already know what I'm thinking! You don't."

"So then tell me." Lindsay stepped closer and crossed her arms. "Are you homophobic?"

"No."

"Are you *sure*?"

"I'm not homophobic, Lindsay."

"Then why does it matter if people think you're gay?"

Valerie ignored the question, instead snapping, "No, you know what I want to know? Why do you care what I think? What do you get out of this? And why ask me what you asked me last night? Did you just want to humiliate me?"

"How was it humiliating? It's a stupid game. Nobody took it seriously but you."

They both fell silent at that statement. Valerie glared at Lindsay, and at last, Lindsay let out a sigh and shook her head, announcing, "Alright, you know what? I'm too drunk for this. You have fun in here. Maybe I'll just go find someone to make out with until I sober up."

She made her way toward the door, and Valerie snapped, "Oh yeah? A boy or a girl?"

"A girl," Lindsay replied without missing a beat, and then opened the door and left the room without saying another word, slamming it shut behind her.

CHAPTER TEN

Valerie spent most of her Sunday lying in bed. She was both emotionally and physically exhausted after the events of Friday and Saturday night, and her mind was still reeling long after her conversation with Lindsay. She couldn't figure out if Lindsay had just made the comment about kissing a girl to antagonize Valerie, or if she'd really meant it. It was true that Lindsay seemed like the type of girl who'd talk frequently about boys if she liked them.

Valerie remembered being surprised when she'd realized that it was herself Lindsay had grown closest to rather than Amber, because she'd expected Lindsay to be very similar to Amber. And she was, in a way. The two of them ran in the same social circles. But there was something about the way Lindsay carried herself that differentiated the two of them, and Lindsay didn't seem to like to talk about the same things that Amber did. Boys were one of those things. Valerie had just thought Amber was overly boy-obsessed. But maybe it was Lindsay who *hadn't* been boy-obsessed at all.

Lucas had mentioned seeing Lindsay dancing with a girl to get guys' attention. Was it possible Lindsay had just wanted to dance with a girl, and the guys' attention was just the result of that? But if Lindsay liked girls… and Valerie spent so much of her free time hanging out with Lindsay… did that mean Lindsay liked her?

The thought of that made Valerie's stomach flip, but not in a nauseating way. She wasn't homophobic, after all. If Lindsay had a crush on her, it had the potential to make things weird, but Valerie wasn't going to hate her for it. In fact, she'd be kind of flattered, as long as it didn't become common knowledge around her school.

Once *that* idea was in her head, her stomach started acting so weirdly that it made it impossible to eat. Her heart pounded faster and faster the more she thought about Lindsay, and she finally forced herself to put the girl from her mind. She could deal with Lindsay on Monday, and if they could just get past what happened the night before, then things could return to normal. As frustrated as she was with Lindsay after her comments and actions on both Friday and Saturday, Valerie was not the type to hold a grudge. Fighting made her anxious, and fighting with Lindsay was already stressing her out after only twenty-four hours.

Evidently, Lindsay felt the same way, because Sunday night Valerie got a text from her. It simply said, *"We need to talk."*

"Drama?" Valerie replied in suggestion.

"Yeah… or did I just imagine last night?" Lindsay replied. Valerie realized she had misunderstood.

"I meant in the class!" she texted back.

"Oh! Oops. Yes!"

And so it was settled. The next day, Valerie got into class early and when she'd made sure Ms. Merriweather had seen her, she went and waited in the light booth, where she and Lindsay often tended to hang out during class. This would change soon, after the roles were chosen and the class actually started practicing the play, but for now, they were free to talk there in private while everyone else ran over lines.

Lindsay arrived several minutes later, sighing as she set her things down and sat on the spare chair across the booth. "Sorry I was late for class," she mumbled. "I'm a bit…" She trailed off, shook her head, and then when she finally made eye contact, Valerie saw that her eyes were reddened on the edges.

"You've been crying," she observed, resisting the urge to go to Lindsay and comfort her. "Are you okay?"

Lindsay forced a smile. "I'm fine. I guess I just, um…" There was a long pause while Lindsay tried to pull herself together. "I miss my family, my old friends. It's just... hard being here sometimes." She sniffed, running a hand through her hair and then asking, to Valerie's surprise, "Can you please not tell anyone what I said to you Saturday night? I don't think they'd take kindly to it here."

"I won't," Valerie agreed, trying not to react to having her suspicions confirmed.

"Please don't hate me," Lindsay added quietly, sniffing again. "I didn't mean to make you uncomfortable. I just thought I was doing the right thing."

"I don't hate you," Valerie reassured her, and finally stood up and crossed the booth. Lindsay stood up as well and immediately pulled Valerie into a hug, burying her face in Valerie's neck. Valerie wrapped her arms around Lindsay and pulled her as close as she could, and they stood there together for a moment. It was then that Valerie's mind caught up with the rest of what Lindsay had said, and she pulled away slightly to look at her.

"Wait, you were doing the right thing? What do you mean?"

Lindsay looked at her for a moment, eyes wide, and then shook her head. "I shouldn't have mentioned it; I'm sorry. It's not my place to say. I'm just glad we're not fighting."

Valerie released her, stepping away with an air of defensiveness. "I'm confused. You just told me you liked girls, right?"

Lindsay nodded, almost shyly.

"So that's what this is about. But you just said that you thought by doing what you did to make me uncomfortable this weekend, you were doing the right thing."

"That's... not the best way of wording it," Lindsay mumbled. "And frankly I'm not sure we should have this conversation."

"I think we should," Valerie insisted.

Lindsay hesitated, sighing deeply. "Valerie..." She trailed off, and then Valerie motioned for to continue. She sighed again. "Okay, just from my point of view, try to imagine... I get here, and you and your friends are talking about how your best friend's just kissed this guy you're clearly

93

disgusted by, and about how you have this great guy who likes you, but you don't feel anything when you kiss him. I mean, you used the word 'mechanical', Val."

Valerie immediately knew she didn't like where this conversation was going, but Lindsay was talking so quickly, and Valerie was almost engrossed in her words, as much as she didn't want to hear them.

"I mean, the way I've seen you look at *Tara*, Valerie... and you know you never mention guys. And then with the way you and I have been attached at the hip... Maybe it's a stretch, but I just thought-"

"You were right," Valerie cut her off at last. She felt sick now. "This wasn't your place to say."

"I'm sorry, Val..."

"I have to go," she said simply, moving to gather her things. "I don't feel well."

"Valerie," Lindsay tried again, but Valerie was already on her way out of the booth. She rushed out of the auditorium and headed straight for her car, throwing her things inside and then climbing into the car and resting her forehead on the steering wheel. She wished she could just un-hear everything Lindsay had told her, or that she could just pretend not to understand what had been said. But she'd gotten the message loud and clear: Lindsay had thought she was a lesbian from the first day they'd met. And Valerie wasn't so sure Lindsay was wrong, now.

She'd felt nothing for Lucas, and she couldn't understand why. She'd *known* she wasn't attracted to him, and the only reason she'd entertained the idea of dating him was for her friends' benefit. She'd never gotten the hype about boys in general, and she'd spent countless sleepovers eye-rolling with Tara while Amber and Kat gushed over their boyfriends. But at the same time, she'd always felt ready to date someone... just not any of the boys she knew.

And she'd not been happy at all when Tara had started dating Oliver. She'd attributed that to feeling left behind and left out, but when Tara had tried to include her, she'd still spent more time disliking Tara and Oliver together than trying to make a romantic effort with Lucas. So maybe she hadn't been upset because she was the only one without a boyfriend. Maybe she'd been upset because Tara *did* have one.

Her hands tightened on the steering wheel and she felt like crying. She hated that Lindsay had made her think about this. She'd been perfectly fine just not dating anyone. Now here she was, genuinely contemplating the idea that she might like girls.

She'd really just never given a thought to being gay before. At Riverbank, gay people weren't necessarily treated like complete pariahs, but they were still outcasts. Still considered "weird". And Valerie wasn't weird; she was just like anyone else. So she couldn't possibly be gay.

But Tony wasn't that weird either, and neither was Nathan. And Lindsay was one of the most normal girls she knew. Lindsay was *cool* at their school. But she probably wouldn't be if everyone knew the truth about her. And Amber would hate her.

Amber would probably hate Valerie, too.

Valerie straightened up and shook her head, brushing her thoughts aside. She'd never done anything with girls before, and Lucas was just one guy. In a world full of billions of boys, how could she possibly rule out all of them after kissing only one? Surely there was someone she'd like. But with those odds, she had to admit it was possible that there were some girls out there she'd like as well. So maybe she was bisexual. Maybe nearly everyone was, to some degree, and most people just had a strong preference for the opposite sex.

She thought back to kissing Lucas. She hadn't liked it, but it definitely had to be a stretch to reject *all* guys because of one, right?

Then she thought about Tara. She tried to imagine what it'd be like to kiss her. Her stomach fluttered slightly, but there was something distinctly uncomfortable that filled her chest. Tara was her best friend. As pretty as Tara was, maybe they *had* at least partially crossed the threshold into sisterville over the course of the past month, now that Tara was dating Oliver and Valerie was spending most of her time with Lindsay.

She thought of Lindsay next. Lindsay, who actually liked girls, and was pretty and popular and kind, even if she had gotten herself involved in something Valerie wished she hadn't. Lindsay was probably a good kisser. She had the kind of confidence boys went crazy over.

She felt the butterflies in her stomach flap harder this time, and her heart began to beat faster. She thought of how nice it was when Lindsay hugged her, and how comfortable she felt when it was just the two of them hanging out together. She tried to picture kissing Lindsay, the way she'd imagined kissing Tara. Then she had to abort that thought when her cheeks began to flush. Suddenly, kissing Lindsay sounded a lot better than kissing Tara *or* Lucas.

She swallowed hard and tried to shake the thought off. She needed to take a day to think about all of this. She knew that being gay wasn't a choice, but she couldn't help but feel that if she decided she didn't like girls, maybe the thoughts would just never come back. But she wanted to at least make an educated decision.

She reached for her phone and saw she had a massive apology text from Lindsay. Remembering Lindsay was probably still in the light booth, she lifted her phone to her ear and called her.

Lindsay answered on the first ring. "Val, I'm so, so sorry."

"You're really really sorry?" Valerie questioned, emphasizing the second "really".

"You have no idea how bad I feel. I really didn't mean to say what I said, seriously."

"Do you feel bad enough to come meet me by my car and skip school with me?" Valerie questioned simply, and then waited.

She didn't have to wait long. Lindsay seemed perplexed, but she replied, "...Okay?"

"See you in a minute," Valerie replied, and then hung up.

She had a plan in mind, and was still busy outlining it when Lindsay showed up. Valerie unlocked the car doors and let her into the passenger's seat. "I'm confused," Lindsay admitted. "Are you okay? What's going on?"

Valerie sat in silence for a moment as Lindsay watched her with concern. Finally, she forced herself to ask the question on her mind. "How did you know you liked girls?"

Lindsay's expression immediately softened. "Oh, Val... I'm so sorry..."

"You don't have to apologize anymore. I just want to know."

Lindsay sighed, then sat back in her seat and took a minute to collect her thoughts. "I was thirteen, I think... and I had this friend. Her name was Kylie. She had an older brother and she knew where he hid this bottle of wine he'd gotten from a friend, and so one night when I was over, we stole it and drank a ton of it. And she decided that since we'd both never kissed anyone we'd be bad at it when it came time to kiss a boy, so... we kissed. And I really didn't see the point of kissing boys after that." She laughed a little, and added, "Then we turned fourteen and she got a boyfriend and I was crushed, so that helped cement it a bit as well."

"You've never tried kissing a guy?" Valerie asked.

Lindsay shook her head. "Not beyond pecks. And I didn't need to. Just like straight guys know they don't want to kiss other guys, I know it's not what I'm interested in either."

"You kept it from us for a month..." Valerie realized, looking over at her with surprise.

"That's nothing," Lindsay replied, shrugging. "I kept it a secret for ages back at home. Didn't tell my mum until just last year."

"Wasn't that hard?"

"Yeah. But I wanted to be sure she and my dad would still love me." Lindsay let out a sigh. "I'm not saying it's easy. But I'm happy with myself, you know? My family loves me, and I've had my fair share of dates, so a couple of comments here and there is hardly going to make me wish I'd spent the past three years letting guys I wasn't interested in have a go at me." She reached over and nudged Valerie. "But you aren't me, you know? And I don't know everything. I saw what I saw, but... you know yourself the best, okay?"

"I feel like I don't know anything about myself anymore," Valerie admitted.

"Well... maybe we need to help you get a better idea of who you are," Lindsay suggested. "And I bet I know just the place to start."

With that, she reached into Valerie's purse, found the keys to her car, and then leaned over and slid them into the ignition.

CHAPTER ELEVEN

Lindsay's scream echoed across the field as Valerie rushed forward, planted her foot, and swung her other leg forward toward the small soccer ball resting on the grass in front of her. Lindsay quickly turned her body away and tucked her arms in against her chest, trying to make herself as small as possible despite that fact that she was supposed to be defending the net behind her. The ball soared... completely off to the side, missing the right goalpost by several feet.

Lindsay straightened up and joined Valerie in watching the ball roll away. "Football star, you are not," she admitted.

"Soccer," Valerie corrected with a small smile.

Lindsay produced a folded sheet of paper from one pants pocket and a pencil from the other. Then she crossed out where she'd written "football". Above it, "cosmetology", "bowling", and "knitting" were both already crossed out as well. "Next is 'laser tag'."

"I thought I told you not to write that one down!" Valerie protested. "And anyway, I can't afford it. We blew all our money on three games of bowling."

Lindsay let out a mock-sigh. "I thought you were rich. That indoor swimming pool your neighborhood has access to makes you seem pretty rich. Speaking of, I could use a good swim, if you'd let me borrow one of your suits."

"Okay," Valerie agreed. "But this is the last thing we're trying. I'm sick of being bad at things."

"You weren't bad," Lindsay insisted as they moved to retrieve the soccer ball and then headed back to Valerie's car. "They're just not your calling."

"Well, I don't really see how finding my calling will help me with the fact that I'm having a massive sexuality crisis here," Valerie sighed out. It made her feel sick to her stomach to even say the words.

"Then you're missing the point," Lindsay explained. "There's more to you than who you date. And you have way too much free time; you're gonna drive yourself insane with overthinking this if we don't get you a hobby."

"So you're trying to distract me?" Valerie questioned. "That doesn't seem productive."

"No, I'm trying to show you that 'Valerie discovered she is good at X today' will have a much bigger impact on your life in the long run than 'Valerie discovered she may like girls today'. Being gay is only one small facet to the complex organism that is myself, and if you do like girls, it will be equally irrelevant to ninety-nine percent of your life. Being good at swimming, however, could impact everything. Maybe you'll get into college on a swimming scholarship, get good enough to go the Olympics, and become the female Michael Phelps: a world-renowned Olympic swimmer. Much more impactful than just kissing a girl, right?"

"Okay, okay, I got it," Valerie retorted, rolling her eyes. "You're trying to make me feel better, yada yada." Lindsay grinned over at her as they began the drive back to Valerie's house, and Valerie added, "No need for any more massive speeches."

They picked up two bikinis from Valerie's house and then headed just down the street to the indoor pool, where Valerie entered the code to get through the front door. They changed in separate stalls in the locker room, and then headed out to the pool together wrapped up in towels. It was deserted, which was unsurprising given the time of day.

"This is awesome," Lindsay admitted. "I bet the water's really warm."

"It is," Valerie confirmed, walking over to a nearby table and setting her stuff down. She hesitated only briefly before removing her towel. Lindsay was busy dipping her toes into the water, and she looked over at Valerie with a grin.

"So warm…"

Without warning, Lindsay dropped her towel and jumped in, resurfacing a moment later and wiping her hair from where it clung to her face. "Come on!" she urged, and Valerie sighed, moving to sit down at the edge of the pool. She dipped her legs in, enjoying the warmth for a moment before Lindsay swam over and grabbed at her arm, yanking her in.

Valerie went under the water and came up sputtering, then glared at Lindsay even as the other girl moved her hair out of her eyes for her. When her vision was cleared, she saw Lindsay was still smiling, unfazed.

"So… ready to find out if you're Olympics material? How about a lap around the pool?"

"I'm not doing a lap around the pool," Valerie told her simply, already moving back to relax against the wall. They were in a shallow area, where the water came up to their shoulders.

Lindsay shrugged. "Suit yourself. But now you'll never know what could've been…"

Before Valerie could respond, Lindsay ducked underwater and swam away, moving through the water much more naturally than Valerie felt she ever could.

Valerie herself only swam around a little, mostly staying in the same shallow area while Lindsay somersaulted, dived, and dipped in the water, clearly not new to swimming.

"You're good at everything," Valerie eventually complained. "It's annoying."

Lindsay paused just as she was about to make a running leap into the pool, then put her hands on her hips and stood there, dripping wet in her borrowed bikini. Valerie resolutely kept her eyes on Lindsay's face as the other girl replied, "I am not."

"You've acted before," Valerie begun, counting off on her fingers. "You're a great swimmer. You make friends with everyone you meet. I mean, you've been here for a month and everyone loves you."

"Not everyone," Lindsay corrected.

"Well, almost everyone. And we can stop acting like we both don't know you're completely gorgeous…" She trailed off and sighed. "The only people who don't like you are jealous of you."

"Well, I'm also terrible at every sport *other* than swimming, as today has proven," Lindsay pointed out. "And today is also living proof that I often stick my nose where it doesn't belong. Sometimes I'm not a very good friend, and then there's the whole gay thing, which shouldn't be considered a flaw, yet is anyway because people are jerks."

"How are you not a good friend?" Valerie asked.

Lindsay jumped into the pool, and Valerie had to wait until she resurfaced for a response. "I left you to fend for yourself at Hannah's party."

Valerie pulled a face. "So? I can take care of myself."

"That doesn't mean I shouldn't have helped," Lindsay retorted. "I knew what the situation would be like for you and I decided to get drunk and go dance with other people anyway."

"You came and found me."

"Yeah, once I finally realized I was being a bad friend. But it took a while."

Lindsay swam closer as Valerie relaxed against a wall, and Valerie pointed out, "None of my other friends showed up either."

"They didn't know what I knew."

Valerie's eyebrows furrowed as Lindsay finally stopped just in front of her. "And what did you know?"

Lindsay shrugged. "That you'd be uncomfortable around guys. That you might feel pressured to dance with them. But this girl asked me to dance… and I'm sure it was for the attention, on her part… but she was cute, and so I said yes, knowing what I knew."

"Did you at least have fun?"

Lindsay considered it. "It was alright, I guess. Better than with guys."

"Better how? You've danced with guys?"

Lindsay nodded. "Sometimes. When there aren't any girls around and there's no pressure to do anything but dance. Girls are softer, gentler..." She trailed off, and something in her expression changed as she finished, "I really like that."

Valerie swallowed hard, suddenly aware of how close she and Lindsay were. "Okay," she forced herself to say, just to be talking.

"If there's another party, I can show you," Lindsay offered. "I know it might be scary at first, but people will just think we're messing around. They always do."

"You'd dance with me," Valerie repeated suspiciously, not quite convinced.

"Why wouldn't I?"

"I don't know. Because I'm awkward and..."

"Pretty?" Lindsay finished, giving her a small smile. "You are, Val. Guys notice you. You just don't care to notice them back."

She moved even closer, and reached up to tuck a wet strand of hair behind Valerie's ear. Valerie tried and failed to swallow. The lump in her throat felt enormous and her heart thundered in her chest.

Lindsay's hand left her ear but maintained contact with her skin, her finger tracing her jaw at an achingly slow pace until eventually she cupped Valerie's cheek in her hand. Their gazes locked and Valerie felt her entire body buzz with anticipation. The butterflies in her stomach were at an all-time high and she was worried she'd faint if her heart didn't slow down soon. She'd never, ever gotten close to feeling anything like this before.

Lindsay made it worse by extending her thumb up and brushing it over Valerie's bottom lip. Valerie immediately closed her eyes, exhaling slowly, and she felt the water rush past her sides as Lindsay moved in closer. She was surprised to feel Lindsay's lips by her ear a moment later.

"I really, really wanna kiss you right now," Lindsay admitted. "Is that okay?"

Valerie hesitated. This was so much for just one day. But there was no doubt that her body was reacting to Lindsay in a way it had never reacted to anyone else before. They'd done nothing but stand together in close proximity and she'd felt a hundred times more than she'd ever felt with Lucas. If this wasn't attraction —wasn't proof she had a crush- then she didn't know what was.

She nodded, and finally found the ability to swallow. Lindsay was already moving away from her by the time she'd even started to nod, though. Their bodies grew further apart, and Lindsay made eye contact with her and said, "No experiments, okay? You have to be sure." Then she kissed her on the cheek, sending a warm feeling spreading throughout Valerie's insides, and fell backwards into the water, twisting her body around and swimming away.

CHAPTER TWELVE

The semester wore on at an achingly slow pace. Valerie tried her best to split her time between Lucas, Lindsay, and her other three friends, but found herself increasingly giving hanging out with Lindsay top priority. She couldn't help it; it was too easy for them to relate to each other, and she was learning a lot about herself from Lindsay. Her massive urge to be friends with Tara back in Kindergarten suddenly made a lot of sense, and she'd long since realized why she'd always felt pressure to look nice around other girls her age. She'd thought at first that it was some form of competitiveness, but Lindsay's explanation of what she herself had felt while exhibiting similar behaviors had hit the nail on the head for Valerie.

It was particularly hard spending time with Lucas at first, but at last she sensed that his smiles were becoming less and less faux around her, and that he genuinely was doing a good job of moving on to another girl. Whom, exactly, she had no clue, but whoever it was, she was highly thankful for their presence in Lucas's life.

Auditions for "A Winter Wonderland" were held, and the final cast was posted outside the auditorium door on a Friday afternoon, just before the final bell rang. An hour later, Valerie's phone buzzed on her nightstand. It was a text from Tara, and it said, *"COME OVER NOW. 911."*

Tara wasn't the type to be overly dramatic, so Valerie immediately knew something was wrong, and hurried out to her car to make the drive to

Tara's house.

When she arrived, Tara's mother told her, "Lindsay's out with a friend at the moment, but Tara and Kat are up in Tara's room."

"Thanks, Mrs. Davis," she replied, and proceeded to climb the stairs to Tara's room. She knocked on the door and it immediately swung open. Valerie registered muffled sobs coming from inside even as Tara sighed with relief upon sight of her.

"Thank God," she mumbled, and yanked Valerie closer, whispering, "Kat's a wreck. She lost that part in the play to Lindsay."

"Shit," Valerie hissed out, completely unsure about how to handle Kat, who was lying on Tara's bed with her face pressed into a pillow.

"Nick drove her here. He said he spent half an hour trying to cheer her up. He got the other lead."

Valerie's eyes widened in understanding, and then she winced as Kat let out a particularly loud sob. She hesitated for a moment, and then moved to sit down next to Kat on the bed.

"Kat, it's Val," she said gently as Tara paced back and forth, watching them. "Tara just told me what happened."

"He doesn't even care that he's kissing her," Kat cried, her speech muffled by the pillow.

"Nick? I'm sure he does. You know he'd rather kiss you," Valerie tried, exchanging a lost look with Tara. "And I bet Lindsay only got the part anyway because of her accent. You have way more acting experience."

"You don't really believe that," Kat protested, rolling over onto her side and sniffing loudly as she stared at Valerie. "You're just saying that to try and make me feel better."

Valerie didn't know how to reply to that, so she asked instead, "I thought you didn't mind the competition?"

"I didn't. I don't," Kat retorted. "I just… I guess I didn't know how much it'd suck until it actually happened. Now I'm stuck being the understudy while she gets to kiss my boyfriend."

"Kat's third-billed now," Tara pointed out. "She got the next biggest role in the play, after Lindsay and Nick."

Valerie couldn't help but laugh at that, and even Kat gave them a small smile as she dabbed at her eyes with a tissue. "So you're totally gonna steal the show. Don't worry about it. And Lindsay will teach you how to do a British accent, and Nick will probably complain constantly about having to kiss her."

"Well, I doubt that," Kat mumbled. "She's way prettier than me."

"Of course she's not," Tara argued, jumping in there. "And Nick adores you. He won't even enjoy it."

"And neither will Lindsay. I promise," Valerie assured Kat.

"How can you promise that? He's hot; she's hot. Sounds like it'll just be a smorgasbord of hot make out sessions for them while I sit in the corner and practice my shivering for my role as a poor little girl in rags who can't find her stupid cat."

"At least you're not playing the cat," Tara pointed out. "Kat the cat. That'd be awkward."

As Kat glared at Tara, Valerie wished for a moment that she could tell her friends that Lindsay liked girls, and therefore would definitely not like kissing Nick. But she'd promised Lindsay she wouldn't say anything, and Lindsay had promised in return that she'd keep the fact that Valerie was questioning her own sexuality a secret. There was no way Valerie was going back on her promise.

"Nick loves you," she finally said. "Everyone knows that. Even Lindsay knows it. It'll be fine."

The next Monday, she was only able to snag a few minutes in the light booth with Lindsay. The roles being assigned signaled the end of sitting around doing nothing in Drama and the beginning of official play rehearsals. But before they began, she couldn't help but ask Lindsay, "So isn't it a little weird that you've never really kissed a guy before and now you're kissing the boyfriend of a girl who's not only my friend, but also kind of your friend now, too?"

"Absolutely," was Lindsay's simple response, and then she flashed Valerie a grin and left the light booth to go take the stage instead.

Valerie'd highlighted the lighting instructions throughout her copy of the script, but she wasn't needed for the first few practices, as they mostly consisted of organizing where the actors would come from and where they would position themselves throughout the duration of the scenes, a process which Ms. Merriweather called "blocking".

As the scenes were blocked onstage and the students recited their lines, Valerie quickly saw why Lindsay had beaten out Kat for the main role. Kat was an amazing actress, but Lindsay glowed. She brought life to everyone she interacted with onstage, as though watching her acting pushed everyone else to do their best as well. Nick was decent, too, but Valerie couldn't help but think that the two leads should've been Lindsay and Kat, and absolutely would've been, had one of them been a boy or had the two leading roles both been female. The latter idea was particular intriguing to Valerie, who couldn't help but wonder why there weren't more gay plays, or books, or movies out there. At least, she hadn't heard of any.

And just like that, she was sent down a wormhole of LGBT facts and pop culture phenomena. She soon learned, with the help of the internet and Lindsay, that gay marriage was legal in less than half of America's fifty states - a fact which she was baffled by, as she'd been sure it was legal in all fifty - that Olivia Wilde should pretty much always play bisexual, and that a certain lovable tennis player's dramatic death by breast cancer was never, *ever* to be spoken of.

She marathoned show after show in her spare time, taking breaks between them to check out whatever lesbian movie Lindsay recommended. Some of them were funny, some sad, some terrible, and some actually quite good.

One Saturday night, Lindsay came over to Valerie's to spend the night, and after the rest of Valerie's family had gone to bed, they sat down together on the living room couch for a quiet screening of a movie about a lesbian spy who falls for her arch-nemesis. December was nearing its end, so they were smack-dab in the middle of winter, and even with the heat on, a blanket was absolutely necessary to keep warm. That left them huddled together on the couch watching two pretty girls flirt with each other on the television. To ease the tension, Valerie tried to make conversation.

"What did Tara think of you coming over here?" she asked. She'd gone to Tara's house to pick Lindsay up herself, and although Tara hadn't seen her, she'd assumed Lindsay had told her where she was going.

"She thinks I'm out with a friend, actually," Lindsay corrected. "She was trying to be all coy about it, asking who I was going out with and everything. In all actuality, we're not spending time together until tomorrow, though."

"A friend?" Valerie echoed. "Is this *the* mysterious friend I've heard about you hanging out with?"

Lindsay let out a laugh. "He's not mysterious!"

"It's a 'he'?"

"Don't act so surprised," Lindsay insisted. "Yes, I've made a friend outside of your clique of girls. I think Tara thinks I'm shagging someone tonight."

"Shagging. Like getting laid," Valerie stated, but raised a questioning eyebrow.

"Yes. So when I don't come home until tomorrow, I get to insist I wasn't having sex tonight, and then she won't believe me and I'll be the talk of the school."

"All of this to hang out with me," Valerie acknowledged, outwardly impressed even as Lindsay sent her a sweet smile.

"Of course." Lindsay glanced to the television and turned serious, nudging Valerie with her elbow. "Oh, this is a good part. Watch. And stop stealing the blanket!"

"It's too small," Valerie laughed out, but focused her gaze on the television even as she felt Lindsay scoot closer to her. Their shoulders brushed and then didn't separate, and Valerie only half paid attention as one of the girls on the TV screen tried to kiss the other, only for the second girl to chicken out at the last second and run the other way. "Awkward," she muttered, and felt Lindsay shake with silent laughter beside her.

She shifted slightly, still facing the television screen, but she couldn't help but glance to where her arm and Lindsay's arm extended from their touching shoulders to down under the blanket. She knew their hands had be close to touching, and no sooner had the thought crossed her mind then she felt Lindsay's hand brush across the back of hers. She breathed in sharply, just loudly enough that she thought maybe Lindsay heard it.

A minute later, the backs of their hands brushed again, and then again a few seconds after that. Valerie stayed stock-still, barely paying attention to the movie now. It was like she could feel the electricity between Lindsay's hand and hers, but she felt silly even thinking about it like that. They were just *hands*. They were two seventeen-year-old girls; surely this was a little juvenile.

Lindsay moved her hand again –purposefully, Valerie now understood- and this time, when the backs of their hands touched, Lindsay gently slid her hand underneath Valerie's wrist, then brought her hand back toward Valerie's again. Their palms touched and Lindsay slid her fingers through the gaps between Valerie's, lacing their fingers together and then squeezing lightly. Valerie's pulse quickened.

Lindsay stopped there, probably sensing Valerie's nerves. They held hands until their palms were sweaty, and after the movie was over, Lindsay slept on the couch and Valerie retired to her bedroom, where she got very little sleep, if any at all.

The next morning, Valerie's mother made them breakfast and asked them about their plans for the day.

"I'm going out with a friend," Lindsay told her honestly.

"Ooh, and is this friend a boy?" Mrs. Marsh asked. Valerie rolled her eyes silently.

"Yes," Lindsay told her, and didn't have time to say anything more before Valerie found herself face to face with a pointed look from her mother.

"Lindsay's hasn't even been here for two months and she's already going out on a date."

"Oh, it's not date," Lindsay was quick to correct. "We're just friends. Val's even welcome to come, if she wants."

Valerie let out a sarcastic laugh. "Uh, definitely not. I'm not third-wheeling."

"You wouldn't be third-wheeling. You'd be keeping me company," Lindsay assured her. "I like having you around."

"You should get out more," Valerie's mother concurred. "I've been worried about you. You just sit around on that computer of yours, watching who-knows-what on that thing. Get some exercise."

"We're going to the school gym, actually," Lindsay cut in there, shooting Valerie a triumphant look when her mother turned away from them. Valerie glared back at her. "My friend's one of the school's football players so he said he can get us in. There's supposedly a vending machine inside with Gatorade at half-price."

"I could go to the store and get Gatorade," Valerie brushed off.

"But can you get a workout at the store? Probably not."

"I don't want a workout."

"Nonsense," Mrs. Marsh said, ending their argument. "Your friend wants you to go out, Valerie, and she's still new to your school. Stop holing yourself up in here and keep her company."

With that said, Mrs. Marsh took their plates to the kitchen, leaving Valerie free to glare at Lindsay from across the table. Lindsay just smirked in response, and told her, "Don't be so pessimistic, Valerie. Maybe female bodybuilding's your calling."

"Maybe shacking up with a gross beefcake from the football team is yours," she retorted, which only made Lindsay laugh at her.

CHAPTER THIRTEEN

As it turned out, Dustin wasn't a gross beefcake. He was thin despite being muscled, and was hardly even a football player, actually. He played second-string quarterback, which meant he hardly got to spend time on the field at all, and was really only a part of the team by title alone. The result was that Valerie actually hadn't really heard of him, but she could tell immediately that he was nicer than most of the football players, mostly because he didn't seem annoyed that Valerie was joining him and Lindsay. In fact, he seemed happy to have her along.

"It seems like he just genuinely wants to be your friend," Valerie later told Lindsay as they waited at the door for Dustin to come let them inside the gym. He claimed to have his own special way of getting inside, but insisted upon keeping it a secret.

"Told you," Lindsay replied. "He's just a nice guy. We met in my Civics class."

"Isn't that a freshman class?"

"Yeah, I didn't say he was smart," Lindsay admitted. The door in front of them opened before Valerie could reply, and Dustin grinned at them.

"Welcome, ladies."

They entered the gym and Lindsay wrinkled her nose as Valerie waved at the air. "It smells like sweat in here, Dustin."

"Yeah, one second…" Dustin looked around for a moment until he spotted a bottle of air freshener on one of the benches. After a massive spraying session, he clapped his hands together and looked to Lindsay for instruction. "So what do you wanna try first?"

Why Lindsay was choosing now of all times to try getting into shape, Valerie wasn't sure, but she seemed to be taking it seriously, because she immediately selected the small weights nearby. Valerie refused to join her, and took a seat on one of the benches while Dustin walked Lindsay through basic weight-lifting.

That turned out to be a very good decision. Lindsay was dressed in a tight tank top and equally tight shorts, with her hair pulled back into a messy ponytail, and it was extremely hard not to watch her lift weights. It wasn't long before Valerie gave up on being subtle and just stared openly at her, and it wasn't long after *that* that Lindsay noticed and shot her a wink. Embarrassed, Valerie tried to pay more attention to Dustin, and as a result, she learned a lot more than she cared to about toning biceps and triceps and quadceps and however many other –ceps there were.

Eventually, Lindsay got the hang of it and Dustin turned his attention to Valerie, and then, much to her horror, approached her and declared, "This machine beside you is called the deadlift. You just grab onto the bars and pull up, lifting with your thighs, not your back. Like this." He demonstrated, squatting down and then grabbing the bars with his hands, then standing straight up. The weights came up with him, and then dropped back down with a clang when he released the bars. "Now you try."

"Oh no, that's okay," she replied quickly, but he was already busy reducing the weight on the machine.

"Don't worry, I'll walk you through it," he insisted, waving her over. Grudgingly, she got up and moved to him. To her surprise, he turned her around so that he was standing directly behind her, and then gestured to the bars before her. "First, you're gonna bend your knees just slightly. But make sure you have a wide enough stance to lift with."

She planted her feet far apart and then squatted in her best impression of a sumo wrestler, which made Dustin laugh. "Not like that. Here." To her surprise, his hands went to her hips and he held her in place, then tapped at her thigh and held his hand a few inches away from it. "Move out until your thigh is at my hand."

As she obeyed, she saw Lindsay stop lifting weights to stare at them. Growing a little amused, she let Dustin's hand make contact with her thigh, and then repeated the motion with his other hand and her other thigh. Out of the corner of her eye, she noticed Lindsay still watching.

"Keep your back straight," Dustin directed, placing one hand gently on her shoulder and another on her back. "And then grab."

Under his guidance, she grabbed the bars and then straightened up, coming to a full stand as she lifted the weights. "Perfect!" She could hear the grin in Dustin's voice, and smiled a little herself. "Now just do four more reps, and repeat that three times for a total of fifteen reps." Her smile died instantaneously, and then she scowled when she heard Lindsay laugh at her.

Thankfully, it wasn't long before they finally gave up on the gym and went for ice cream just down the street. She and Lindsay found a table while Dustin took their money and went to go order for them.

"So why did we just go to a gym, again?" Valerie asked.

"It's December, which means it's almost January," Lindsay explained. "I'm getting a head start on my New Years' resolution: to get into shape."

"That's literally everyone's New Years' resolution," Valerie pointed out.

"I never said I was unique."

They sat in silence, watching Dustin order, until Lindsay spoke up again. "So I guess that mystery's solved, then," she said matter-of-factly, and when Valerie looked confused, she clarified, "He's into brunettes."

"What?"

"What else could that have been? I've never seen someone so handsy on a first date before."

"This is not a date," Valerie hissed, much to Lindsay's amusement.

"It would be if I weren't here. And I didn't see you complaining." She raised an eyebrow in silent question. "What do you think of him?"

Valerie shrugged, confused. Dustin was nice enough, and had managed to avoid coming across as creepy despite his earlier behavior, but she'd thought Lindsay... well, she and Lindsay certainly weren't just friends, were they? Yes, some time had passed since Lindsay had asked to kiss her, but

113

they'd held hands last night.

Valerie sighed quietly, realizing how juvenile last night still seemed. They weren't in middle school. She'd held hands with other girls before. Other girls who were just her friends. Maybe she'd been overthinking it, and Lindsay had decided that Valerie was a waste of time. Crushing on a girl in sexuality limbo was probably frustrating, assuming the way Lindsay had felt before could even be considered a crush. They hadn't really talked about their feelings at all since that day in the pool, actually.

"Well, he definitely seems into you," Lindsay continued, pulling Valerie from her thoughts.

"So what do you think I should do?" she asked.

It was Lindsay's turn to shrug, but she resolutely avoided looking Valerie in the eyes. "Whatever you want to do, Val. It's your life. Your decision."

"What if I don't know what I want?" she replied, but Dustin showed up before Lindsay could respond.

"One medium chocolate cup and one small vanilla cup," he declared, handing them their ice cream and then sitting down at their table with his own cup. "And here's your change, ladies."

"I like this place," Lindsay decided, glancing around them. "We should come here more often. This could be, like, our new place to hang out."

"The three of us?" Dustin clarified. He grinned at Valerie. "I could definitely be down with that."

She forced a smile back, but her mind was still on Lindsay. She felt hurt that Lindsay could just brush aside whatever they had between them. Because there definitely *was* something, at least on Valerie's end. And she could sense things weren't one-sided with them, no matter how nonchalant Lindsay was trying to be about it now. Sure, Valerie wasn't sure if she preferred boys or girls or both equally or one ninety-percent of the time or *whatever*, but that didn't change that one look from Lindsay could give her butterflies.

Dustin took them both back to Valerie's house around four o'clock, and Lindsay turned down his offer to give her a ride back to Tara's house. Valerie was pretty certain Lindsay was putting off an inevitable interrogation from Tara.

They went up to Valerie's room to shower and change, and Valerie sat on her computer while she waited for Lindsay to finish up in the bathroom, surfing Facebook but not really paying attention to the screen. The more she thought about the possibility that she'd misread the situation between her and Lindsay, the more her stomach churned. By the time Lindsay was out of the bathroom, she felt sick.

Lindsay noticed, and almost immediately asked her, "Are you okay, Val? You look a little pale."

"'M fine," she managed to mumble, but Lindsay only drew closer and sat down next to her on the bed.

"You don't look fine," she pointed out, pressing a hand to Valerie's forehead. "But it doesn't seem like you have a fever."

"Why do you want me to go out with Dustin?" Valerie blurted before she lost her nerve. Lindsay paused, looking confused at first, and then concerned.

"When did I say that?"

"Well, you implied it."

"No I didn't. I said you should do what you want."

"So what if I wanted to go out with him? You'd want me to do that?"

Lindsay opened and closed her mouth for a moment, then shook her head abruptly. "I think you misunderstood…"

"Yeah, obviously," Valerie retorted, her voice sharp. "But I'm not sure exactly *what* I misunderstood."

"What's that supposed to mean?"

"I don't know. You tell me."

Lindsay let out a short, unamused laugh, and glared at Valerie. "Why are you being so passive aggressive all of a sudden? Look, if you want to hook up with Dustin, be my guest. If you don't, then don't."

"If you don't care, then…" Valerie hesitated, but pressed forward, "…then what was last night?"

Lindsay stood up slowly, taking her time to answer. She turned away slightly before she answered, "Whatever you wanted it to be."

"No, that's dodging the question. I want a straight answer."

Lindsay gave another dry laugh. "No pun intended?"

"I'm serious, Lindsay. You're holding my hand and telling me you want to kiss me...?"

"I said I wanted you to be sure."

"Sure about what?" Valerie asked, more confused than ever. She watched Lindsay close her eyes and let out a quiet sigh.

"Sure that you like me, and that you can handle this." She looked to Valerie again. "This isn't a movie, Val. People are cruel. It'd be a lot easier for you to date someone like Dustin. That's all I'm saying."

"So it's okay for you rule out guys without ever hooking up with one, but I should kiss every guy I know before I kiss you?" Valerie bit back, crossing her arms. "How is that fair?"

"That's not what I'm saying," Lindsay insisted. "I just don't want you to get hurt. You have friends and a life here. And I'll be gone in a few months. I don't want to leave you here confused and alone and with feelings you don't understand."

"Well, I'm not alone, but the rest of that already sounds accurate."

"I'm sorry. I know I started this," Lindsay apologized. "I didn't mean to come in here and screw up your life."

"You didn't screw up anything."

They fell into silence after that. Lindsay kept her eyes on anything but Valerie, and Valerie finally spoke first.

"I'll be friends with Dustin, because he's your friend. But that's all."

"Okay. That's fine. If that's what you want," Lindsay mumbled.

"What do *you* want? Do you even like me?" Valerie questioned.

Lindsay let out a short breath, and the hint of a smile appeared on her lips "Yes. Of course."

Just hearing the confirmation eased the chaos in Valerie's stomach and jump-started the thrumming of her heart in her chest. "Good," she replied, and felt a little lame as soon as the word was out of her mouth. "I mean…"

"It's fine," Lindsay cut her off through a chuckle. There was another pause, and then she changed the subject. "So, um… I'll probably need a ride soon."

Valerie felt her heart sink a little at the realization that they were done talking about whatever it was they had between them, but she nodded all the same. "Okay. I'll take you home."

CHAPTER FOURTEEN

"Thank God *someone* has some free time around here. I'd have never forced myself to get this done without someone to go with me."

Valerie forced a smile as she trailed Amber, who was practically marching from store to store in the local mall in search of somewhere that sold condoms. They were pretty much her regular gift to whatever guy she found herself with when Christmastime came along. It was a different one every year.

"Seriously, I don't know how Kat and Tara are getting their Christmas shopping done," Amber continued. "Or Lindsay. Wait, do most British people celebrate Christmas?"

"Unless Scrooge was the main character of 'A Hanukkah Carol', then yes, I think that they do."

Amber shot her a look of confusion. "You are so strange. Anyway, what should I get Tara? Clothes aren't an option, by the way. Not after I spent like thirty bucks on that *adorable* scarf for her last year and she never even wore it."

"Maybe you can double up on condoms for her and Oliver," Valerie joked dryly. Amber looked to her with wide eyes.

"Oh my God, do you really think they're having sex?"

Valerie cringed. "I don't know...? Why would I think about that?"

Amber scoffed. "Ugh, come on. You are so immature sometimes. Just because you don't think about sex doesn't mean the rest of us don't."

"I think about sex," Valerie retorted indignantly.

"With who?" Amber countered. "Not Lucas, that's for sure." She smirked. "And with yourself doesn't count, Val."

"Ha ha. Look, are you almost done? I'm actually supposed to meet Lucas here really soon."

"What? Why?"

"He wants me to shop with him, too. And I need to buy your gift." She looked down to the bags in her hands. She'd gotten a box of cigars for Lucas, courtesy of Amber's fake ID, a DVD of Kat's favorite musical, Wicked, on Broadway, a blown up family photo in a frame for her parents, a new leotard for Abby, and one-half of a necklace for Tara that said "best friends" on it. The other half was for herself. She still needed to get something for Amber and Lindsay.

"Oh, I need to buy yours, too," Amber realized. "Okay, you can go meet Lucas. Tell him I said 'hi', though."

"Okay," Valerie agreed. "Is Hannah giving you a ride back?"

"Yeah, she'll be off work soon. I'll be fine. Ciao!" Amber blew her a kiss and they parted ways, and it wasn't long before Valerie found Lucas at the food court.

"Amber says 'hi'," was the first thing she told him, just to get a rise out of him.

It worked: His nose wrinkled unpleasantly and he mumbled, "Whatever." Then he noticed the bags in her hands. "Hey, is there a present for me in there?"

"You'll have to wait and see," she replied, ducking him when he tried to peek inside one of the bags. They bought a milkshake each at the food court and then talked as they browsed the nearest shops.

"So who're you shopping for?" Valerie asked.

"You, my parents, and a couple of the guys," Lucas told her, shrugging. "It won't take long."

"None for a secret girlfriend?" she pressed.

He laughed. "I don't have a secret girlfriend, Val. You're so paranoid."

"I refuse to believe it," she insisted. "I see you on a daily basis; I can tell when you're in love."

"Okay, I am *definitely* not in love with anyone."

"But there is someone."

"There's a no one," he told her cryptically, his eyes focused on a video game store across the hallway. "No strings attached is the way to go, I'm telling you. The easiest way to get over someone is to get under someone else."

"You're such a cliché. Sleeping with a random to get over me."

He punched her lightly and she swatted his hand away. "Lindsay doesn't play video games, does she?"

"You'd know better than me," he pointed out. "You saved her for last?"

"I couldn't find anything to get her."

"Well, what does she like?"

"Swimming. England. Um… tea?"

Lucas let out a loud laugh. "Holy crap, you two are attached at the hip and you have no idea what she even wants for Christmas?"

"Shut up."

"I never pegged you for the type to obsess over the perfect gift," he admitted. "But it's very sad, so I'll help. Besides, she asked me about a gift for you."

"She did?"

"Yeah. And so I'm assuming she probably asked Tara, too."

"What did you tell her?"

"Tweezers to pull the stick out of your ass," he told her idly as they entered the video game shop. "And also to make sure you finally get laid."

"I have no words for you."

Lucas clucked his tongue in response, locating the video game of his choice and then snatching it off the shelf. "Awesome. Brody'll love this."

They left the shop after Lucas paid and made their way down a new hallway. They passed jewelry stores and clothing stores and electronic stores and everything in between, but nothing felt right for Lindsay.

"So are you going to tell me to get Lindsay laid, then?" she eventually joked dryly as Lucas bought his second gift. He laughed.

"No. Lindsay's not a virgin."

"She told you that? Since when are you two *that* close?"

"I mean, she hinted. And since I stopped hitting on her. What, did you think she was?"

"Well... no. But we never really talked about it."

"Hmm," he replied simply.

Soon, Lucas was done shopping with the exception of his gift for Valerie, and went with Valerie to find a cute top for Amber. After making her purchase, she still felt completely lost about what to get Lindsay, and ended up settling on a winter beanie she saw in the same store. It wasn't much and she felt lame for not finding something better, but it was cute, at least.

She waited in her car for fifteen minutes after that, while Lucas found a gift for her, and they drove home together while Valerie grilled Lucas on his mystery hookup. By the time they got home, she was no closer to finding out who it was than she had been back at the mall. Lucas gave nothing away, and simply mock-blew her a kiss in his best impression of Amber before hopping out of her car and heading inside his house.

Her mother was waiting for her when she got inside her own home, and she looked somber. Valerie set her bags aside and asked, "What's up?"

"I talked to my boss at the hospital today," her mother told her. "I've been offered a promotion if I work the night shift on Christmas Eve."

"Oh," she said shortly. "So it'll just be Dad, Abby, and I until how late in the day?"

"I'll get back at noon. But your father... he won't be here, either. The newspaper's had to lay off a lot of employees lately and so they're a little short-staffed at the moment. They've been getting their stories finalized closer and closer to the deadline as the days go on. So with there being no paper on Christmas Day, this is a chance to help alleviate some of the pressure by starting early on the paper for the 26th. At this point, he needs all the time he can get."

"Wait. I'm confused," Valerie replied, picking up her bags again. "What's happening on Christmas Eve, then?"

"Well, Abby's going to spend it at a friend's. So I was wondering how you'd feel about staying the night at Tara's? I talked to her parents and they're open to the idea."

"How do I feel about it?" she laughed dryly. "I feel like I can't believe we aren't even spending Christmas together."

"Valerie, you know your father and I work very hard to make time for you and Abby. You've being doing your own thing lately, and I tried to give you some space."

"Leaving me here alone on Christmas Eve is not space."

"You know that's not what I mean," her mother sighed out.

"Whatever," Valerie countered, storming off to her room.

Once there, she texted Tara to thank her for the offer, but added that she didn't want to intrude on her holiday with her family. Tara's response was to point out that Lindsay was already intruding anyway, which only made Valerie even surer that she didn't want to be at the Davis's for Christmas. She felt bad that Lindsay had to be the odd one out, though.

Their winter break came, but for Valerie, Lindsay, and Kat, that didn't mean an end to going to school. Their play was due to take place in three weeks, during the second week of January, which meant practices were frequent, and vacation from school was no excuse to stop them.

Two days before Christmas, only six of the students from their Drama class were invited to rehearsals. Nick, Kat, Valerie, and Lindsay were four of them. Tony's not-quite-boyfriend Nathan was the fifth, and the sixth was a younger freshman girl. As they soon found out, Ms. Merriweather had decided upon the theater version of a "closed set" for the day, and had invited the minimal amount of people needed to rehearse Lindsay's and

Nick's kissing scene. Kat, Nathan, and the other girl all had several lines in the scene that needed to be structured correctly around the kiss, and Valerie was needed to ensure the lighting was done perfectly from start to finish.

As Ms. Merriweather gave Lindsay and Nick stage-kissing instructions, Valerie sat in one of the auditorium chairs with Kat, whose feelings she could empathize with more than she'd admit. Kat did *not* look happy, and Valerie had a feeling she'd been dreading this very moment from the instant the roles had been announced.

"Why do they have to kiss?" Kat mumbled quietly even as Valerie frowned at Nick beside her. "Can't they just show their love through hugging or something?"

"I'm sure it'll be just a peck," Valerie insisted, trying to be rational.

"If I see tongue…" Kat warned, and didn't finish her sentence. That was probably for the best.

"Okay, places everyone!" Ms. Merriweather called, and Valerie headed up to the light booth while everyone else took the stage. They ran through everything leading up to the kiss several times before Ms. Merriweather announced, "Alright, Lindsay and Nick, follow all the way through this time. We'll just do it a couple of times today, to make sure you look natural, and then we'll move on with the rest of the scene. Start over. Val, make sure you're on time with your spotlight!"

The scene was replayed. Valerie cringed her way through the first part, which was bad enough on its own. Kat found her cat, which turned out to be Nathan, and in some sort of terrible plot twist, the other girl arrived with one-hundred thousand dollars in tow, to be awarded to Lindsay and Nick for the altruistic deeds they had done over the course of the play. Lindsay and Nick celebrated, and then Nick gave a giant speech about how the money was great and all, but what truly made him happiest about the events of that day were that he'd gotten to meet and spend time with Lindsay. Cue kiss.

Both Nick and Lindsay leaned forward. Valerie's gaze shifted from where Kat stood nearby, jaw clenched, to where Lindsay was cupping Nick's cheek, her lips just an inch from his. Valerie's stomach flopped and she felt her fist clench unconsciously at her side.

"Valerie!" Ms. Merriweather called, bringing the kissing scene to a screeching halt just before Lindsay and Nick's lips touched. Valerie's gaze snapped to her teacher. "Where's the spotlight?!"

"Sorry!" she called, her voice cracking slightly. Nick looked mildly relieved onstage, Kat was letting out an aggravated sigh, and Lindsay looked to her feet, hiding a smile. The students reset, and Valerie had to watch the whole cringe-worthy scene all over again.

Finally, it was time for the kiss. Valerie flipped the switch for the spotlight and took the lights down on the rest of the stage, leaving all of the focus on Lindsay and Nick as they closed the gap between them and kissed.

It was convincing. It was *too* convincing.

Valerie could practically feel Kat's anger radiating from across the room, but she just felt sick to her stomach. The kiss couldn't have lasted for more than a few seconds, but it still felt like an eternity before Ms. Merriweather called for them to stop. Then they had to run through the whole scene a second time and kiss again before it was finally time to move on.

Kat was ice cold as they packed their things and prepared to leave an hour later. Lindsay made the mistake of trying to apologize, and got an immediate brush-off. Kat practically stormed out of the auditorium when they were finally dismissed, and Nick trailed after her, insisting fruitlessly that he'd felt nothing and it was only for the play.

"Well, that was fun," Lindsay deadpanned when it was just her and Valerie walking to Valerie's car together. "So now Kat hates me, and I'm getting the feeling that Amber and Tara aren't massive fans of me either."

"They don't hate you," Valerie told her, although she wasn't so sure that was true at this point. "Kat's reasonable. She'll come around."

"Well, I wish Tara would, too," Lindsay retorted. "Christmas is gonna be so awkward. I'd rather just let her spend time alone with her family, you know?"

"Well, it won't be as awkward as mine. I'll be all alone."

Lindsay looked to her, alarmed. "What? You're kidding!"

"Nope. Parents are both working, so Abby's going to a friend's house. Tara's parents offered to have me but I didn't want to intrude."

"That's terrible. So you're just gonna open presents by yourself?"

"I guess so. Mom'll be back at noon on Christmas Day, at least. Anyway," Valerie continued, eager to talk about something else, "was kissing Nick as bad as you expected?"

"Kind of," Lindsay admitted. "It was like a mix of weird, gross, and nothing. But don't try to change the subject. No one should spend Christmas alone."

"It looked convincing."

"C'mon, Val. Not you, too."

"No, not me," Valerie confirmed. "I'm just saying. It looked natural. Like it came naturally to you. I mean... you looked like..." She hesitated, not realizing how she'd planned to finish that sentence until it came time to say the words: *A good kisser.* She flushed, and could tell by that way a grin slowly made its way onto Lindsay's face that she'd noticed the darkening of her cheeks.

"I looked like what?"

"Never mind."

"Oh, come on. Tell me."

Valerie sighed. "A... it's not-" She struggled for words, flushing darker when Lindsay's nose crinkled happily and her smile widened even more.

"You're cute when you're nervous," Lindsay commented idly, as if it was a perfectly natural observation to make.

Valerie sputtered for a moment and finally retorted, "I'm not telling you what I was gonna say."

"That's okay. I think I've got the general idea."

Struggling to rein her blush in, Valerie hastily changed the subject back to Christmas, deciding it was better than the current line of conversation. They got into her car and she said, "I still have to give you your Christmas gift." She'd wrapped them all days ago and had taken the time to hand them all over to her friends and family to open on Christmas Day, with the exception of Lindsay's, as she'd gone back and forth on whether or not to return it before finally resigning herself to the fact that she really didn't have any better gift ideas. "It's in the trunk of my car..."

"Give it to me on Christmas Day," Lindsay told her simply, and then turned the car radio up before Valerie could argue.

CHAPTER FIFTEEN

On Christmas Eve, Valerie's house was predictably deserted. She spent her first few hours alone finishing up the last season of her latest marathoned show home to a lesbian or bisexual female character, and was just about to go to bed and wallow in self-pity until she fell asleep, when the doorbell rang.

Confused, she crossed her house and opened the door to see Lucas and Lindsay on the other side, grinning widely at her. Lindsay had two presents in her hands, and Lucas gripped two massive bottles of wine.

"We decided to bring the party to you," Lucas explained, and then ducked inside without further ado. Valerie watched, baffled, as he collapsed on the couch, and Lindsay stepped over the threshold and smiled at her, offering her both presents.

"One's from me and the other's from Lucas," she explained. "I knew I'd be out of place back at Tara's, and Lucas can go back home anytime, so we talked about it and decided we'd spend our Christmases here."

"You didn't have to do that," Valerie told her, but was touched nonetheless.

"Sure we did. It's what friends do. And Tara's family totally understood, so don't worry about there being any hard feelings. Frankly, it seemed to me like Tara was happy to get some time with just her real family. She's missed Kara more than she lets on, I think, and I'm just another reminder that she's gone."

"Let's get drunk!" Lucas called from the living room. Valerie looked from him to Lindsay, raising an eyebrow, and Lindsay grinned.

"Also, we can't really do *that* with parents around, so… added bonus."

"I'm gonna ask a question, and it's gonna be weird because I know you'll say 'no'," Valerie warned, and then lowered her voice and leaned in closer to Lindsay. "But just for the sake of asking… We haven't entered some bizarre world where Lucas has temporarily turned you straight, have we?"

"Let me respond to that ridiculous question with one of my own: Have you already been drinking? Let me smell your breath."

"Sorry. He's just been really secretive about seeing someone, and you guys suddenly seem to know things about each other."

"Give me some credit; not all of my social interactions involve you," Lindsay explained lightheartedly. "Lucas is nice when he isn't trying to get into my pants. Which is rare, but still."

"Okay, seriously, I'm opening this!" Lucas interrupted. There was a "pop" a minute later as the cork was removed from the wine bottle. Lucas went into the kitchen, presumably to retrieve glasses, and Lindsay grinned at the dubious look on Valerie's face.

"He's leaving later," she explained. "But I'll be with you in the morning to open presents."

Valerie smiled warmly. "Thank you."

"Like I said, what are friends for? 'Friends' is being used as a very loose and not necessarily platonic term here, by the way."

"You're not my friend? What's that supposed to mean?" Valerie retorted, feigning offense. Lindsay pinched her arm playfully and moved to join Lucas as he returned to the living room, juggling three wine glasses. One of the bottles of wine was already missing a few inches of liquid, which explained the mild slur already present in Lucas's speech.

"Okay, so how about I down this whole thing and then we play Spin the Bottle?" he proposed, waving one of the wine bottles in front of himself with a grin. "Except I don't want to be embarrassed when Valerie hates kissing me, so basically we both just make out with Lindsay and everyone's happy. But mostly me; I'd be happiest."

"*Or...* and here's a wild idea," Lindsay proposed, "we *don't* do that."

"Seconded," Valerie chimed in. "Lucas, you're overruled."

"Damn."

They started slowly on the wine, sipping it as they talked about the events of their breaks and occasionally pausing to watch a good show or Christmas special if they could find one on the living room television. Almost inevitably, the conversation turned to whether or not to play Truth or Dare, and Lucas, of course, was the one to bring it up.

"C'mon... it'll be fun!"

"The last time I played that game, it got really awkward really quickly," Lindsay protested, sharing a knowing look with Valerie. "There are a lot of things I'll play, but that's not one of them."

"Would You Rather?" Lucas suggested next. "Or Strip Poker. Or we could just do body shots but with wine."

"Literally no one does that," Valerie protested the latter. "Like, it's not a thing."

"We could make it a thing. Let's spice this Christmas party up."

"That's not a statement you hear every day," Lindsay deadpanned, taking another sip of her wine. She checked the clock on the wall and declared. "It's like, three in the morning. I think you need to go to bed."

"No I..." Lucas cut himself off to yawn, and then frowned. "Well, at least open my present to you before I go, Val. It's awesome." He stumbled to his feet and moved to retrieve it from where Valerie had placed it under the Christmas tree, then came back and handed it to her. "Here. I want you to open it while I'm here."

"Okay," she agreed, excited to have an audience of two, even if it was just for one present. She looked from Lindsay to Lucas, the present in her lap, and imprinted the image into her mind. In just two months, they'd made a bigger difference in her life than anyone else she'd ever met, albeit in two completely opposite ways. And she was forever thankful to them for it.

She pulled the wrapping paper apart and saw a small box underneath. As she moved to open it, Lindsay got up and went to go retrieve her own present to Valerie from under the tree. By the time she'd sat down again, Valerie had the box open and was staring down in confusion at five small charms: A makeup brush, a bowling ball, a diving board, a soccer ball, and some sort of laser gun.

"It was Lindsay's idea," Lucas explained. "It cost a lot so I helped out and we split it."

"Here," Lindsay cut in, offering Valerie the second present. Valerie opened it, and suddenly Lucas's gift made sense. Lindsay had bought her a silver charm bracelet. "A lot changed that day that we spent together," she said. "I wanted you to always remember it, even after I'm gone."

"And I don't really know what she's talking about, but I assume that was the same day you randomly weren't around to give me a ride home after class," Lucas added, offering her an exaggerated smile and a thumbs-up. Valerie chuckled, but barely saw it through bleary vision.

"Thank you guys," she mumbled, wiping at her eyes. "I got you cigars and a stupid hat because I suck."

She heard laughter from both of them, and then found herself sandwiched in between them in a drunken, off-balance hug. "I'm excited for my hat," Lucas joked when they all finally separated. "But it's about time for me to go. See you tomorrow."

Both girls nodded their agreement, and Lucas took his leave, but not before stealing the fuller wine bottle. He let himself out and Lindsay watched the door until he was out of sight, then turned back around to Valerie. They both let out sighs, as though a weight had been lifted from them.

"Want me to put it on?" Lindsay asked gently. Valerie was nodding before the question had even been finished. She held out her arm and waited while Lindsay slid all of the charms on and then clipped the bracelet around Valerie's wrist. "There you go."

"I'm not gonna forget you," Valerie told her, eyes on her bracelet as she twisted it around and around her wrist. "You know that, right?"

"I know," Lindsay admitted quietly. "I feel like I've known you for years. It's weird. I don't even miss my friends back home nearly as much as I thought I would."

"Stay here forever. Don't switch back," Valerie joked, stepping forward to pull Lindsay into a hug. She heard Lindsay sigh, and felt her breath on her neck. Valerie shuddered just noticeably.

"I think Kara and Tara would have something to say about that," Lindsay pointed out, pulling away from Valerie at last. Valerie immediately missed the closeness, and reached out and took Lindsay's hand in hers. Lindsay looked surprised by the action. "I think you had more wine than you thought. You're not normally this forward."

"I'm not drunk," Valerie insisted, stepping closer. "I just *like* you."

Lindsay smiled, but told her, "You're a little tipsy, Val."

"I resent that accusation."

"I think Lucas isn't the only one ready for bed," Lindsay declared, and promptly turned Valerie around and steered her toward her bedroom.

Rather than protest, Valerie simply asked, "Are you sleeping on the couch tonight?"

"That was the plan."

"Don't," Valerie insisted. "It's Christmas. My bed's big enough."

"I should sleep with you because it's Christmas?"

Valerie nodded simply as they arrived inside her room, spinning around to face Lindsay again. Her vision swam just enough that she needed to clutch Lindsay's shoulder for support, and Lindsay gave her a knowing look. "Please? I won't try anything."

"Okay," Lindsay agreed, to her surprise. She borrowed a pair of Valerie's pajamas and then crawled into bed with her, and Valerie leaned over and turned off the lamp on her nightstand, leaving them lying together in complete darkness. Lindsay scooted closer until her front was pressed up against Valerie's side, then slung an arm across Valerie's stomach. They laid there for a while before Lindsay finally declared, "Your heart's beating like you just ran a mile. Jesus."

"It does that," Valerie replied hoarsely, wide awake and staring up at the ceiling. Lindsay's hand slid up to feel directly over her heart, which set Valerie's body alight with electricity. She knew her heart rate was only climbing higher.

"Val," Lindsay said quietly. Her breath tickled Valerie's ear.

"Hmm?"

"I think I'd kiss you right now if we were sober."

Valerie's heart was pounding so hard she could feel it in her ears. "That's... good," she replied lamely, and then winced at herself.

"I just want to make sure we're both totally in our right minds when it happens," Lindsay explained, and then asked, referring to her heartbeat, "God, are you ever gonna slow down?"

"Your hand's on my boob," Valerie explained. Lindsay moved it away wordlessly, her arm resting across Valerie's stomach again.

"Better?"

"No."

Lindsay chuckled against her shoulder and then gently kissed the skin there, leaving Valerie's whole body buzzing for the rest of the night.

The next morning, they woke up at ten, and Valerie elected to open most of her presents after her mother got home. With Lindsay watching, she *did*, however, open her presents from Tara, Kat, and Amber. Tara'd given her a box of Valerie's favorite and very hard to find coffee grounds, which she was absolutely elated by, Kat bought her a giant poster from her favorite musical, Les Mis, and Amber got her an expensive-looking winter coat.

She sent off a few thank-you texts and got several responses from them. Tara was adamant that they both wear their necklaces on a daily basis, which Valerie appreciated given that they hadn't been able to spend as much time together in the last couple months as they'd used to.

When she'd finished with her first few gifts, Valerie handed Lindsay her wrapped-up hat, deadpanning, "I'm sure the suspense is killing you."

Lindsay giggled as she unwrapped the hat, then grinned when she saw it. "Val, this is so cute! I'll definitely wear it!" She put it on, then, and Valerie smiled.

"That actually looks adorable on you."

Lindsay's grin widened, and she kept the hat on until it was time for Valerie to take her home.

In the car, Lindsay told her, "Tara's having a small get-together on New Year's, by the way. I was supposed to tell you. Lucas is invited, too, and I think Tara wants me to bring Dustin, which I'm happy to do because it'll finally show her that we're just friends."

"So we're having a party with Tara, Oliver, Kat, Nick, Amber, Lucas, and Dustin? I see no way that this could go wrong."

Lindsay laughed. "Right?"

After Valerie dropped Lindsay off and headed back home, Lucas came over. He didn't seem excited about the party, either, but Valerie talked him into coming, aware that his presence would probably make things less awkward. He opened his present, then, and looked genuinely confused when it actually *was* cigars.

"I thought you didn't like that I smoke?"

"Well, you like it. Christmas is about making other people happy; it's not about me."

"No, it's about Jesus," Lucas argued. "Jesus wouldn't like me smoking these, you know."

"Jesus is busy with more important things, I would think."

Lucas winked at her, grinning, and held up his cigars in thanks. "Alright, I'll see you in a few days. Time to finally have some down time now that every day isn't a shopping day."

"Bye," she told him, and let him out through the front door.

Her mother got home soon after Lucas's departure. They opened presents together, and her mother put the family picture Valerie had gotten for her up on their fireplace mantle. By the time they were done with their presents, Valerie was almost certain that this Christmas was the best she'd ever had.

She spent most of the next few days sleeping and watching TV shows online, and with the exception of another Drama rehearsal, most of her social interaction took place through texts.

Kat's dad dropped her off at Valerie's the night before Tara's party, as

133

they'd agreed to spent some time alone together over the break. They spent most of their night in Valerie's room, talking. Of course, the topic of Lindsay and Nick inevitably came up.

"It's just hard to see why there *wouldn't* be anything between them, you know?" Kat pointed out as Valerie did her best to be attentive. "He's perfect, and Lindsay's *so* pretty. Why would anyone choose me over her?"

"You have to stop being so paranoid, Kat. There's someone out there for everyone. Just look at your dad, or Tara and Oliver. And Nick's clearly meant for you. Lindsay isn't interested, I swear, and I'm sure she'll find someone else she likes."

"Oh yeah? Like who? Because Tara says she's been hanging out with Dustin from the football team, but that Lindsay keeps saying they're just friends. And if that's true, then she's free to crush on Nick."

Valerie shrugged, not quite looking Kat in the eyes. "I don't know. There could be someone else."

Kat's eyes widened. "Not Lucas, though."

"No, definitely not Lucas. Look, Kat, you and Nick are fine, okay? Just trust me."

Kat eyed her for a moment, then smirked and declared, "Valerie Marsh, you know something about Lindsay's love life that you're not telling me."

"I don't!" Valerie insisted, and immediately realized it sounded too defensive. As Kat grinned at her, she reached for her cell phone and sent a panicked text to Lindsay: *"Kat's grilling me about ur love life. What do I say?"*

"Are you texting her right now?" Kat asked her disbelievingly. "Okay, make it more obvious you're hiding something."

"It isn't my place to say," Valerie admitted.

"So you do know something."

"We really should drop this, Kat."

Her phone buzzed and she read the text: *"Is she gay-friendly and can she keep a secret?"* Her eyes widened in surprise as Kat sighed across from her. Was Lindsay implying what it sounded like she was implying?

Valerie shot back a quick response: *"Only if you can keep her secret about living with her gay dad and his bf."*

She felt bad for revealing Kat's secret, but it was only fair if Lindsay was going to give Valerie the go-ahead to reveal hers.

"You're totally getting her permission to tell me right now," Kat said knowingly. Valerie glared at her as her phone buzzed again. She opened Lindsay's text.

"Oh, wow. Well, b honest about me if u want. But only if u think she won't tell. I trust ur judgment."

Valerie was very careful about how she approached this. "You can't tell anyone," she began nervously, although she wasn't sure why she was so nervous. Kat had long since proven she had no problem with homosexuality. "And you have to let me tell Lindsay about your dad."

"Secret-bartering?" Kat questioned, raising an eyebrow. "Is this one really worth telling her mine?"

"You'll have to take that chance," Valerie replied.

Kat sighed again. "Fine. Now tell me. Which guy at our school is she hooking up with?"

"None of them." Valerie hesitated briefly, and then declared, "She likes girls."

Kat's eyes widened to the size of saucers. "No! Are you serious?"

Valerie nodded, unable to hide her amusement at Kat's reaction. Then she winced as Kat hit her.

"How long have you known and not told me, you bitch?"

"I don't know… since right around auditions for the play? Maybe a little bit before that? She made me promise to keep it a secret."

"Wow. So Nick's been kissing a lesbian. Ha! She's really hot, though." Kat looked thoughtful. "I think I just got a little bicurious."

Valerie felt a small flicker of jealousy flare up within her, and before she could stop herself, she replied, "Lindsay wouldn't be into that."

"How do you know?"

"Because I know she doesn't like experiments with straight girls." Valerie realized now, as Kat studied her intently, why she'd been so nervous about revealing Lindsay's secret. It wasn't a far jump to something Valerie absolutely did not want to get out, and right before her very eyes, the wheels turned in Kat's head and she made the jump.

"So you guys have spent a lot of time together since Lindsay got here, huh?" Kat asked carefully.

"Shut up," Valerie mumbled, mortified when she felt her cheeks getting warm. That only made them flush harder, and Kat sat with her in silence for a long moment, then reached over and took her hand, simply squeezing it once and then holding it.

"It's okay," Kat finally told her. Valerie pulled her hand away and used both hands to hide her face as she shook her head. She felt Kat's palm on her back a moment later, rubbing back and forth. "Val…"

She was overwhelmed. With Lindsay, she'd felt like they were in some sort of safe bubble together, and she could do what she wanted and figure herself out safely and with no judgment. Now that Kat knew, it made it all real, and no longer safe. People were going to find out, and they were going to talk about her. She knew she wasn't ready for that.

"I won't tell anyone," Kat said suddenly, almost as if she could read Valerie's mind. "Not even Nick. We'll blackmail each other, all three of us. If I spill about you and Lindsay being together, you guys can both tell everyone about my dad. And vice-versa."

"We're not together," Valerie couldn't help but mumble. She wiped a few stray tears from her cheeks and sat up, sniffling while Kat's eyebrows furrowed in confusion.

"But I thought…"

"We've come close, sort of," Valerie replied, shrugging. "Sometimes I think it'll happen, or that it might soon, and then it doesn't."

"Maybe she has major commitment issues," Kat suggested. "Remember my ex Kyle? I mean, he wasn't technically my ex, but, well, that was because he never actually dated me. Total commitment-phobe."

"I don't know." Valerie shrugged again. "I'm just confused all the time now."

"Well, we have our activity for the night," Kat declared, rubbing her hands together excitedly. "Tell me everything. We're gonna analyze the hell out of her every move."

Valerie felt a reluctant smile tug at the corners of her lips. "Kat..."

"I'm serious. You've never had a boyfriend to do this with before, and I don't discriminate. If you can suffer through stories about boys you don't care about for years, I can definitely spend a night talking you through your will-they-won't-they relationship with a gorgeous girl. And God, Val, you're gorgeous too... you guys would be so hot together. Like, I'm jealous of your lesbianism right now."

"Look, I don't even know if I'm... like Lindsay," Valerie admitted. "I just didn't like Lucas, and I know I like her. Does that make me gay?"

"Well, I'm not an expert on any of that," Kat told her. "But it seems to me that if you like Lindsay and she likes you, you're a little occupado in the romantic department at the moment, and so there's no reason for you to really care about who else you might like, is there?"

Valerie hadn't considered that before. "That's... a really good point."

"I know, I'm a genius. Now, have you kissed her?"

As Kat sat with her, patiently listening, Valerie told her everything. She started with the knowing looks Lindsay had shot her on the day they'd met, while she'd been talking about Lucas, and then she told Kat about the party, Lindsay's admission of liking girls in the light booth, and the subsequent day they spent together. When she got the part about the pool, Kat scoffed.

"God, what a tease."

From there, Valerie told her all about her search for gay media, and the way Lindsay had spent countless hours on her couch, watching gay TV shows and movies with her. She briefly touched on the hand-holding and did her best to cover their more flirtatious moments over the course of the past two months, and then she finished by telling Kat about how Lindsay had joined her for Christmas when she'd discovered Valerie would be spending it alone.

"Okay," Kat said on an exhale when Valerie was finally finished. "So if you lose interest, I'm dumping Nick and dating her, just so you know."

Valerie smiled, aware she was joking. "So what does it mean?"

"Hell if I know, but that was adorable. She's said she likes you, though. What's keeping her from going for it?"

"I don't know," Valerie admitted. "Lack of opportunity?"

"No way. I think maybe she's just trying to take things super slow to make sure you're comfortable," Kat suggested. "You have to show her you want the V, girl."

Valerie both laughed and cringed at her wording. "It's so weird to think about it that way."

"What, you don't wanna have sex with her?" Kat questioned disbelievingly. "I know that's not true, because I'm straight and I'd probably have sex with her under the right circumstances. I mean, not really since she's into you and you're into her, but in some alternative universe where you and Nick don't exist and I was maybe a little tipsy-"

"I got it, Kat," Valerie laughed out. "And... I mean, I would. I *think* I would." She thought of Christmas Eve, and of Lindsay cuddled up next to her in bed with her hand on her chest. "Okay, I would," she decided emphatically, making Kat laugh.

"Then let her know. Not that you would sleep with her; she has to work for that. But that you aren't scared to get with a girl."

"But I don't know that I'm not scared."

"But do you *want* to?"

"Yes. With Lindsay," Valerie told her.

"So hide the scared part and fake some bravery," Kat suggested. "You'll see her tomorrow at Tara's party! Oh my God, I'm so being your wingman. New Year's kiss, Val! It's perfect!"

"In front of everyone?" Valerie questioned, alarmed.

"I'll make sure you get some time alone," Kat assured her. "This is gonna be awesome."

They spent a few more hours talking before they went to bed, and Valerie felt almost light-headed as she laid awake and thought of everything that had just happened. It felt surreal. Kat had been so perfect, so *accepting*.

Could other people really be like that? Her parents? Tara?

Kat shifted beside her in the bed, and Valerie rolled over to face her friend when she realized they were both still awake. "Thanks, Kat," she said quietly. Kat reached over and found her hand, squeezing it briefly.

"Anytime, Val."

CHAPTER SIXTEEN

Kat insisted upon getting dressed up for Tara's party the next day.

"I want Lindsay's jaw to drop when she sees you," Kat commented as she straightened Valerie's hair in front of her bedroom mirror. Valerie took a sip of the soda in her hands. "Along with her panties." And *out* went the sip of soda.

They did makeup and chose outfits over the course of the day, and Kat put the finishing touches on her own hair just in time for them to leave.

"You two look nice," Mrs. Marsh told them on their way out. Beside her on the living room couch, Valerie's dad looked impressed, as well. "All of this for Tara? Are you sure there aren't boys coming?"

Kat fielded the question, thankfully. "My boyfriend will be there, but it's just a small get-together. Five girls and four guys."

"Okay. Have fun, girls! Don't be ninth wheel, honey," Mrs. Marsh joked.

"Oh, I will be," Valerie replied, rolling her eyes as she and Kat took their leave.

Once they were in the car, Kat asked, "Did I say the right thing? I wasn't sure…"

"You did fine, Kat. I know they care, but my parents only half pay attention to who I hang out with, anyway."

"They like Lindsay, though?"

"I think so. They definitely don't dislike her."

"Good."

They pulled up to Tara's house to find three cars already in the driveway. Inside, Tara, Oliver, Lindsay, Amber, Lucas, and Dustin were all dressed up and gathered in the living room. Valerie did the math, realizing Lucas had to have gotten a ride from Oliver, Amber, or Dustin. From the looks of things, the solution appeared to be Amber, as she was hanging all over him on one of the couches while he glared at everything in existence.

Tara took notice of Valerie and Kat first, breaking off her conversation with Oliver to stand up and greet them. "Hey, guys! You both look so pretty!"

While Tara proceeded to question Kat about Nick's whereabouts, Valerie shifted her attention to where Dustin and Lindsay had been talking on one of the other couches. Now they were both staring at her. She kind of liked the look on Lindsay's face.

Dustin, however, was the one to stand up and approach her first. "Hey, Valerie. You look really nice."

"Thanks," she replied, forcing conversation. "You do, too."

Lindsay appeared at his side a moment later, and simply offered her a small smile. As pretty as Valerie *felt*, she knew Lindsay had to have her beat. Her hair was silky and straight, and her top had a deep neckline that was only slightly more distracting then the form-fitting skirt that stopped a few inches above her knee. On top of that, she was wearing heels that made her legs look much longer than they actually were. Valerie's mouth felt dry.

"So do you have a New Year's resolution?" Dustin questioned, distracting her. "Both Lindsay and I are gonna try to get into better shape. You could join us if you want," he joked.

"Actually, I have something different in mind," she admitted, glancing to Lindsay briefly. She really wished Dustin wasn't here at the moment.

"Really? Like what?" he asked.

"Well... I haven't been assertive enough lately," she explained, hiding a smile when she saw Lindsay pause with a glass in her hand halfway to her lips. "So I'm going to try and be better at that."

"It's always fun to get what you want," Dustin agreed. She was pretty sure he was trying to flirt with her, but her attention was still subtly on Lindsay. She was downing whatever was in her glass. It was probably alcoholic, given that Tara's parents were at a party of their own for the night.

"Oh, I intend to have a lot of fun."

Lindsay abruptly burst into a fit of coughing, and Dustin looked to her, surprised, and quickly moved to pat her on the back. They drew the attention of the whole room, and at last, Lindsay waved him away dismissively.

"Sorry," she croaked, and when everyone was assured she was fine and had returned to their own conversations, she shot Valerie an alarmed look. Valerie shrugged, having no explanation she could give in Dustin's presence. She was only doing what Kat had instructed her to do, and despite it being out of character, it seemed to have at least partly worked, because Lindsay's eyes stayed trained on her for a large portion of the night.

She spent a little more time talking to Dustin, and from there she elected to save Lucas from Amber, who was getting a little too handsy.

"Please let me kiss you tonight," he begged her as soon as Amber was out of earshot. "I know you'll hate it but I hate *her*."

"Who says you have to kiss anyone?" Valerie pointed out. "There's an odd number."

"Uh, yeah, and it's five girls and four guys," Lucas pointed out. "So a girl's getting left out, unless someone wants to get lesbionic tonight."

"I'll take care of it," Valerie reassured him. "Just stay out of the way."

As midnight grew closer, she did her best to introduce Amber and Dustin and get them acquainted, while Lucas ducked in and out of the house frequently to ensure that Amber didn't get much time to talk to him. Kat, meanwhile, seemed to make it her personal mission to monitor all of Lindsay's actions and inform Valerie about the way she'd been given the once-over at approximately 11:34 pm, but luckily that stopped after Nick arrived.

Valerie took a bathroom break with just a few minutes to go until midnight, and Lindsay followed her down the hallway and waited for her to come out.

"Hey," Valerie greeted her, surprised to see her waiting.

"So Kat won't stop staring at me," Lindsay told her bluntly. "I can't tell if she thinks I'm a freak or she wants to sleep with me."

"Definitely the second one, if those are the only options," Valerie responded. "But neither. She's trying to play matchmaker. I kind of told her everything."

Lindsay raised both eyebrows. "Wait…about you, too?"

Valerie nodded. "I told her I didn't know what I was, but that I knew I liked you. We were up late last night just talking. And she promised not to tell anyone anything, lest we spill about her dad."

"Val, that's great!" Lindsay complimented, pulling her in for a hug. Valerie hugged her back, grinning. "How do you feel?"

"Nervous," she replied honestly, pulling away. "Anxious. But a little less scared that everyone will hate me. She was great."

"I'm so proud of you," Lindsay told her sincerely, giving her a warm smile. She looked Valerie up and down, then, and asked, "So Kat's playing matchmaker, huh? It's working."

Valerie held back a blush, remembering Kat's words from the night before. She needed to stay confident. "Good."

"Dustin definitely thought you were talking about him with that whole New Year's resolution line I'm positive Kat told you to say, though," Lindsay warned. "You should probably watch out for that."

"That was all me," Valerie lied. "And besides, I've got him acquainted with Amber, and Lucas is planning to mysteriously vanish from 11:59 to 12:01."

"Huh," Lindsay said, her expression thoughtful. "So Tara and Kat will definitely be kissing Oliver and Nick, and now you've got Amber kissing Dustin. And Lucas is gone. I think I see where this is going."

"Hey guys, get in here!" Tara called from the living room, but before either of them could respond, they heard Kat speak next.

"Don't worry about them, Tara. I think I heard Lindsay say she didn't feel very well. Val's probably making sure she's okay."

"They're gonna miss the countdown," Tara pointed out, but didn't pursue the issue.

Lindsay looked amused as Valerie mustered up the courage to take her hand, but that expression didn't last long. By the time Valerie had pulled her down the hallway, up the stairs, and into Lindsay's room, all traces of amusement were gone. Valerie shut the door behind them and bit her lip as she clicked on Lindsay's television and found the correct channel. The newscaster announced that the ball in Times Square was due to begin its drop in thirty seconds. It was 11:58.

They stood in silence for a moment, until Lindsay spoke. "You don't have to act brave if you're scared, you know."

Valerie realized her hands were shaking, and struggled to subdue them. "I'm fine."

"What are you scared of, Val? It's just me." Lindsay took her hand and brushed her thumb over the back of it. "You don't have to kiss me."

Valerie stayed silent for a few seconds. Fifteen, according to the timer on the television. "What if I don't like it, and what if I do?" she finally questioned rhetorically. "What does it mean if I do? What happens after a kiss ends that you actually *like*? All really, *really* scary thoughts."

"So don't kiss me," Lindsay insisted. "Wait until you're ready."

"I *am* ready. I've been ready to kiss someone I actually had feelings for since practically age thirteen. I've just never felt like that about anyone until now."

"Fifty, forty-nine, forty-eight," echoed from downstairs, and Valerie glanced at the television to see the ball slowly descending in Times Square.

"And wow is that countdown just making this more terrifying," she squeaked, swallowing hard. Lindsay rubbed her hand again as she forced herself to make them face each other. "Okay, so I'm terrified. But... you're one of the nicest people I've ever met, and so non-judgmental and pretty and caring and so even if it's going to go really really badly, in thirty seconds I'd really like-"

She barely had time to register long eyelashes and tiny freckles before a hand was on her cheek and Lindsay's lips were pressed against hers. She would've gasped if her lips weren't a little occupied the moment, and she felt as though the millions of little butterflies in her stomach had burst as she melted forward and reached out to tangle her hands in Lindsay's hair, pulling her closer.

It came naturally to her, kissing Lindsay. They were instantly in synch with each other, and there wasn't any awkward nose-bumping or excessive saliva or rough chin stubble. Lindsay was soft and gentle and careful and made Valerie's legs feel like mush. And Lindsay's lips... they tasted like vanilla lip gloss in the best kind of way, and they knew what they were doing.

They kissed long enough that Valerie lost track of time, and when Lindsay finally moved to pull away, Valerie followed her lips and kissed her again, surprising Lindsay this time. Their second kiss was a little less gentle and a little more rushed, with something deeper brewing under the surface. Valerie's sudden urge to tear all of Lindsay's clothes off gave her a pretty good idea of exactly what that something was.

A knock on Lindsay's bedroom door broke them apart, and Lindsay looked to Valerie, alarmed.

"Relax, guys, it's me," Kat called through the door. "Um... you should probably come back downstairs... everyone's starting to think Lindsay might need a trip to the hospital since she's supposedly been puking her guts up for ten minutes now."

Valerie's gaze shot to the clock on Lindsay's nightstand. It was 12:07. Beside her, Lindsay started laughing. "Be right out, Kat!" Valerie called, and then rounded on Lindsay, only to realize her legs were still jello. She collapsed on Lindsay's bed and let out a slow breath, swallowing hard. Lindsay sat down beside her, and after a moment of silence, spoke first.

"So that was interesting."

"People do this regularly," Valerie realized, thinking of how obsessed Kat was with Nick, and now Tara was with Oliver. "I get it now."

"Get what?" Lindsay asked, looking to her with amusement.

"Dating. Kissing. Sex. Everything. I feel... like I just discovered the meaning of life."

"Making out with pretty girls is absolutely the meaning of life," Lindsay concurred. "Now come on, Aristotle. Tell your legs to start working so we can go pretend we're straight."

"They're not listening," Valerie protested even as Lindsay helped pull her to her feet. "How are you okay?"

"My legs are okay," Lindsay responded simply. Valerie realized the hand still gripping hers was shaking noticeably, and slowly began to grin. "Shut up," Lindsay told her, heading off a snarky comment before it could be made. "At least it'll make me look sick."

They went downstairs together and Valerie helped a faux-sickly Lindsay sit down on the couch as everyone else looked on with sympathy. Kat, of course, was the exception, and had to hide her mouth for most of the ensuing conversations about how sorry everyone was that they'd had to miss the ball drop and hoped Lindsay would get better soon, and was it the wine or the cheese that she thought made her sick. Lindsay fielded the questions well enough, and then slowly made a miraculous recovery over the course of the night. By three in the morning, she was well enough to go to Valerie's house.

Lucas joined them on the ride home, complaining about Amber and how she'd chased him out to the backyard to kiss him, and Valerie realized that Dustin had been the odd man out for the night. She felt embarrassed for him, but not guilty.

Her house was quiet when she and Lindsay entered. The rest of her family was asleep already, and so it wasn't difficult to sneak up to her room with Lindsay in tow, and it was even less difficult to let Lindsay lock the door behind them and to change into something more comfortable.

They didn't stay in their underwear, electing instead to put on pajamas, however flimsy they might've been. And then Lindsay was kissing Valerie on her bed and Valerie's head was swimming.

"Let me know if it's too much," Lindsay told her at one point, which was basically the most useless piece of instruction ever given that everything Lindsay did and everywhere she kissed or touched was simultaneously too much and not enough.

Kat wanted every little detail the next day, and even called her while Valerie was still with Lindsay in order to get them. That was interesting.

"I can tell you some other time, Kat," she insisted as Lindsay kissed her neck. A small nip followed and she squirmed throughout Kat's response. "This Monday. The day school starts back up. I swear." She hung up and glared at Lindsay, who sat up with a grin and trailed a finger from her neck down to the center of her chest.

"This isn't stopping anytime soon, you know," Lindsay pointed out. "It's a new couple thing."

Valerie blinked up at her, unsure if she'd just heard correctly.

"New couple?"

The smile on Lindsay's face died. "Oh... I'm sorry, I just thought-"

"No," Valerie cut her off. "It's good. We just... didn't exactly talk much last night."

Lindsay's grin returned, and she leaned down and kissed Valerie until they could feel their hearts pounding hard against their chests. Breathless, Lindsay whispered, "I'm so glad I met you."

Valerie wound her arms around Lindsay's back and pulled her closer, kissing her again, and they stayed that way for the next few hours, tangled together with racing hearts and wandering hands.

CHAPTER SEVENTEEN

"First base?"

"Do you have to word it like that?" Valerie mumbled, glaring at Kat from her spot in front of the light board in the booth. Lindsay and Nick were the only ones onstage right now. They were blocking the final scene, thankfully. They'd gotten behind and the play was due for its first performance in just five days.

"What's wrong with saying first base?"

When Valerie didn't reply, Kat smirked knowingly. "Oh," she said, drawing the word out. "I get it. I'm trivializing it when it meant a lot to you because you're super head-over-heels for her, aren't I?"

"A little bit." Valerie half listened to Kat, keeping her eyes trained on the stage. She couldn't miss her lighting cue or Ms. Merriweather would freak out and make them restart the entire scene.

"Sorry. Well, I think we can establish that you two kissed. You looked high when you came downstairs at Tara's."

Her gaze abruptly shot to Kat. "I did not!"

Kat nodded. "Totally baked. You were so dazed. Amber asked me if Lucas was dealing you pot after you guys left. I told her you were probably just traumatized after watching Lindsay repeatedly hurl her guts up. Aren't I a great friend?"

"The best," Valerie replied half-heartedly. "Anyway, yes, we kissed."

"But was it like a peck, or...?" Kat trailed off expectantly.

Valerie wasn't sure how to respond. She'd never been in this situation before. It was hard to even wrap her mind around the fact that she was someone's *girlfriend* now. She was another girl's girlfriend. "Oh God, we're dating," she breathed out as it finally sank in. Kat gasped, then wrapped her arms around Valerie, squeezing her tight.

"I'm so happy for you! Who asked who out? Wait, yeah, who *does* do the asking when you're both girls?" She looked confused, then seemed to shrug her own question off. "Seriously, though, Val…"

"We kissed," Valerie told her shortly, and then hesitated, "We kissed a lot."

When she didn't say anymore, Kat raised both eyebrows. "Wait… did you two have sex?"

"Of course not," Valerie sputtered, flushing darkly. "No. God, we've been dating less than a week, Kat."

"But you've known her for much longer," Kat pointed out. "And you've liked her for much longer than a week. I don't think it's a stretch."

"It is for me." Valerie let out a deep sigh. "Just over two months ago I thought I was straight, and I was going on a date with and kissing Lucas. Now I have a girlfriend and I don't know what the hell I am. So much has changed."

"Not so much," Kat disagreed. "You tried to be with Lucas, and now you're with Lindsay. You just know more about what you like now. You're still the same Val I know and love. Just with a hot girlfriend. And once Amber pulls her head out of her ass and you decide to tell everyone about your relationship, I see many quadruple dates in the future."

"Yeah, right. Amber'll hate me," Valerie told her, long past accepting it. "I'm just glad we're going to different colleges. It'll make things easier."

"If she can't accept you for who you are, then she was never a real friend for you to lose anyway," Kat declared. Valerie shot her a small smile.

"Thanks, Kat."

"Valerie!" Ms. Merriweather roared from the stage.

"Shit!" she hissed, and hastily flicked one of the light switches. "Sorry, Ms. Merriweather!"

Valerie's afternoons were chock full of rehearsals for the next week, and then it was finally Friday night. Amber, Tara, Oliver, and Lucas all bought tickets for the first showing that night, but when Valerie asked Kat about her dad and Kenny, she explained that they always bought tickets to the Saturday matinee, when none of her friends ever showed up. Valerie, now more than ever, empathized with Kat's situation. Kat was straight, but in a way, she was living in secrecy the same way Valerie and Lindsay were.

Lindsay, Valerie soon learned, invited Dustin to the Friday night show, as the two of them had maintained their friendship easily despite Lindsay stealing away Valerie on New Year's after "getting sick". He sat in the back, dangerously close to the light booth, and when Lindsay asked Valerie to help do her makeup backstage before the play, Valerie took the opportunity to ask, "So you're still really good friends with Dustin? Why?"

"Because he's nice. And funny," Lindsay replied simply. "Why wouldn't I be?"

"Because he kind of seems like he likes me?" Valerie pointed out.

"And you like me," Lindsay told her, lowering her voice. "So his feelings are pretty moot at this point. Just let me know if he hits on you or makes you uncomfortable and I'll take care of it."

"Really?" Valerie asked, smiling as Lindsay murmured a positive response, trying to stay still as Valerie applied her mascara. "It's kind of sexy imagining you kicking his ass for flirting with me."

Lindsay pursed her lips and kissed the air, and Valerie giggled as she switched to the other eye. "Beneath this small, feminine exterior beats the heart of a warrior princess."

"Well, Xena, you have absolutely gorgeous eyes," Valerie told her quietly, moving away to get a better look when she was done with the mascara. "Wow. You are so wasted on Nick tonight."

"Don't get jealous when I kiss him tonight," Lindsay warned, her voice a whisper. "I'll be imagining it's you to make it more convincing."

Valerie grinned at her. "Okay. Make sure you let Kat know that."

"I will. Rock the lights."

They bid each other goodbye and Valerie left the backstage area under Ms. Merriweather's instructions, moving to get settled in the light booth just minutes before the play was due to start. On her way there, she caught sight of Tara and Amber, who were sitting with Lucas and Oliver. They all gave her thumbs up and she smiled back at them.

The play went off without a hitch, not counting the failings in the script itself. Lines were remembered, deliveries were on-point, and no one tripped and fell onstage. The audience "whoo"-ed appropriately at Lindsay and Nick's kiss, and Kat didn't even looked fazed as it happened. Valerie strongly suspected that had a lot to do with the fact that Lindsay was dating one of her closest female friends.

For her part, Valerie flicked switches on and off at all the right times, and that was that. It wasn't hard, but she still got her own polite applause at the end of the play.

They performed it again on Saturday afternoon, and then again on Saturday night and on Sunday afternoon. After the last performance, everyone went on a group trip to the ice cream place nearby, where Dustin had taken Lindsay and Valerie just a few weeks prior.

Valerie found herself saving a booth for Kat, Nick, and Lindsay, but Kat evidently made the executive decision to leave Lindsay and Valerie to their own devices, and sat somewhere else. That left an open side at their booth, which was eventually occupied by Tony and Nathan, after the rest of the parlor was filled and after Lindsay offered the vacant space to them.

"You guys did really well," she complimented them. Valerie nodded her agreement, trying her best to be friendly. She wondered idly if Lindsay knew that Tony and Nathan's relationship held a very similar status to their own, and if the two boys had actually given dating a try yet.

"Are you kidding; *you* did awesome," Nathan replied. He seemed much more open and comfortable in his own skin, as opposed to Tony, who just sat quietly and nodded. Tony was the Valerie of himself and Nathan, Valerie realized. And Nathan was much more like Lindsay. "And you and Nick nailed the kiss. I'm surprised Kat isn't angry at you."

"It's just acting," Lindsay replied, shrugging. "I powered through it."

"Through kissing Nick?" Nathan asked, laughing. "Honey, that's not a struggle. He's hot."

"Not my type." Lindsay shrugged again, and Nathan chuckled.

"Alright. Suit yourself."

After the ice cream, Valerie grudgingly dropped Lindsay off at Tara's house. When she got home, Lucas came jogging out of his house, and hopped into her car before she could even get out.

"Were you waiting for me? Look, Lucas, I'm not in the mood to give you a ride right now. We just got back from doing the last show."

"I know," he replied. Something about his tone made Valerie take him seriously. He looked like he had something important to say. "I need to tell you something. I want to preface it by letting you know that I'm a terrible person."

Valerie let out a sigh. "You're sleeping with Amber."

Lucas's gaze snapped to her. "What? How did you know?"

"I figured it out after New Year's," Valerie told him, shrugging. "She bought condoms for Christmas, which she always does when she's sleeping with someone. And I knew you were sleeping with someone, and then she was all over you at New Year's. Plus, she's always talked about how she thinks you're attractive. It doesn't take a genius to figure it out. So when did it start?"

"It was stupid," Lucas told her immediately. "At that party her older sister threw. I was drunk and upset and she was drunk and hitting on me after you went off with Lindsay, and I guess... in my stupid state of mind, I thought maybe hooking up with her would make you jealous, since it was your friend. Then she was actually *good-*"

"Ew, no. Skip ahead," Valerie input, cutting him off.

"Alright. Anyway, we kind of just fell into it. At first, it was nice, because even though I find her totally repulsive as a person —no offense meant to your taste in friends, of course- it was a distraction and when I was with her, I wasn't thinking about... getting rejected. And I knew she liked me. But long story short, I'm sick of her and I'm actually having to spend time with Amber the person rather than Amber the sex partner. How do I end it without incurring her wrath and potentially losing my genitals as a result?"

Valerie was quiet for a long time. Finally, she let out a breath. "You know, Lucas, I always joke about how you're a jerk, or a douchebag. But I was always joking. I know that you don't have the best home life, or the best recreational habits, but I knew you were a nice guy. This isn't okay."

"I know," he agreed immediately. "I just... I thought it was just sex for her, too. It took me until New Year's to realize it wasn't. It's only been a couple of weeks."

"You're gonna have to just be honest with her," Valerie concluded, shrugging her shoulders. "Although… I'd leave the part out about me. You'll just have to tell her you didn't want a relationship. You have to start being honest, Lucas."

"I don't wanna hurt anyone."

"Sometimes people have to get hurt. But they mend, and they get over it. And you get to be happy. Just because someone isn't gonna like what you have to say is no reason to keep it quiet and make yourself miserable." Valerie took a moment to reflect on her own words, and realized that this conversation was hitting way too close to home.

"Yeah, well… having to say something sucks," Lucas mumbled, sighing. "You ever have something you want everyone to know, but you just wish they could know it without you having to say it?"

"Yes." Valerie closed her eyes and sighed, too.

"This feels like that, you know? Like, if I could just… *say it-*"

"Lucas, I'm dating Lindsay," she breathed out, and then immediately winced when he fell completely silent. The tension mounted in the car as she heard him shift to face her.

Finally, he spoke, his eyes wide. "…*What?*"

"Lindsay and I…" She shook her head and finally finished, "Please don't make me say it again."

"You're gay," he stated, and then paused, like he wanted to make sure the words made sense on his lips. "You like girls."

"I don't know," she told him honestly. "I like her."

"I knew it wasn't me," he whispered, almost happily. Immediately, Valerie glared at him.

"Hey!"

"I'm just saying. Wow. This makes a lot of sense, actually. Lindsay wasn't into me, either."

"Clearly, if a girl turns you down, she must be gay," Valerie deadpanned. "God, why did I decide to tell you about this?"

"You and Lindsay, huh?" Lucas marveled, shaking his head in disbelief. Valerie wasn't sure he'd even heard what she'd just said. He closed his eyes and smiled. "Let me just take a moment to get a mental image of this... there we go..."

She punched his arm as hard as she could, jolting him out of his stupor. "Not funny."

"I'm sorry, but she's hot. You're hot. It's pretty hot."

"This is exactly the kind of reaction I'd hoped for when I told you. Thank you, Lucas," she snapped sarcastically.

At hearing that, he turned serious. "Hey. I'm here for you, okay? Seriously. And I'm totally keeping my mouth shut about this if that's what you want. Does anyone else know?"

"Just Kat," Valerie admitted.

"And how long have you...?"

"Since New Year's."

"Ah." He nodded his head. "So it's new. Well, I'm proud to be the second person you've told. And if ever need someone to beat up a homophobe, or give sex advice... ow!"

"Seriously, Lucas." She glared at him, and he raised his hands defensively.

"Okay. I'm done. Sorry. Hotness overload. Anyway, I'll just be on my way, then. I've gotta deal with this Amber situation, so."

"Don't be a douche about it," she warned him. "Amber's got a very big ego. She'll tear you apart unless you grovel."

"Thanks," he told her seriously, and then climbed out of the car and shut the door behind himself, leaving Valerie alone with her thoughts.

As much as she'd vowed to keep what was going on between herself and Lindsay a secret from the people at their school, one person had already figured it out before they'd even started dating, and now she'd gone and told another after just two more weeks.

At this rate, it was going to get out somehow. She had no doubt about that. And she wasn't sure she'd be prepared to deal with the repercussions when it did.

CHAPTER EIGHTEEN

Valentine's Day was a massive affair at Riverbank High. The instant the week before the holiday arrived, announcements were everywhere about how anonymous roses could be sent to friends or crushes or lovers or *whoever*, pink and red hearts and streamers covered the walls, lockers, and even the bulletin board by the front office, and little candy hearts were suddenly the most frequently seen edible item.

"Love me," Lindsay declared when she ambushed Valerie at her locker that Monday. Then she laughed at the alarmed expression on Valerie's face, and uncurled a clenched fist, revealing the heart candy inside with those same words printed on it. "Very subtle reaction there. I didn't know we had two 'L' words that were taboo in this relationship."

"I have no problem saying the word lesbian," Valerie contested, snatching the heart candy away and popping it into her mouth.

"So is your school always like this?" Lindsay asked, quirking an eyebrow and glancing at the décor around them.

"Every year. It's very important to the staff that we, as students of this fine institution, all have sex with each other."

"Gross. Are we participating in this strange celebration?"

Valerie shifted uncomfortably as a student passed them by, clearly within earshot. But if he heard them, he didn't give any indication, and Lindsay quickly apologized.

"You're fine," Valerie insisted. "I'm just paranoid."

"That'd be like us, though. To end up giving it away when we're so paranoid about Kat and Lucas telling people."

"Yeah," Valerie agreed, forcing a laugh.

"But seriously. Are we making plans?"

"For Valentine's? That depends. What were you thinking?"

Lindsay looked reluctant to speak first. "I don't want to give it away, if I am thinking of something."

"I just want something simple," Valerie insisted. "Just you and me, okay? And... possibly a bed."

Lindsay's expression softened. "Okay. Whatever you feel comfortable with."

Valerie nodded, and she and Lindsay headed to their Drama class together, taking care not to walk too close to each other.

She felt nervous even thinking about a Valentine's Day date with Lindsay. They'd only been dating for a month, and Lindsay had initially been determined to let Valerie make the decisions when it came to progressing in the sexual aspect of their relationship. Valerie was the one in her first relationship, and she was the virgin, after all. But she could sense Lindsay was getting antsy, and she wasn't the only one; Valerie liked Lindsay very much, and she felt ready to take things to the next level. She just wasn't sure how to initiate it.

At lunch, her friends' heads were all in the same places, as Valentine's Day date options were basically all that were discussed. Amber, for once, was the only one not interested in talking about romance. Not after Lucas's pseudo-dumping of her two weeks prior. Valerie suspected she was planning a night of eating chocolate and binge-drinking at home, or else she was planning to get Hannah to take her along to a bar.

Tara and Oliver, on the other hand, were planning a picnic, and Nick and Kat intended to go to a nice restaurant together. When Tara asked Lindsay and Valerie if either of them had plans for the holiday, they both just shrugged and shook their heads as Kat smiled knowingly.

Lucas was equally clueless about his own Valentine's Day plans, as Valerie soon found out, but that was mostly due to the fact that he hated Valentine's Day.

"You know what I hear around the guys, though," he told her as she drove him home one afternoon, "Is that rumor has it the quarterbacks are tag-teaming, with you and Lindsay as the targets. Second-stringer's back with a vengeance."

Valerie sighed. "Really? Why me and Lindsay?"

"Well, that Dustin guy's had a thing for you or whatever for a while now, and when Jimmy found out he was friends with Lindsay, he decided to help him out with you in return for the hookup with Lindsay, so to speak."

"That sounds like the stupidest thing I've ever heard."

"Basically. But look out, because you and your girlfriend are about to be on the receiving end of a very sad wine and dine attempt by two of the dumbest guys at our school. Just a warning."

"Thanks," she replied, and made a mental note to text Lindsay to let her know. She was staying after school with Kat and a few other students to help write the Drama class's next production: the senior play. It was to be written and directed entirely by the seniors of their class.

A couple of hours later, her doorbell rang, and she opened the door to see Lindsay standing on the other side, frowning despite the massive bouquet of roses in her hands. "You were right," Lindsay deadpanned. Valerie realized the roses weren't *from* Lindsay, but had instead been *for* Lindsay. "This one seems pretty relentless. I told him I didn't want them but he wouldn't go away. I also told him I didn't want to go out with him, and he only took 'no' for an answer because I agreed to take the flowers." She sighed, moving to Valerie's kitchen to dump the flowers into the trash. "I might have to be honest with this one, Val. Seriously. I'd only say something about me, though, if I did."

"No way," Valerie protested immediately. "If it gets out about you, everyone will know about me, too. We're together all the time."

"Well, I know you have a problem with people knowing we're a couple, but this isn't about that. It's about me."

"That's not it," Valerie insisted. "I'm really glad I'm with you. I feel really good about this." She reached out, taking Lindsay's hand in hers. "I just don't want other people to ruin it by treating us like crap."

"I don't like hiding that I'm dating you," Lindsay told her. "I'm not used to it. I was waiting to gauge what the reaction would be before I came out here, but honestly, I just don't care anymore. And now I don't even want to keep my own sexuality a secret, but to also keep yours a secret *and* our relationship? It's too much and it's been a month. Why don't we just be who we are?"

"I don't know who I am," Valerie protested. "And I don't feel ready to be crucified just for liking you."

"As opposed to myself, who should be prepared for it since I've actually committed the cardinal sin of being gay," Lindsay countered, oozing sarcasm with every syllable.

"That's not what I mean. I don't... I'm not good with fielding insults. Not like you or Kat."

"Having a snappy comeback doesn't mean it hurts less," Lindsay told her. "I hate it too. But it's worth it to be able to hold your hand whenever I want. Don't you want that?"

Valerie bit her lip. "Of course. But... Can't we wait a little while? Please? This is still so new to me."

"I mean... I absolutely want you to wait if you're not ready," Lindsay told her gently. "But I don't want to wait forever. Can you at least think about it? You told Lucas and it went well, you know? There are other people who will have that reaction."

"And some who won't."

"Well, there are bad seeds everywhere. You just have to ignore them."

Lindsay let out a breath. "But of course we can wait."

Valerie nodded. "Okay. Thank you."

With that settled, they huddled up under a blanket on the couch to watch television together. Valerie rested her head in Lindsay's lap, and Lindsay toyed with her hair, twisting strands around her finger until they stayed curled. "You're so beautiful," she murmured, and Valerie rolled her eyes.

"Not nearly as much as you. Or any of my friends, for that matter."

"That's definitely not true," Lindsay told her. "The first time we met... I still remember it: I walked out of Tara's front door and saw this group of three girls, and my eyes went straight to you. I thought you were so cute. Remember? I guessed you were Amber, the cheerleader. I'd just assumed the prettiest one was the cheerleader." She laughed, and Valerie's eyes widened as her memory was jogged.

"That's right!" she recalled. "And then you hit on me. Wow, I was so oblivious; I didn't even realize you were flirting."

"A lot of people don't even let their minds go there unless they like the same gender," Lindsay replied. "And I know you weren't homophobic before me, but I'm guessing you just didn't give much thought to the idea that someone you were close with could be gay."

"I guess. I just didn't think about it. I mean, homosexuality didn't really come up until Kat started bringing it up. I remember that guy Tony getting picked on in the hallway. She made Nick go defend him. I remember... I wanted to ignore it." Her heart sank as she recalled how anxious she'd been to get out of that situation. Now, she could very well be in Tony's place soon. "Karma's a bitch, huh?" she mumbled.

"Don't say that," Lindsay demanded, nudging her. "People are ignorant sometimes, but that doesn't make them bad. You were just ignorant. Now you're not. I bet you'd put a stop to it now if you saw it."

Valerie thought about it. The first thing Kat had been asked by the football players who'd been picking on Tony was if she was gay too. She wasn't sure she could handle even an implication from someone that she was gay without giving herself away. She'd given it away to Kat already.

"You're a good person, Val," Lindsay murmured, kissing her on the head. It was only a small comfort to Valerie that one of them thought so.

The next day, as she was leaving her last class and heading out into the parking lot, she was surprised to see Amber sitting on a curb alone, her knees pulled to the front of her body with her chin resting on top of them. She normally waited for a ride to work from Hannah on this day of the week, Valerie knew, but Hannah picked her up at the front of the school, and this was the back parking lot.

Curious, she changed direction and headed over to Amber. "Hey. What are you doing here?" she asked, taking a seat beside her. If Lucas saw she wasn't at her car, she knew he could hitch a ride from one of his other friends, but she sent him a quick warning text anyway. If Amber needed a ride, it was probably best that Lucas wasn't there.

Amber shrugged half-heartedly in response to her question. "I don't know. I'm supposed to be at work soon, but…"

Valerie sighed and stood up, offering Amber her hand. "C'mon. You're riding with me. Weren't you due to get a promotion soon? I'm not letting you be late."

Amber stared at her hand for a moment, and then grudgingly took it. Together, they walked to her car, which thankfully didn't have Lucas anywhere near it. Amber brought him up anyway. "I thought you drove Lucas home every day."

"I let him know you were coming along today," Valerie explained, and realized it was the wrong thing to say when Amber's lips turned down into a frown.

"So he ditched."

"No, I told him to leave," she corrected. "I thought it'd make you upset to see him."

They got into their respective seats and Valerie started the car. "It would have," Amber admitted. "This week just sucks, you know? I feel like no one understands, or even cares."

"About what?"

"Me!" Amber retorted loudly, surprising her. "Tara's off in la la land with Oliver, and Kat's got Nick. And you spend every Valentine's Day alone. I really wanted to spend it with Lucas, you know? And I know I see a lot of guys, but... I really liked him. And nobody cares that I'm upset because they're all too busy being *happy*." She sniffled quietly, then sifted through Valerie's glove box for some spare napkins. She found one and dabbed at her eyes. "I want love too, you know? I have feelings just like everyone else. If Oliver dumped Tara we'd all be there for her."

"Well..." Valerie wasn't sure how to even begin to respond to that, but she tried her best. "Do you think that maybe you date so frequently that we don't really know how to tell the difference between the ones who matter and the ones who don't? Which... there's nothing wrong with dating a lot of guys if that's what you wanna do, but when you're with someone that you know you wanna be with for a long time... or at least you hope the two of you will be... it's special."

"That's how I felt about Lucas," Amber explained bitterly. "But clearly he didn't feel the same way about me."

"Well, it's not easy to tell... one hookup from another," Valerie replied, hoping her wording wasn't offensive. Luckily, Amber didn't seem bothered by it.

"But I like hooking up."

"Then keep hooking up. Do what makes you happy. But if you want something more with someone, you should let them know, and you should let us know. That way you can avoid another Lucas, where the guy thinks it's just hooking up and where your friends assume the same because you don't tell us you actually like someone. We all thought you'd be onto the next guy within a few days."

Amber sighed. "Now I'm spending Valentine's Day watching rom-coms and eating chocolate like some loser who can't get a date." She glanced to Valerie. "No offense, Val. But even *you* have someone that wants you, from what I've heard. And Lindsay too. Not me, though."

Valerie didn't respond to that. They pulled up to Mackie's and to Valerie's surprise, Amber leaned over and wrapped her arms around Valerie in a tight hug. When she pulled away, she said, "I know we don't spend a lot of time together with just the two of us, but I'm really glad we're friends, Val. Thanks for the ride."

"Yeah, no problem," she replied distantly, and drove home deep in thought.

Her parents were home when she got there. It was one of those rare days where work was slow and they both collaborated to get a few hours off to come home early. Mr. Marsh made spaghetti for dinner and the four of them sat down at the table together just a couple of hours later. The typical questions were asked about school and friends, which inevitably led to a mention of Lindsay. Valerie only half paid attention to the conversation after that. She was too busy thinking about the talk she'd had with Lindsay the previous afternoon. But now that the people it was probably most important for her to come out to were right in front of her, she had nowhere near the amount of guts she knew it'd take to tell them the truth.

She tried to imagine it in her head. Just saying aloud, "I'm dating Lindsay." That's all it'd take. Three words. She didn't even have to commit to a sexuality. She just had to tell them she was with a girl.

Then she imagined their reactions. She'd never talked about homosexuality with them before, but she knew they occasionally watched television shows every now and then that had a gay character or two, so maybe they'd be accepting, or just neutral.

But what if they weren't? Having a daughter into someone of the same gender was entirely different from just seeing a gay person on television. If they took it badly, she had no idea how she'd handle that. She could be kept from seeing Lindsay outside of school, or forced to break up with her. She knew her parents would never be extreme enough to send her to some sort of brainwashing therapy, but that didn't mean they wouldn't take measures to try and change her mind about liking girls. And even if she was bisexual and there were guys out there she'd be into, that would still mean losing Lindsay.

She sighed to herself as she helped clear the table. As far as she could tell, there was only one benefit to telling *anyone* about her relationship with Lindsay, and that was getting to stop sneaking around together. But there were countless pitfalls. A possible forced breakup if her parents reacted badly, possible loss of friendship with Tara, even though that seemed unlikely... *definite* loss of Amber's friendship. Bullying, teasing, snide remarks from other students...

Valerie would argue that it'd be much better to just wait until graduation and then be open in college, but Lindsay was leaving after graduation. That was another issue. She wasn't even sure what would happen to their relationship after Lindsay went back to England, so why go through hell for what could turn out to be a five-month relationship with the only girl she'd ever end up dating?

No, it definitely didn't seem worth it. Maybe to Lindsay, who already knew she was gay and would most likely be the one to dictate the course of their relationship after graduation, but not to Valerie, who just felt along for the ride most of the time. She cared about Lindsay a lot, but she cared about her friendships and her family, too. Lindsay would just have to accept that she'd have to wait until after graduation, after they'd hopefully found a way to continue to see each other.

Until then, Valerie was staying firmly in the closet.

CHAPTER NINETEEN

Five days later, Valerie got a text after school that made her heart drop.

It was from Kat. *"Idk if you and Lindsay talked about her doing this, but she just started bonding with Tony and Nathan over being gay. Like, everyone that's here knows."*

She stared at the text, reading and re-reading it several times over to try and discern some sort of meaning from it other than the obvious one. Lindsay and Kat were at another writing session with the other seniors from their Drama class who'd volunteered to help write the senior play. There were at least ten people in that group. Eight new people knew about Lindsay.

Her text back to Kat was brief. *"We didn't."*

Alone in her bedroom, she panicked. *Everyone* was going to know. She and Lindsay were constantly visiting each other's lockers, sitting with each other at lunch, talking to each other in classes... granted, she did this with her other friends, too, but none of her other friends were lesbians.

Her phone buzzed with a text from Kat. *"I'm sorry, Val. If it helps, I think that Jimmy guy was seriously harassing her. He's been stopping by here every day."*

She let out a slow breath as she stared down at her phone, trying to calm herself down. Lindsay would let her say they weren't together. She knew that. It was just a matter of making people believe it.

She never responded to Kat, and she spent the next few hours preparing herself for the next day. She stood in her mirror and practiced lying about Lindsay without blushing, and she even went onto her Facebook and changed her "interested in" section, which had been blank, to "men". She was aware that she was being paranoid, but she couldn't help it.

She called Lindsay when she was confident she'd be done with writing, and tried her best to stay calm. As the phone rang, she tried to imagine big, intimidating, dumb Jimmy hovering over her with his massive muscles and stupid grin, asking her over and over to go out on a date with him, no matter how many times she said no. She tried to imagine knowing that if she told people she was gay it would humiliate him, and feeling the temptation to do just that. She tried to be understanding.

It didn't help.

"How could you do this?" was the first thing out of her mouth when Lindsay answered the phone. She heard a sigh from the other end, and could already feel the tears welling up in her eyes. "Do you know how terrified I am right now? I can't go to school tomorrow, Lindsay; what if people know?"

"They don't know, Val," Lindsay replied, her tone gentle. "That's what I've tried to tell you. I told people I was gay. Me. Not you. If they jump to conclusions, I'll lie for you, even though I'd like nothing more than to let everyone know that I'm dating this beautiful, wonderful girl that I absolutely adore. It's gonna be okay."

"But I don't wanna be accused in the first place. I don't wanna have to be even more careful about how I look at you or what I say to you."

"Then be honest," Lindsay suggested.

"I can't do that."

"Why not? Everyone's been nice to me, Val."

"That's the Drama class; they're a little bit of a fringe group," Valerie pointed out, her voice dripping with sarcasm.

"Tara was fine, too," Lindsay replied, making Valerie freeze where she paced across her bedroom floor. "She's not in Drama."

"You told Tara."

"Yes, when I got home. And her parents. They're fine."

"But... Tara knows?"

Lindsay chuckled. "Yes, Val. And before you ask: I told her, she said, 'oh, ok', and then we had a short talk about how it made sense now that I hadn't liked Lucas, or Dustin, or now Jimmy. And then we moved on. Her parents had even less of a reaction; they seemed confused about why I felt the need to mention it in the first place. Very nice family."

Valerie sat down on her bed, only feeling worse now. Tara was her best friend, and knew her inside and out more than even Kat did. She was smarter than Kat, too. Lindsay could lie all she wanted, but there was no way Tara had missed the parallel between Lindsay's attitude toward boys and Valerie's recent dismissal of dating guys like Dustin and Lucas. Not to mention, Tara had already made comments about Lindsay being Valerie's new best friend. There was no doubt that she knew what was going on now. How could Valerie face her?

"I have to go," she said abruptly, and hung up the phone before Lindsay could reply. Immediately it began to ring as Lindsay attempted to call her back, so Valerie shut it off and ignored it for the rest of the night.

She forced herself to go to school the next day. Valentine's Day was just two days away, on a Friday, and as she walked through the hallways, it seemed to be the only thing everyone was talking about. That was good. If Lindsay had truly told only ten people or so, it would probably take at least a week to become school-wide knowledge.

She went to her locker to get her books for her next few classes, and just as she was slamming the door shut, she felt a tap on her shoulder. She turned, expecting to see Lindsay. Instead, she saw Tara, who smiled at her brightly and said, "Hey. Just thought I'd stop by and see if you wanted to skip lunch for a last-minute Calc study session?"

Valerie shifted uncomfortably. They did have a test that day, but it was likely that what Tara *really* wanted was to have a private discussion with her about Lindsay. "Um..."

She was saved by a couple of girls nearby, who distracted both herself and Tara when they squealed and then "aww"-ed at something they saw down the hallway. Both Valerie and Tara followed their gaze, and several students nearby mimicked the action.

Valerie realized it was Dustin they were all looking at, and he was headed straight for Valerie. In one hand, he clutched an adorable stuffed dog, and in the other, a bouquet of roses. He was dressed to the nines in a nice suit, and had clearly made an effort to clean himself up. Valerie guessed that if he'd chosen any other girl in the hallway to approach at that moment, she'd have swooned. Valerie, however, was horrified as he stopped in front of her and shot her a wide grin. "Hey."

"Hi," she said meekly, a little overwhelmed. They had quite the audience at this point.

"I know we don't get the chance to talk much," he began, looking a little nervous for the first time now. "And I know we haven't really hung out alone... but I think you're beautiful."

There was another "aww" from the nearby girls, and Valerie struggled not to look like a deer in headlights. Dustin didn't stop there. "And not just beautiful; you're sweet, and smart, and funny, and if you'd like, I'd really enjoy getting to know you better." He got down on one knee and Valerie blinked at him, baffled as to what on earth he was doing. He offered her the rose, and finished, "Valerie Marsh, will you do me the honor of being my Valentine?"

She stared at him for a moment, her mouth wide open with surprise. Then she glanced to the ring of students that had formed around them, most of which were gaggles of girls who watched the two of them so hopefully that for a moment Valerie forgot she was meant to accept a Valentine's date and not a marriage proposal. "Uh..." was all she could come up with at first, and Dustin's smile faded slightly. She wondered briefly how hurt he'd be if she turned him down. Then she wondered what people would say about her. Lindsay'd turned down Jimmy. Lindsay was gay. Valerie'd turned down Dustin. Valerie spent a lot of time with Lindsay.

She swallowed hard, and then, at last, nodded. Dustin's smile came back, this time as a wide grin. "Yes, I'll be your Valentine."

He stood up and wrapped his arms around her as the chorus of girls clapped and fawned over them. Awkwardly, she hugged him back, and he let her go as the crowd finally began to disperse. "I'll pick you up at eight, okay?"

She nodded dumbly. Right. She'd just agreed to a real date with a real boy on the holiday she was supposed to be spending with her girlfriend. That was a bit of a problem.

Tara, for her part, looked a little confused, and seemed to be deep in thought. Valerie could practically see her reevaluating Valerie's sexually. "That was interesting," Tara finally said. "You like him?"

"He's sweet," Valerie replied, and Tara nodded her understanding.

"Cool. Well, maybe there's a *successful* double date in our future, then," she suggested, and they shared a grin before splitting up to go to their first classes.

It didn't take long for Valerie's grin to fade as she walked to her Drama class. There was no doubt in her mind that Lindsay would be upset with her, and that was *before* factoring in that she'd just accepted a date with Dustin.

She arrived at the auditorium to see that most of the seniors were up onstage. Some had sat down together on the stage floor and were huddled in a group, and those appeared to be writing the play. Others were backstage, examining the props they had available to them. Lindsay was one of those.

Sucking in a breath, Valerie dropped her backpack in a seat and then headed backstage. She found Lindsay sitting alone at a grand piano that mostly went unused, tapping at one of the keys as though testing to make sure it worked. Valerie glanced over her shoulder to make sure no one was nearby, and then slowly approached Lindsay, her anxiety mounting.

Once she was just a few feet away, she stopped and stared. Lindsay didn't look up, but murmured, "I thought you were ignoring me."

"I'm sorry, Lindsay." The words hung in the air, and she swallowed hard. Her apology was sincere, but she knew she was still mid-panic. Fight or flight was engaged, and Valerie wasn't a fighter. "I'm not sure I was ready for this."

Lindsay barely managed a dry laugh. "I noticed." At last, she looked to Valerie. "I asked you to be sure, you know? That you were ready and you wanted this. And when you wanted to kiss me on New Year's I thought it meant that you were. But I guess us kissing in the privacy of my room probably should've been my first clue."

"I *am* sure about my feelings for you," Valerie insisted. "Isn't that enough?"

"You really like how things are going?" Lindsay asked, and then turned away abruptly. Valerie heard her sniff and saw her wipe at her eyes. When she finally turned back, she shook her head. "I feel *so* unwanted, Val. I don't want to be something you hide away. But I've been willing to be that for you because I really like you and I know how hard it was for me to come out. I understand. But now I just want to not hide myself and that's *still* too much for you."

"It's not!" Valerie backpedaled hastily. "I get it, okay? I shouldn't force you to keep being something you're not. And I do want you. I just... panicked. I'll fix everything."

"How?"

Valerie hesitated. She knew she needed to be truthful about the Dustin situation, but she didn't want to upset Lindsay any further. Finally, she let out a sigh and elected to be honest. "Well, first of all, Dustin treated a Valentine's date like a marriage proposal and asked me out. I said yes, but I'll call him and cancel, Lindsay, I swear. I can tell him I felt too bad for him to turn him down in front of an audience, or something like that, and I'll let him know that I'm not interested."

Lindsay shook her head in disappointment and wiped at her eyes again. "But that's not why you said 'yes', is it?"

"Like I said, I panicked. I regretted it right after," Valerie assured her. "I'll call him tonight. And I'll plan something for us. We can spend all afternoon and all night together, if you want that."

Lindsay nodded wordlessly, and gave Valerie a small smile. Relieved, Valerie smiled back.

"Okay? You're wanted, Lindsay. Probably a little too much, even. I just need time."

"Okay," Lindsay agreed quietly, and Valerie let her be, her brain already working overtime to try and figure out how exactly she'd handle Dustin later on.

It occurred to her soon enough that she'd gotten herself into a bit of a predicament. Tara thought she was straight because she'd agreed to go out with Dustin, and now she was cancelling on Dustin. She highly doubted Dustin would go around telling everyone his proposal went south and his date got canceled, but Tara would eventually find out Valerie had never gone out with Dustin unless Valerie spun her web further with yet another series of lies. Eventually, whether directly or indirectly, canceling on Dustin meant coming out to Tara.

She tried hard to make herself okay with that. Kat knew and was fine, and she'd even told Lucas herself with the knowledge that he'd be okay with it as well. She knew Tara would accept her due to her reaction to Lindsay, but there was something difficult about telling Tara. Perhaps because she'd realized she'd had a bit of a long-standing crush on her before Lindsay had come around. But she didn't necessarily have to tell Tara that, so in the end it was still a moot point.

Her biggest problem with coming out and dating Lindsay, she realized, was the complete lack of contradiction time-wise between those two actions. She didn't want to come out until after high school, and she couldn't continue to date Lindsay —at least not in person- after high school. So was she doomed to be in a relationship where Lindsay felt like something to be hidden until graduation, and then in an honest but long-distance relationship afterward?

She knew something needed to give, and she knew it was herself with the problem. Sticking to the "come out after graduation" plan was probably not going to work out. Especially given that she felt like everyone at her high school with any semblance of a gaydar was closing in on her. Despite Lindsay's good intentions, with Lindsay being openly gay, it was only a matter of time before Valerie would be found out, and the only way to stop that would be to take drastic measures, like dating a guy. She didn't want to hurt Lindsay, so that was off the table. The only thing left to do was to gather the courage to be honest before she was forced out of the closet.

She started with fixing the Dustin situation that afternoon, hands shaking as she found his name on her contact list and the phone began to ring. She was nervous not only about turning him down, but also about what this phone call represented. She was throwing her chance away at a heterosexual cover, leaving herself exposed and ready to be pounced on.

The phone rang again, and again. Valerie closed her eyes and thought of Lindsay. She would do this for Lindsay. She just needed to be brave.

The phone stopped ringing, a signal that Dustin had picked up. "Hello?" she heard him ask.

Her mouth opened and closed wordlessly.

"Hello?" he repeated.

She squeezed her eyes shut, silently cursed herself, and then forced her voice into a cheery tone. "Hey! Dustin."

"Valerie," he replied, sounding happy to hear from her. "Hey. I'm really excited for our date tomorrow night. How are you?"

"Great! Um," she hesitated, biting her lip, "so I think tomorrow is actually..." She paused, swallowing hard. Her heart raced and she felt herself freezing up.

"What'd you say, Val? I think I missed the end of that," Dustin replied. He was met with silence. "...Val?"

"I can't do tomorrow night, Dustin," she forced herself to breathe out. "I'm sorry."

There was a long pause on the other end. When Dustin replied, he sounded dejected more than angry. "Why not?"

"I'm so, so sorry. I just... I can't right now. It's not a good time, and-" She realized she was headed straight for a long ramble, and cut herself off. "I'm just... I'm sorry. We can be friends."

"Yeah," Dustin replied shortly. "Friends. Okay, Val."

"I'm sorry," she said again.

"Bye," was his response, and with a click, the call was over.

Valerie felt sick to her stomach as she stared at her cell phone. But not because she'd hurt Dustin, and not even because she'd given up a shot at being "straight".

But because for just a moment, she'd considered rescheduling the date instead of cancelling it.

CHAPTER TWENTY

Valerie's Valentines setup involved rose petals, candles, a stolen bottle of wine, and a dinner, all in the privacy of her own room.

After school, Lindsay came home with her. They had an hour of complete privacy until Abby's arrival, but plenty of time after that before Valerie's parents would show up, as they were going on a date that night.

That led to Valerie snagging the food and wine from her room for an early dinner on her couch, her stomach twisting into nervous knots even as she presented Lindsay with the dish of the night. To her relief, Lindsay lit up upon sight of it, and then started laughing.

"Oh my God, you bought me fish and chips!"

"I thought you might be missing home a little bit by now," Valerie pointed out. "It's been three months."

"Thank you." Lindsay took the food gratefully. "I do miss it. But I Skype with my friends and family sometimes, and that helps. They all know everything about you by now, I think." She grinned, and Valerie flushed, embarrassed.

"You .alk about me? What have you told them?"

"I'm serious; everything," Lindsay repeated. "While you have Kat and Lucas to share with, I just get on the computer and call up someone from back home. I'd love for you meet them one day."

"I know a little bit already," Valerie admitted. "I kind of stalked you on Facebook right after we met."

Lindsay swallowed a bite of her food and looked flattered. "Aw, so I wasn't the only one with an instant crush."

"It's embarrassing," Valerie sighed out.

"I think it's adorable. But anyway, yeah, I do miss home, but I like America, too."

"You're kidding me? This dumb small town?"

"I could live here," Lindsay told her, nodding. "College'll help with the homophobia, once you get there. From what I understand, people just stop giving a shit."

"Or you could go somewhere cool, like Oxford," Valerie pointed out.

"True. If I could actually get in." They ate in comfortable silence for a couple of minutes, cuddling on the couch, until Lindsay finally broke it, albeit a little reluctantly. "I promise this is the only time I'll mention this, but did things go okay with Dustin? I mean, I know you canceled, obviously, but…"

"It was hard," Valerie admitted. "But I did it, and now I'm here with you, and I'm very *very* happy about that." She reached over and drew Lindsay toward her, pulling her into a deep kiss for emphasis. The nervous knots in her stomach tightened. She knew what she'd set up her room for; the only question was whether or not it was going to be utilized, and signs were currently pointing to 'yes'.

They broke apart and Lindsay brushed her nose against Valerie's with a small smile, then pulled away at last to reach for the bottle of wine. "Is your sister going to be home soon?"

"I think so," Valerie replied. "Unless she has Valentines plans, which, as a thirteen-year-old, I seriously doubt."

"You never know," Lindsay point out, pouring them each a glass and then reaching for Valerie's phone, which rested on the coffee table beside them. "But there's an easy way to find out. She'll be out of school by now, right?"

Valerie nodded, and at Lindsay's urging, dialed her sister's number. As the phone rang, Lindsay scooted closer, smirking at her. Valerie looked to her questioningly, and then realized what she was up to. "Don't you dare," she murmured, just as her sister answered the phone.

"What? I'm busy," was the first thing Valerie heard.

"With whom? Are you coming home soon?"

Abby laughed on the other end of the phone. "Ooh, do you have a date?"

"Shut up, seriously, are you?" Valerie asked, just barely managing to duck Lindsay's lips as they aimed for her neck. "Stop it!" she hissed, and Abby heard it, if her gasp was any indication.

"Oh my God, you do! He must be hideous if he settled for *you*."

"Abby, just answer the question."

"I won't tell if you won't," Abby replied simply, and then briefly added, "Ben says 'hi'," before hanging up. Valerie gaped at her phone, and Lindsay watched her, amused.

"What is it?"

"I think my dumb sister has a date with her best guy friend," Valerie announced, watching as Lindsay set aside their food and wine. "I can't decide if I think that's cute or not."

"Best friends who fall for each other are adorable. Now come here." Lindsay tugged at the front of her shirt gently, and they kissed again. At some point, Lindsay tipped backwards and pulled Valerie onto her, her hands tangling in Valerie's hair and drawing her closer as their kisses deepened. Valerie was breathing hard by the time they broke apart, and the knot had grown even tighter.

Lindsay, too, was breathless as she murmured, "Do you want to go up to your room?"

The question held a much deeper meaning than a simple change in location, Valerie knew. Still, she swallowed hard, and nodded.

"Are you sure?" Lindsay asked again, her voice still quiet. Valerie reached out for her hands and felt them shaking, just subtly enough to barely be noticeable.

"You're nervous," Valerie observed gently.

"Of course," was Lindsay's simple response.

"But you've done this before."

"Not with you."

"It's not all the same?"

Lindsay shook her head. "Absolutely not."

The knot squeezed tighter, but Valerie pushed past it, and nodded. "I'd like to…" she trailed off, but Lindsay understood her meaning, and kissed her cheek. Valerie felt Lindsay's smile against her skin.

"It's okay to be nervous," Lindsay told her. "But it's not like in the movies, just so you know. It's not all slow-mo passionate sweatiness. If we don't giggle at some point we're probably not doing it right."

"Okay," Valerie acknowledged. Her voice sounded squeaky to her own ears.

Lindsay took her hand, squeezed, and then together they disposed of the evidence of their date that remained in the living room. Lindsay took the wine with them and led Valerie up the stairs, then motioned for Valerie to be the one to open the bedroom door. Appreciating it, Valerie took a moment to collect herself mentally, and then pushed the door open.

The lit candles were just as she left them, providing the only source of light in the room given that Valerie had made sure to draw her curtains shut and to close the blinds on her windows. Flower petals formed a trail to her bed, and Lindsay took it all in, awestruck.

"Val, I can't believe you did all of this."

"I know it's cheesy," Valerie prefaced, but Lindsay cut her off.

"Stop. And come here."

Lindsay closed the door shut and locked it, then pulled Valerie to her and initiated another kiss, hands on Valerie's hips and slowly sliding higher. Valerie felt her head spin when Lindsay's hands touched her sides under her shirt. They'd made out plenty of times by now, but the touching had stayed strictly PG-13. And while Lindsay's hands had journeyed under her shirt before, it was different now, when Valerie knew how far they planned to go.

"We don't have to," Lindsay reminded her after she ended the kiss. "Don't forget that, okay? We can stop." Valerie grabbed Lindsay's hand and led her to the bed without any warning, an act which elicited a surprised but pleased response from Lindsay. "...Or not?"

"Not," Valerie agreed, despite the tension still present in her stomach. She made the first move, getting on her bed and pulling Lindsay to her so that they were pressed together, and then Lindsay was kissing her and her hands felt like they were everywhere all at once, and soon enough, the knot was gone and Valerie couldn't think anymore.

They cuddled for a while afterward, taking turns being the big spoon. Valerie fell asleep at some point, and when she woke up, it was dark out and her house was still silent. She felt Lindsay shift against her and then whisper into her hair, "Do you want me to stay over?"

Valerie nodded wordlessly and huddled closer, an arm slung across Lindsay's stomach. Eventually, she sighed out, "You were good at that."

"You weren't so bad yourself," Lindsay replied, chuckling.

"The best?" Valerie joked.

"Obviously." Lindsay grinned at her. Valerie wondered briefly how many girls Lindsay had been with before her, and then decided maybe she should just ask.

"If you don't mind me asking... how many...?" she trailed off, confident Lindsay got the message.

"What, girls have I slept with?" Lindsay finished. "Three."

"That's all?"

"Hey, three's a decent amount for a teenager," Lindsay pointed out. "But if I'm lucky, it'll stay at three." She leaned down and kissed Valerie's cheek, and Valerie felt an overwhelming warmth course through her.

She moved closer, trying to decrease the already miniscule distance between them, and then nestled her head in the crook between Lindsay's shoulder and neck. Instinctively, she murmured, "I love you."

And then she froze up, realizing what she'd said. Lindsay felt her tense, and reached out to rub a hand up and down Valerie's arm. "I love you," she echoed, and just like that, all of Valerie's tension ebbed. Grinning, she leaned in and kissed the skin stretched over Lindsay's collarbone, and they didn't speak any more after that, eventually drifting off to sleep together.

They snuck out the next morning to get Lindsay back to Tara's, luckily avoiding any of the Marshes on the way out. When Valerie got back home, however, her parents were up, and so was Abby. Valerie waited with baited breath for questions about her mystery guy, but they didn't come. Instead, Abby caught Valerie's eye and lifted her index finger to her lips. Valerie got the message loud and clear: "I won't rat you out if you don't rat me out."

"Oh, if only you two girls had each had gotten to have a special night this year," Mrs. Marsh lamented later over breakfast, catching the eye of her husband and sharing a smile with him across the table. "It's a shame neither of you has given dating a real shot yet."

Valerie resolutely kept her mouth shut and her eyes on her plate, and across the table, Abby did the same.

"What did you two do yesterday afternoon, by the way?" Mr. Marsh questioned curiously.

"Studied," both daughters replied in unison, and then exchanged proud looks with each other when neither of their parents were looking.

The high of Valentine's Day and of taking her relationship to the next level stayed with Valerie until eight in the morning on Monday, when she entered the halls of Riverbank High and began to walk to her locker.

She passed two of the football players and caught a murmur of "Such a waste...", but didn't think much of it until she was at her locker and she overheard a much larger bit of conversation between two girls in her Lit class.

"She's, like, pretty though. You'd think she'd be able to get a guy."

"Maybe in England the guys don't like blondes."

The girls shared a laugh and Valerie grit her teeth, tensing up. She fought off the urge to snap at them, and turned away, slamming her locker door shut. She fast-walked to Drama, trying her best to ignore the comments, but it was like her ears had been tuned specifically to hear every little whisper about Lindsay that they could pick up.

"So hot... maybe she'd let me watch."

"Do you think she likes you? She keeps asking you to help her out with that Geography project..."

"Lindsay Walker's *gay*? No way!"

"Gross, why is she shoving it down everyone's throat? Just keep it to yourself."

Valerie pushed the auditorium door so hard that it flew open and thudded into the wall, drawing the attention of everyone in the hallway and everyone from her class. She hurried inside the auditorium and was immediately met by a concerned Kat, who knew her well enough to know exactly what was going on. Seconds later, Kat was in the light booth alone with her and Valerie was practically hyperventilating.

"Val, it's okay. It's okay. Calm down," Kat told her, rubbing her hands up and down Valerie's arms. "Lindsay's a strong girl. She'll be fine."

"I won't," Valerie choked out. "I don't want to hear people talk about her like that, and it's all the same stuff they'll say about me."

"I know it's hard. Today's the first day it's finally gotten around school. I bet by tomorrow it'll be old news and no one will even mention it anymore."

"Is she okay? Have you seen her?" Valerie asked, looking out through the front of the light booth toward the stage. She didn't see Lindsay.

"She's fine," Kat assured her. "Just taking inventory of our prop swords. We'll need them for our play."

Valerie had no idea what she was talking about, given that she wasn't at all involved in the writing process, but she forced herself to relax a little, taking Kat's word for it. "People in our class are going to realize why I'm upset," she realized.

Kat forced a laugh. "Hardly. They're too busy with their own drama to use the brainpower to make that much of a leap. You're fine." She hesitated. "But it probably would help if you were calm by the time we got out of here."

Valerie opened her mouth to respond, but her phone buzzed in her purse and she reached down to check for texts. When she saw who it was, her heart sank. "Amber."

"Just don't open it," Kat advised, but Valerie had already pressed the button to pull up the text.

"Heard about Lindsay :(Gross, r u ok?"

She showed it to Kat, who pulled a face but admitted, "It could be worse."

"Yeah, wait until Lit," Valerie mumbled, and left the booth to go find Lindsay.

Just as Kat had said, she was backstage with the swords and a clipboard in her hand. She caught sight of Valerie and immediately shot her a warm smile. Valerie couldn't help but return it. This was the first time they'd seen each other since Saturday morning, although they'd spent the whole weekend texting and talking on the phone.

"How are you?" Lindsay asked, and Valerie raised an eyebrow.

"I think *I* should be asking you that."

"Not really." Lindsay shrugged. "I mean, I'm not happy about what people are saying, but it's them with the problem, not me. I'm confident enough in who I am that I won't let other people affect what I think of myself."

"Good. But don't expect me not to be insulted on your behalf."

"Just as long as you don't get yourself into trouble," Lindsay joked, and they fell into comfortable silence. Lindsay went back to counting swords, and even as she scribbled numbers onto her clipboard, she began, "So Friday night…"

Valerie looked to her sharply, and sat down on a small bench used in their last play. Lindsay looked to her fondly as she tried to sound casual. "What about it?"

"It was really nice. The best Valentines I've had in a while."

"Me too," Valerie agreed, though it went without saying.

Lindsay set her clipboard aside and joined Valerie on the bench. "Listen, whatever happens here at school… whatever people say… you're more important to me than a dumb reputation. I know you feel like the pressure's on, but I don't want this to change you and me." Valerie nodded her agreement, and Lindsay took her hand. "Even if these next few weeks are hard, please don't give up. High school only lasts for three more months."

"Okay," Valerie murmured, but deep down, she wasn't completely sure she was making a promise she could keep.

CHAPTER TWENTY-ONE

Amber was surprisingly nonchalant when Valerie and Kat met up with her for Lit that day, but Valerie soon learned that that was only due to Kat's presence. The instant Kat left her seat to go take a bathroom break, Amber leaned over to Valerie and hissed, "I can't believe about Lindsay. She seemed so cool and normal. Were you shocked?"

"A little," Valerie told her honestly.

"I heard from Jimmy, actually. That *would* explain why she turned him down, I guess."

"Well, he's also kind of a jerk," Valerie couldn't help but input. Amber continued on as though she hadn't heard.

"But I just can't believe she kept it a secret for so long. Normally I can spot them a mile away, you know? But she's actually decent-looking and doesn't have short hair, like most of them do. She's not, like, dykey or anything. Still, it's gross."

Valerie gripped the pencil in her hand tighter, struggling not to snap it in half. Beside her, Amber continued talking, oblivious.

"It's weird, though. I've never met a gay person who was actually cool and like, seemed normal and stuff. Maybe she's just saying it for attention."

"Amber," Valerie interrupted at last, "if she wanted attention, I would think she'd do something that would result in a little less criticism."

"Well, she won't get much from the guys," Amber pointed out. "They'll all think it's hot." She gasped, as though having an epiphany. "I bet that's what happened! She was playing hard to get with Jimmy, saw that he was starting to talk to me, and decided to say she was a lesbian to get his attention again!"

"Clearly," Valerie replied dryly. "Because only being attracted to and dating girls is definitely the best strategy for getting a boyfriend."

"Well, it is if she isn't *actually* a lesbian," Amber countered. Valerie pressed her lips together firmly to keep from responding. A moment later, Kat returned, saving her.

She relayed the conversation to Lucas during Chemistry, who thought it was hilarious, and that helped cheer her up a little bit. But at lunch, things went south again.

As usual, Valerie sat with Lindsay, Kat, Amber, and Tara, but this time Amber didn't let the fact that Kat would be listening stop her from talking about Lindsay. Especially when Lindsay was right there to be interrogated. The second all five girls were seated, Amber got straight to the point.

"So Lindsay, when did you become such an attention whore?"

"Excuse me?"

Lindsay glared at Amber as Kat and Tara watched on, bewildered, and Valerie put her face in her hands.

"I'm just saying that this is awfully convenient. C'mon. We all know you're not really a lesbian."

"You really wanna have this conversation, Amber?"

"Of course. You're just jealous because Jimmy isn't sticking around to play your games."

"I turned *him* dow-" Lindsay cut herself off and shook her head. "Okay, I can't believe I'm arguing about this with you."

"Amber, as hard as it may be for you to believe this," Kat cut in with a roll of her eyes, "Lindsay's gay. I've known for over a month now."

"You have?" Tara input, sounding a little offended. "She only told me just a few days ago. Lindsay, how come you told her and not me?"

"Uh…" was Lindsay's response. She glanced to Valerie uncertainly, and beside Valerie, Kat took a deep breath.

"Because… my dad's gay. Since we're all coming out here, or whatever. Valerie accidentally found out a while ago, and she kind of arranged for Lindsay and me to share with each other."

"Wait, so how long did *you* know?" Tara asked, looking to Valerie.

"Um… I don't know?"

"This is messed up," Amber interrupted, shaking her head at them. "Two boys can't raise a kid, and neither can two girls. Children need a mother and a father."

"I've been just fine with two fathers," Kat snapped.

"That's debatable," Amber shot back. "Besides, the Bible says it's a sin."

"The Bible also says having sex before marriage is a sin, and yet here you are," Kat retorted. Valerie had a feeling she'd been holding that one in for a while.

Lindsay snorted, clearly caught off-guard by Kat's response, and Amber's face went red. Tara was wide-eyed.

"Bitch," Amber snarled. "I seem to remember *you* coming to *me* for advice on that very same topic."

"Yeah, and it ended up being useless. No wonder Lucas dumped your ass," Kat snapped. Even Lindsay's smile faded at that. Amber's lip trembled and her face went even redder, and a second later she was hurrying away.

"Kat, that was uncalled for," Tara murmured.

"She deserved it," Kat protested. "Think of all the things she's said about gay people and how much they hurt the three of *us*." She gestured to herself, Lindsay, and Valerie, then froze when she realized her mistake. Valerie wanted to disappear on the spot as Tara blinked at them.

"The three of you," she repeated simply, then looked to Valerie. "I thought you were with Dustin."

"She is," Kat rushed to correct. "I just meant because Valerie's good friends with us. When we hurt, she hurts."

"Totally," Lindsay interjected half-heartedly.

Tara raised an eyebrow, looking almost amused now. Then she smiled. "The poor guy must've been crushed when you canceled on him."

"I'm sorry," Kat apologized, immediately turning to Valerie, who was almost as red now as Amber had been. "I wasn't thinking."

"Don't worry, Val," Tara reassured her. "I love you and it's only slightly weird that you're with... you know." She gestured to Lindsay, wary of the people around them, although none of them were paying attention. "And only because she's been functioning as my sister for the past three months. I won't tell a soul." Valerie nodded wordlessly, only slightly reassured, as Tara stood and said, "Well, I should probably go comfort Amber. I'll see you guys later."

She left, and Kat immediately apologized to Valerie again. "That was so inconsiderate of me. I deserve whatever you say or do to me. I would've *killed* Nick if he'd told you guys about my dad before any of you knew."

"Kat, it's fine," Valerie mumbled. "At least she's okay with it."

But even as Kat sighed in relief, glad Valerie wasn't mad at her, Valerie couldn't help but add a tally to her mental count. Three people now knew about her and Lindsay. Thankfully, they were the three she would've picked were she forced to, but they were still three people.

The week crawled on and by Friday, everyone knew about Lindsay. Some were supportive, and some were like Amber, who now refused to eat lunch with their group or to talk to Lindsay or Kat, but most were neutral or just plain ignorant, a category which included the "it's hot; can I watch" crowd and the girls who approached Lindsay wondering how on earth she could "choose" to go for girls when she was pretty enough to get any guy she wanted. Kat got some heat for her dad after Amber spread that around, as, well, but she'd picked a good time to tell people, as all the focus remained on the bigger deal: Lindsay.

But at any rate, as Lindsay had predicted, the novelty wore off, eventually. Lindsay wasn't physically picked on like Valerie had seen happen to Tony, because even the most homophobic of the boys at their school didn't want to be seen hitting a girl, and so if any abuse came her way, it was mostly through guys claiming one night with them would turn her straight or girls gossiping about how she probably had a crush on all of them.

"They must think I have impossibly low standards," Lindsay said of the latter group one day, while she was rummaging through a bin backstage during Drama class while Valerie watched. "Aha!" she finally declared, withdrawing a fake mace from the bin and grinning. "There it is."

"Okay, seriously, what is this play even about?" Valerie questioned.

"Maybe if you actually took part in some of the after-school writing sessions, you'd know," Lindsay pointed out.

"I'm not a writer."

"Neither am I, and have you ever tried?"

"No, but I wouldn't be good at it."

"You'll never know unless you try. C'mon, it'll be fun!"

"Hey, Lindsay!" a new voice called, and a second later a third girl joined them. Her name was Sarah, and she was one of the seniors in their class. She was usually in charge of costume design, and rarely actually held roles in plays. "What do you think of this for the male lead?" she asked, holding up a renaissance-y outfit.

"Looks great," Lindsay complimented. "You're the expert, though. You don't have to run everything by me."

"Well, I value your opinion," Sarah replied simply, tossing her blonde hair over her shoulder and smiling at Lindsay in a way that made Valerie's fingers twitch into a half-fist.

Right. Sarah was also bisexual. But she'd been open about it since their freshman year, so she was long past being old news by now.

"Well, consider my opinion your opinion, then," Lindsay replied easily, and Sarah flashed her another grin before leaving to go look for more costume material. Valerie looked to Lindsay, who avoided her eyes a little too purposefully.

"What was that?"

"What was what?" Lindsay asked innocently.

"Does she go to the writing sessions?"

184

"Um… actually, I think she hasn't missed one yet, as a matter of fact," Lindsay surmised.

"Then I'll see you both this afternoon," Valerie bit out, marching away to go ask Kat if she could take a look at the script.

When she let Lucas know he'd need to find a new ride that afternoon, he asked to come along to their writing session, much to her surprise.

"Brody can't give you a ride?" she questioned, referring to his usual backup transportation. Lucas refused to ride the buses except in absolute emergencies.

He shook his head. "Nah."

"Why not?"

Lucas seemed hesitant to answer. "He's, uh… out of commission for a few days."

"What does that mean?" Valerie countered, beginning to get a little suspicious.

"He's just having a little problem with one of his shoulders. He dislocated it, I think," Lucas explained, an edge to his tone.

"And how did that happen?" Valerie was pretty sure she already knew the answer. She noted the bruises on a few of Lucas's right knuckles.

"I *may* have wailed on him."

"He's your friend," Valerie reminded him incredulously. "Why would you do that?"

"He was talking shit about…" Lucas trailed off, aware of their classmates, but Valerie got his meaning loud and clear. She took a deep breath, and then, to Lucas's surprise, leaned in and kissed him on the cheek, and wrapped her arms around him in a tight hug. "…Thanks?" was his response.

That afternoon, they walked to the auditorium together, and Lucas asked her, "So why are you doing this all of a sudden? I thought you didn't want to write it."

"Lindsay convinced me…" Valerie's jaw tensed. "And Sarah."

"Sarah, Sarah…" Lucas murmured, trying to put a face to the name. His eyes widened. "Wait, Sarah with the-?"

"Two ex-girlfriends? Yeah."

"I thought she had more than two."

"Well, I remember two," Valerie retorted, and then let out a groan. "Lucas, how can I compete with that? I won't even hold her hand in public and this girl's probably an expert on all things gay."

"Well, there's a certain endearing aspect to getting to instruct you in the teachings of Sappho, I would think," Lucas pointed out. "Maybe Lindsay wants that over an oldie. Plus, you've got a three-month jump. Sarah, if she's interested now, has only just started to make her move because she only just found out Lindsay likes girls. But alas, she is too late, for Lindsay loves a baby-dyke."

"Don't call me that," Valerie murmured, elbowing him as they approached the auditorium. They entered, and saw Nick, Kat, Tony, Nathan, Lindsay, and Sarah amongst the group of ten or so students gathered by the stage.

"Wait, Sarah's bi, right?" Lucas mumbled, and Valerie gave him a subtle nod. "Okay, I got this. I'm so your wingman right now." He increased the volume of his voice and waved, greeting the group. "Hey guys! I hope I'm allowed; I kind of didn't have a ride home."

"Take the bus, dummy," Lindsay suggested, but looked at him affectionately as he shook his head.

"Never. Anyway, what do we have here?"

"We're doing a medieval love story, just like Romeo and Juliette," Nathan explained, grinning. "We're almost done with the second act but we want it to be three."

"The story's about a peasant guy whose peasant sister is in love with the prince of their kingdom and is due to marry him," Kat began explaining. "But the prince is a bit of a dolt and he ends up encroaching on the territory of a witch, who curses him in a way that makes him unable to be married. The only way to break the curse is to brew another potion, and one of the ingredients is the pure soul of a princess.

"So the lead guy has to go find the princess. But, of course, he's gonna fall in love with her and not want to take her back to have her soul used in the potion. We have a lot of the plot planned out, but there are still some kinks to work through."

"Awesome," Lucas retorted, clapping his hands together. "Let's get started, then."

"He's not even in our class," Valerie heard one girl mumble to another, and couldn't suppress a grin. However, it quickly faded when she saw Sarah approaching Lindsay with a sparkling pink dress in her hand.

"I just found this backstage. How perfect would it be for the princess?"

"Oh my God, that's so pretty," Lindsay gushed, nodding. "We're using it."

Keeping one eye on them, Valerie allowed herself to be ushered over by Nathan to the group surrounding the script. "Maybe a fresh pair of eyes will be a good thing," Nathan suggested. "Okay, so the witch has given our male lead an expert fighter to travel with, in order to avoid thieves and highwaymen along the path to the princess's castle, where she's asleep and awaiting her true love to kiss her awake."

"And this main guy's gonna be her true love," Valerie surmised.

"Exactly. But the thing is, the witch is obviously the only one who should be able to brew a potion, so we have her telling this guy and his bodyguard where to go. But if she cursed the prince in the first place, why would she do that? We need her to have an ulterior motive."

"Because she wants the princess dead," Valerie suggested. "She's glad to kill her."

"But why would she want her dead?" Tony asked.

Valerie thought about it for a moment, the wheels turning in her head. She had to admit, this type of creativity was something she hadn't really done before, and it was kind of fun. "Maybe she has some sort of vendetta against her parents. How old is the witch? Maybe *she* was in love with the princess's dad! But he married the now queen instead of her, and so she wants revenge."

"We had the witch being able to change her appearance, which means she can be any age, so that's a good idea," Nick complimented. "And the witch obviously knows ahead of time that this guy is the princess's true love. But we have to find a way to make sure they get out of this alive while also giving the main guy's sister and her prince fiancé a happy ending."

"Well, what's the curse do?" Valerie asked.

"We haven't decided that yet."

"It should turn him into an animal. Then onstage he can just wear a mask." She perked up, grinning. "And the potion... the antidote one should be exactly the same as the one that turns him into the animal, only with the pure soul added. So when the princess's soul doesn't get added because of course she has to survive, you're just left with another animal potion. And the sister drinks it to be the same animal as the prince. That's kind of a happy ending..."

"Uh, that's genius," Nathan replied, scribbling it down in the script's margins. "How are you coming up with this stuff?"

Valerie laughed. "I don't know. It just doesn't seem hard."

"You need to come write with us every day," Nick insisted. Beside him, Kat grinned encouragingly.

"Yeah, you're good at this, Val."

"Maybe," she told them, and then remembered Lindsay and Sarah. She looked up to see Lucas engaged in conversation with Sarah, who looked a little less than interested, to say the least. Lindsay, meanwhile, surprised Valerie by tapping her on the shoulder.

"How's the writing going, guys?"

"Valerie's helping us out a lot," Nick explained. "I don't know how skilled she is at putting pencil to paper, but she's got some good ideas."

"Maybe you've found your calling, after all," Lindsay told her, grinning.

"Maybe," Valerie echoed, turning away from Lindsay to look back down at the script again, her expression thoughtful. She glanced to Nathan and asked, "Could I take this home?"

"Of course," Nathan agreed. "Just bring it back tomorrow morning and let us know if you change anything."

With Nathan's permission, she left with the script in her backpack, and drove Lindsay home while Lucas rode in the backseat. When she finally got back to her own house, she went straight to her room and took out the script, then read over what had already been written.

It was pretty basic: Peasant family is made up of a mother, daughter, and son. News arrives via messenger that the daughter's fiancé, the prince, has been cursed by a powerful witch. The son is sent to find the witch to see if he can talk her into breaking the curse, and she tells him the only way is to brew an antidote that contains the pure soul of a princess. She provides a bodyguard and then the son and the bodyguard are off to get the princess, encountering several obstacles along the way. The son gets to the princess and kisses her awake at the end of act one, and in act two, the son and the princess get separated from the bodyguard during a highwaymen attack and take refuge in a nearby city. The story stops there, with a note that says act two should end soon and that there should be one more act after that.

Valerie perused the script several times over, making notes here and there and filling in plot holes in her head. By midnight, she had the entire general plot planned out, and was pretty confident she'd covered all of the plot holes.

She finally took a break to check her phone, and saw she had a text from Lindsay and a text from Amber. Amber wanted to know if she felt like coming with her and Tara to the mall the following afternoon, and Lindsay was wishing her goodnight.

She responded to both texts and finally set the script aside, eager for once to go to school the next day.

CHAPTER TWENTY-TWO

Drama was quite the affair the following day. Everyone wanted to know what Valerie had come up with, and they were all pleased with the outline she presented. With Valerie having given them a skeleton of a workable plot, the group started writing out the rest of the individual scenes, and editing scenes that needed slight alterations.

Valerie joined Lindsay backstage again, and Sarah was in and out every ten minutes or so, either to make small talk with Lindsay or to show her a new outfit. After the third visit, Valerie asked, dryly, "You do know she's hitting on you, right?"

Lindsay smiled over at her. "Yes, and I also know you're jealous. But it got you to try something new, and you turned out to be really good at it, so I consider it a good thing."

"I'm sure you do."

Lindsay laughed at her tone. "Oh, come on, Val. You really think I'm gonna leave you for some girl who didn't give me a second glance until she knew I was gay?"

"Well, people know she likes girls," Valerie pointed out. "If you wanted someone open…"

"She's cute," Lindsay told her simply. "And maybe in an alternate universe or something, I'd have been interested. But I like you way too much to pay any attention to anyone else. Even if you're terrified of admitting you aren't straight."

"I'm sorry you have to deal with me," Valerie sighed out, only half-kidding. "I wish it was as easy for me as it was for you."

"Everyone's different," Lindsay pointed out. "And I'd done it once before, so."

"Plus you won't have to live here after three more months," Valerie remembered. Lindsay didn't respond to that. "Do you ever want to talk about that?"

"Maybe sometime," Lindsay answered in a tone that Valerie could tell meant "no".

Sarah entered moments after they fell silent. "Lindsay, please tell me you're trying out for the princess. I found the cutest crown!"

"Actually, I think I'm gonna go low-key on this one," Lindsay replied. "I've had enough of stage-kissing Nick. Kat will rock the princess, I'm sure."

"What part do you want, then?" Sarah questioned. Valerie watched them, eager to hear Lindsay's answer as well.

"I haven't really thought about it, actually. Maybe the witch?"

Sarah giggled. "I don't think you're scary enough."

"I'm plenty terrifying, c'mon."

Sarah shook her head, trying hard not to grin. "No, you're not. I think you're adorable." She immediately looked embarrassed at what she'd said, and then glanced to Valerie, who struggled to keep a straight face but wound up with a tensed jaw. "Sorry," she murmured, clearly a little pink-faced, and abruptly vanished behind a curtain, heading back towards the front of the stage.

Valerie looked to Lindsay, still tense. "I don't know if this is funny to you, because it's really not to me."

Lindsay took one look at her, huffed, and then immediately strode across the backstage area, directly toward her. Valerie's expression morphed to one of apprehension and confusion just before Lindsay pushed her backward the couple of feet it took for her back to hit the wall, then pinned her there and tangled her hands in Valerie's hair, kissing her with fervor. Valerie, caught off-guard, gripped Lindsay's hips with her hands and pulled her closer, head swimming.

They were broken apart by a loud series of clangs as Tony knocked over at least six different props in an effort to hurriedly duck back behind the curtain he'd come from. Both girls caught sight of him, and he stood there awkwardly, swallowing hard.

As Valerie turned away and ran a hand through her hair, trying to keep her anxiety contained and her tears at bay, she heard Tony murmur, "I just...um, I didn't mean-"

Lindsay's voice followed. "Tony, please don't say anything about this."

"I won't. I wouldn't. I'm sorry, I really didn't mean to... I left my jacket here."

"Make sure no one else comes back here."

"Okay." Valerie heard quick footsteps and then a rustling as Tony moved to get his jacket, and then more footsteps followed as he ducked back through the curtain and announced, "Sorry, just knocked over some stuff. It's fine."

Lindsay, meanwhile, reached out and touched her shoulder, her voice gentle. "Val-"

"I don't know if I can do this," she heard herself say. "Lindsay, I don't think I can."

"What are you talking about, Val?" Lindsay used the same gentle tone, and walked around Valerie so that they were face to face. "Do what? Date me?"

"I don't know." Valerie shook her head, trying hard to fight back tears that kept welling up. "It feels like every time I think I might be okay, someone new finds out. The only person I had any control over was Lucas, and now not only do practically all my friends know, but *Tony*? I hardly know him!"

"Tony's gay, too," Lindsay reminded her. "He more than anyone else would know that outing someone isn't okay. You know your secret's safe with him."

"And Kat. And Lucas. And Tara," Valerie listed off. "How many more do I get to add to that list before someone tells? And I'm not ready for that. So maybe we should just stop before it gets worse, and then you can be happy with Sarah and I can just go date Dustin or something and everyone gets a happy ending."

"Everyone but you," Lindsay corrected. "You know that's what this is about, right? If you're doing any of this for me, you're doing it for the wrong reason. You should date people to make yourself happy, and you should be honest with your friends and family because it'll improve *your* life. So if breaking up with me will make you happy, then go for it, but I love you and I want to be with you for as long as I can."

"I don't want to break up," Valerie admitted. "I just want to live in a happy safe bubble with our adopted half-British half-American children."

Lindsay cracked a smile. "That's very specific."

Valerie sniffed, then wiped at her eyes. "I've thought about it."

Lindsay chuckled and pulled her in for a hug, trying to calm her down. When class was over, they left together, and Valerie struggled to not think too much about her tally increasing to four.

Her trip to the mall that afternoon with Amber and Tara would've been a nice distraction, had Amber not chosen to use it as an excuse to bash Lindsay and Kat while they weren't around. She seemed to take the most offense to Kat, to Valerie's relief, as it at least provided some evidence that there were people Amber could hate *more* than gay people. That was at least a start.

As Amber rambled, Valerie found herself frequently locking gazes with Tara, which would follow with them sharing an eye-roll together, and then struggling not to laugh while Amber ranted obliviously nearby. It was the most Tara had felt like her best friend in over three months now.

A couple of weeks ticked by, and Valerie was astounded by how well she and Lindsay maintained contact with Dustin. She'd figured he'd be bitter toward at least Valerie after her rejection, and there was always the chance he'd be homophobic and stop spending time with Lindsay as well, but the three of them got ice cream two times in sixteen days, and according to Lindsay, she and Dustin talked regularly in Civics. Valerie sometimes wondered if it was awkward for Lindsay to be friendly with Dustin, the same way she felt it'd be awkward for herself to be friends with Sarah. But maybe it was different, given that Dustin and Lindsay had been friends before Valerie had ever come into the picture.

Sarah, for her part, was remarkably relentless. She wasn't quite the female Jimmy, but she was a pretty blatant flirt, and Valerie spent a lot of her time in the auditorium clenching her fists at her sides when she wasn't busy consulting Nathan and the other writers of their play. Valerie was pretty certain that Lindsay didn't put a stop to Sarah either because a part of her liked the attention, because a part of her liked seeing Valerie jealous, or because she hoped that that jealousy would spurn Valerie to openly claim Lindsay as her girlfriend.

That last one would be a big hurdle to get over, she knew, although she still aimed to try for coming out sometime before graduation. She finally managed to broach the subject of homosexuality with her parents near the end of February, using another state's recent legalization of gay marriage as a jumping point, and while her father had seemed mostly neutral to it, her mother rolled her eyes at the very notion that homosexual relationships be considered equal to heterosexual ones. Of course, that didn't mean she'd hate Valerie forever, but it definitely meant she wouldn't be happy about it.

That didn't stop her from having Lindsay over whenever they could spare some alone time. In fact, after Tony, Valerie's paranoia led to even less time spent together in public, which meant more time together in private.

Sex was a big part of that, which was a little weird to Valerie, mostly because she was confident she'd been the last of her friends to lose her virginity and it was still strange to think of herself as "sexually active". It seemed like a term reserved for the fictional promiscuous teens she was told horror stories about in sex ed class, not for a seventeen-year-old girl in love with her first girlfriend.

And she was definitely in love. She'd never been before, but she knew the feeling now that it had happened. The way just seeing Lindsay's smile could make her heart skip a beat, or the way the beats could triple in speed instantaneously when Lindsay's hands reached for the button of her pants. If what she felt for Lindsay wasn't love, then frankly, she was terrified of what real love was like, because she already felt like she'd die if she had to live a life that didn't have Lindsay in it. Just thinking about what her life would be like after graduation made her feel sick to her stomach. She was dreading Lindsay's departure and Kara's return, but every time she tried to ask Lindsay about it, Lindsay just said, "We'll see how it goes." That meaningless sentence gave her literally no new information, and did nothing to comfort her.

As March's halfway point drew nearer, the pressure on Valerie seemed to mount higher and higher. With not only Lindsay's sexuality being common knowledge, but Kat's father's, as well, and with Valerie hanging out with the both of them whenever she wasn't with Amber, Tara, or Lucas, she couldn't help but be paranoid that things were about to go very, very badly for her.

She threw herself into the play to take her mind off of it, and even joined in on writing some of the actual scenes. As it turned out, she was actually good at that, too. She wasn't sure that being good at writing and plotting would help her choose a college major in the fall, but it certainly gave her a potential career to strive for. It was, as Lindsay had said, as though Valerie had finally found her calling. She suggested a Journalism major, which didn't sound half-bad to Valerie.

College letters came in as well. Valerie got into everywhere she'd applied to, miraculously. That included Cloverdale University, which was what she'd wanted. Amber would be headed off to her sister's college in the fall, and Kat had her choice between two of the three liberal arts schools she'd applied to. Both Amber and Kat were staying relatively local, just as Valerie was, but Tara had gotten into Brown University, an Ivy League school in the northeast. It was weird to think that in just over two months, Valerie would be losing both Lindsay and Tara. And when she realized that, she immediately felt bad for the small amount of time she and Tara had spent together lately.

They held a sleepover at Valerie's the next weekend, just the two of them, and as they relaxed on Valerie's bed and ate ice cream, Tara admitted, "You know, a part of me did kind of wonder about you, you know... with girls. Right before Lindsay showed up. I never told you that."

"Why?"

"Well, I never thought there was any reason to bring it up, really."

Valerie smiled. "No, why did you wonder?"

195

"Oh." Tara shrugged. "I don't know, really. It wasn't that you'd never had a boyfriend, because obviously I hadn't either. But... you know, I'd never put much thought into how the gay people at our school must feel, because it didn't affect me, but when it came up with Kat, I was willing to talk about it. I started wondering why you kept avoiding the subject. And then the whole thing with Lucas happened, and I know one bad experience with a guy doesn't make someone a lesbian, but I just thought-"

"I don't..." Valerie cut her off, and then tried to get her wording right, "...call myself a lesbian. I don't know what I am."

"What, you're attracted to guys?" Tara asked, arching her eyebrows as she swallowed another spoonful of ice cream.

"I don't know. I haven't thought about it that much."

"Well, Lindsay does make it kind of irrelevant," Tara told her, laughing. "I guess that's one way to think about it, though. Go from person to person, and if you like them, you like them, and if you don't, you don't. There's no reason to get hung up on who you could *potentially* like, is there?"

"Most people do it," Valerie pointed out, and sighed. "What if I really am a lesbian? Do you that'd make being honest with everyone worse than it'd be if I were bisexual?"

"No," Tara told her, shrugging. "I don't think a lot of people at our school even understand the difference."

"How relieving," Valerie deadpanned. "They'll all hate me equally, regardless."

"Not all of them," Tara reassured her. "I know Oliver wouldn't. He's been friendly to Lindsay anytime he's come over."

"He seems nice," Valerie agreed. "And you really like him."

Tara smiled. "Yeah. I'll miss him at Brown. And all of you guys, of course... Amber keeps saying I need to get a move on with him before I go."

"What does that even mean?" Valerie laughed out. "Like get married?"

Tara colored. "No, no... well, we haven't had sex."

Both of Valerie's eyebrows shot up. "Seriously?"

"Yeah. I mean, we've only been together for four months. You and Lindsay haven't...?" She caught sight of Valerie's expression and her eyes widened. "Oh. Wow, really?"

Valerie nodded. "But wait with Oliver if that's what you feel comfortable with, though." She sighed. "I wish I had more time, too, so I know how you must feel."

"You know what we need," Tara proclaimed. "A double-date."

Valerie groaned, falling back on the bed as Tara giggled in front of her. "No more!" Abruptly, she sat back up. "Okay, do you know what I've been through? That date with Lucas, *another* kiss with Lucas, a nasty college guy grinding on me at Amber's, a hangout with Dustin and Lindsay that started with myself being the third wheel and ended with *Lindsay* being the third wheel, and your New Year's party, where I spent the night trying to hook up Amber and Dustin so that Amber wouldn't kiss Lucas and Dustin wouldn't kiss me. I am so unfortunate when it comes to romance in social situations that Lindsay and I would probably be broken up by the end of a double-date with you guys."

Tara chuckled, but her expression looked thoughtful. "You know, I feel like we've missed so much of each other's lives in the past few months. I'd hardly heard about any of that. Since when did your life get so dramatic?"

"Since Lindsay showed up," Valerie joked, and Tara laughed as they finished up their ice cream.

They spent a few more hours talking after that. Valerie asked if living with Lindsay had gotten any better, and Tara admitted that it had, especially after her parents found out Lindsay was gay. Tara's parents were how Valerie suspected her dad would be: fine with gay people, as long as it wasn't their own kid. Her mom, on the other hand, was a different story, and Valerie'd only become more and more aware of the subtle homophobia her mother exhibited as the weeks had gone on. It was evident in even the smallest comments she made and the language she used, and it never ceased to hurt Valerie's feelings every time it happened.

That led back to where every conversation Valerie seemed to have eventually ended up: to talking about coming out and potential reactions. Tara, like Kat and Lindsay, was in favor of it, as long as she was ready.

She was beginning to wonder if she'd ever be.

CHAPTER TWENTY-THREE

"Valerie and Mystery Guy sitting in a tree, K-I-S-S-"

"Are you ten years old? Shut up; I thought you wanted our parents to *stop* babying you."

Abby stuck her tongue out at Valerie as she rode in the passenger's seat of her car. "I can lose a little maturity for two minutes if it means making fun of you. And you better start being nice to me, because now that Mom and Dad know about Ben, what's to stop me from telling them about how *you* spent your Valentine's Day?"

"Because they may know you're dating him, but they still don't know you snuck off with him. So keep your mouth shut and I will, too."

"Tell me who the guy is," Abby demanded.

"No."

"Why not?"

"Because it's none of your business."

"Is it Lucas?"

"No. Now stop asking."

"You don't hang out with any other guys," Abby pointed out. "Unless it's that one that picks you up from our house sometimes, but he's always with Lindsay, too. Is he dating Lindsay?"

"No. Lindsay and I are both just friends with him. Drop it, Abby."

Abby let out a sigh, and Valerie's grip intensified on the steering wheel. Abby had been at this for several days now, ever since their mother had gone to pick her up early from school for a dentist appointment and spotted her holding hands with Ben. And Mrs. Marsh, being Mrs. Marsh, had easily pried most of the details from her younger daughter.

Thankfully, Abby hadn't given up any information about her secret Valentine's Day date for fear of being punished for lying to her parents, and so Valerie still had a form of blackmail. But Abby admittedly *did* still have the upper hand, and so here Valerie was, escorting her sister to a Riverbank High basketball game, where she planned to meet Ben. Just the idea of going to the game bored Valerie, but to middle-schoolers like Ben and Abby, a high-school basketball game was a thrilling opportunity for a date.

"Make sure you stay where I can see the two of you," Valerie told her dully. "Otherwise I'll let Mom know about this."

"If you tell her, I'll tell her about your Valentine's date," Abby warned.

"Then I'll tell her about *yours.*"

Abby's eyes narrowed, and Valerie quirked a threatening eyebrow, ending their argument.

The game was held in the school gym, and Valerie was left to her own devices as Abby immediately left her to go sit by Ben, who was waiting with a hotdog in each hand. Taking care to keep track of their location, Valerie took a seat in the stands and waited by herself the game to start.

She wasn't alone for long. Dustin entered the gym just a few minutes later, scanned the stands for a place to sit, and then hesitated when his eyes landed on her. Not wanting to seem unfriendly, she offered him a thin smile, but he took that as permission to come sit with her. The result was an awkward greeting, followed by tense silence. They'd hadn't really talked without Lindsay around since Valentine's Day. Now, without her around to break the tension, Valerie couldn't think of anything to say.

Dustin, fortunately, did. "So I didn't know you were a basketball fan."

"I'm not," Valerie admitted. "My sister wanted to meet her boyfriend here." She pointed to where Abby and Ben were seated in the front row of the stands, and Dustin nodded his understanding.

"Ah. Well, that makes two of us, I guess. I'm not a fan either. But my little brother's on the team and our record's so good that they're letting him play for most of the game today. He's normally a sub. Must run in the family."

"Oh, so your brother lost out to a hulky douchebag with parents who have connections, too? What are the odds?"

Dustin let out a good-natured laugh. "Ouch. Better not let Jimmy know what you think of him."

"I think Lindsay spoke for most of the girls at our school back in February," Valerie pointed out.

"I guess." They both fell silent for a moment. Valerie regretted bringing up Valentine's Day as the silence grew tense, and then she regretted it even more when Dustin spoke again. "So I know things have been kind of weird... but we never really got a chance to talk about... *that.* Just the two of us, you know? Lindsay's always breaking the ice."

"She's good at that," Valerie murmured, her eyes finding her feet.

"Yeah. But not so good at letting me have an explanation." He sighed. "Look, I know you don't owe me anything, but I thought we were getting along, and then you just kind of canceled on me out of nowhere, and we never had a conversation without Lindsay around after that."

"I had other things going on," Valerie told him, rushing to come up with an explanation that didn't involve telling him the truth.

"And what about now?" He stared at her, waiting. She tried her best to avoid his eyes.

"I don't know... it's not a good time."

"Will it ever be?" When she didn't automatically respond, Dustin shook his head knowingly. "It's Lucas, isn't it?"

"I don't have feelings for Lucas," Valerie countered, aggravated. "God, why does everyone assume there's something going on between us?"

"Well, if you're hanging out with a guy that isn't me, it's him."

"Maybe I'm allowed to have guy friends," she snapped at him, feeling a flicker of anger in the pit of her stomach. She was so tired of having to defend herself. Of feeling obligated to explain every little romantic decision she made. What was wrong with just being left to live her life in peace?

"But that's all it ever is?" he questioned. "Just friends. With every guy in existence? How do you know it can't be more until you give someone a shot?"

Angrily, she whipped her head around, glaring at him. "And how do you know I haven't already given someone a shot?"

He raised both eyebrows, and she immediately regretted her outburst. "I haven't heard about you getting serious with anyone."

"Well… even if I had, it's not like it's any of your business."

"Okay," Dustin sighed out, relenting. "That's true. But I'd still like to know what's going on with you. And what I did to make you turn me down on Valentine's Day. You just don't see me as more than a friend?"

"That's all," Valerie confirmed. "And it might make you feel better that I gave the same speech to Lucas after multiple awful kisses."

Dustin looked amused by that. "Well, I can guarantee I'm a better kisser than him."

"I'll take your word for it."

She looked away from him and back toward the basketball court, where the game had just begun. To her surprise, Abby was no longer in her seat, but had at some point elected to climb back up the stands until she wasn't far from Valerie and Dustin. She smirked at them and crossed her arms.

"I thought you said basketball game dates were lame, Val?"

"We're not on a date," Valerie told her, rolling her eyes. "We ran into each other. Go back to Ben."

"Sure you did," Abby replied, her voice dripping with sarcasm. "Just like he totally *wasn't* the guy you spent Valentine's Day with. We'll go with that." Abby over-exaggerated a wink and Valerie swallowed a lump in her throat, not daring to look at Dustin. She could feel him tensed up beside her.

Abby, oblivious, spun around and returned to the first row. Valerie let out a deep sigh. "Dustin…"

Before she could say anything more, he stood up abruptly and descended the stands, his back to her. A moment later, he'd disappeared from the gym completely. Valerie held back a groan and put her head in her hands, but didn't go after him.

Dustin never returned to the gym, and Valerie drove Abby home a few hours later. Abby pressed her for more details in the car.

"So was he the guy? Are you dating him? And don't bother lying."

"Yes. Are you happy?" Valerie knew Abby wouldn't believe her even if she denied it, anyway, and frankly she was sick of making excuses to people. It was too much effort.

"Are you gonna introduce him to Mom and Dad?"

"They already know him."

"Yeah, but as Lindsay's friend, not *your* boyfriend. And are you sure Lindsay doesn't like him? Aren't you worried?"

"She doesn't like him," Valerie dismissed. "And you better keep this quiet. I have two secret dates to blackmail you with, now."

"Relax. I was just curious. I can't believe you finally have a boyfriend, though. I'm four years younger than you and I *still* got one before you."

"Congratulations," Valerie deadpanned, and promptly turned on the radio to drown out whatever Abby said next.

Lucas was on her living room couch when they entered what they thought would be an empty home.

"I see you've just resorted to breaking and entering now when you want my attention," Valerie observed, raising an eyebrow upon sight of him.

"Hey Lucas, Val's dating someone!" Abby called out to him, much to Valerie's annoyance. Lucas looked to Valerie with shock.

"You told her?"

"Yes, all about my complex love affair with Dustin," Valerie retorted, shooting him a warning look. He pulled a face.

"Ah. Yes, that one. Well, you couldn't hide it forever. Not from your own sister, at least."

"He's kind of cute," Abby decided. "I'm not sure how my lame sister managed to convince him to go out with her, though."

"She plays hard to get. Trust me, I'd know," Lucas retorted. Abby disappeared upstairs, and he immediately grinned at Valerie. "Your life sucks."

"I'm aware," she sighed out, collapsing on the couch beside him and reaching for the remote.

"Hey! I'm watching this," Lucas countered, slapping her hand away.

"What are you even doing here?"

"My parents are fighting," he explained. "The yelling was giving me a headache."

"I'm sorry."

"It's no big deal. I'd rather have them then be gay with homophobic ones."

"Shhh," she reminded him, gesturing toward the stairs. "And it's only my mom, anyway."

"So when are you telling them?"

"I have no idea."

"They're gonna think you're with Dustin, now."

"Not if Abby keeps her mouth shut," Valerie pointed out.

"What has her so convinced you're dating him in the first place?"

"He was at the game and she saw us together. And she also revealed that I spent Valentine's Day with someone else, so there's that."

"So your sister thinks you're dating a guy who probably hates your guts but is friends with your secret girlfriend who's becoming less and less of a secret as the weeks go on and is also being relentlessly hit on by an openly bisexual girl who, ironically, is ignoring all of *my* advances." He grinned. "This is fun, let's do another. I bet we can fit Amber in somehow."

"Fitting Amber in opens up an entirely new can of hookup worms," Valerie pointed out. "Let's not." She sighed, and leaned over to rest her head on Lucas's shoulder. "Why couldn't I have been born one-hundred years into the future, when none of this would've mattered and just the idea of homophobia would've been hilarious to everyone?"

"Hey. You wouldn't have met me, if that were the case." He paused. "And Lindsay. That's probably important, too."

"She could've married Sarah."

"Nonsense. Their kids would be too blonde."

"A clear travesty."

"Exactly."

She tilted her head to grin up at him, and a moment later, the front door clicked and then swung open. Mrs. Marsh walked in, took one look at them, and then raised both eyebrows, pleasantly surprised. "Oh... was I interrupting something?"

"Not at all," Lucas answered as Valerie lifted her head off of his shoulder. "I was just about to leave."

"Oh, don't mind me," Mrs. Marsh insisted, waving him off. "Stay as long as you like. I'll be heading to bed soon, anyway."

"No, I have to go." Lucas stood up and sent Valerie an apologetic look when his back was to her mother. "I'll see you tomorrow, Val."

"Sure," she replied. He left, and Mrs. Marsh locked the door behind him.

"You two looked cozy."

"Stop, Mom."

"It was just an observation, sweetie. You know I've always thought Lucas was a nice boy..."

"Then *you* date him," Valerie countered, heading into the kitchen to fix herself a snack. Mrs. Marsh followed her.

"Honey, I don't understand why you get so defensive about stuff like this. There's nothing wrong with having a crush."

"Except I don't. Lucas and I are just friends."

"Val," Mrs. Marsh began knowingly, "I was in high school once, too. I understand what it's like. Dating boys can be scary and confusing-"

"I'm not confused!" Valerie insisted, whirling around to face her mother. "Mom, just stop. Please. Stop pretending like you know what's going on with me. You're never even home."

She could tell immediately that she'd struck a nerve. Mrs. Marsh blinked at her, momentarily stunned, and her voice was quiet when she spoke next. "Valerie, I work very hard to try and give you the best life that I can. So does your father. You know that."

"But what if my life isn't the life you want for me? Would you still support me then, or is everything conditional?"

"I don't understand... the life I don't want for you? Of course it's not conditional. I want you to be happy."

"You make comments, Mom, and you don't know who you're hurting when you make them. And maybe you don't pressure me with school, like Tara's parents do with her, but you make it clear you have an expectation that I'm not meeting."

Mrs. Marsh let out a disbelieving laugh. "Valerie, that's ridiculous. I put very little pressure on you. Just because I've made it clear that I'd be happy to see you with someone-"

"With a boyfriend."

"Yes. Of course. With a boyfriend."

They fell silent, and Valerie let out a breath she didn't know she'd been holding. She could feel her heart starting to beat faster, and a lump developing in her throat. She looked down and saw her hands were shaking. She was so close to saying it. If she didn't take the opportunity now, then when would she have it again?

"But... what if I don't want a boyfriend?"

Mrs. Marsh frowned at her. Valerie gripped the countertop in front of her to try and keep her hands steady. "Well... then I suppose you should wait until you're ready to date. But I met your father in high school, you know, so I think now's a perfectly good time to start-"

"No, Mom," Valerie cut her off, closing her eyes tightly. "What if I don't want a *boy*friend?"

She was met with a deafening silence. Her heart rate spiked, and she forced herself to open her eyes. She could feel her whole body shaking, she was so nervous, and Mrs. Marsh just stared at her, eyebrows furrowed.

And finally: "…That's not funny, Valerie."

The shaking reached her voice this time. "I'm not kidding."

Even as her mother continued to stare and the shaking continued, Valerie felt a sense of relief, albeit small, fill her chest. She'd done it. It was over with, and tomorrow she would be able to tell Lindsay, Lucas, Tara, and Kat what she'd accomplished. They'd all be there to support her, at least. She wouldn't have to worry about Abby thinking she was with Dustin, or her parents thinking she was with Lucas. The secret was out.

Mrs. Marsh stepped toward her, her expression unreadable. Only the countertop rested between them as her mother looked down at her and replied, "You're young, Valerie. Impressionable. And I think, perhaps… a little confused."

"I'm not confused," she retorted without hesitation.

Mrs. Marsh raised a hand to pinch at the bridge of her nose, and sighed. "Who is it that has you thinking like this? Honey, this is not you. This isn't my daughter."

"I am your daughter." Valerie ignored her question. "And you have no idea how terrified I've been to tell you this. I'm standing here shaking and I have no idea whether or not you hate me, or…" she trailed off, nearly stuttering over her words, and felt tears prick at the corner of her eyes. She forced them away even as her mother's expression softened. Now, she was simply looking at her daughter with pity.

"Honey, I don't hate you. I don't. I just… I know this isn't you. I'm your mother; I raised you. And I raised you well. Not to be like this. What will your father say?"

"If he's a good father, he'll tell me he's happy if I'm happy."

"And you're happy?" Mrs. Marsh countered, unconvinced.

"If we can be okay, and me and Dad, and Abby, and… everyone else I care about, then I think I am."

"How can I be okay with this? When you could have a husband and kids…"

"I can have kids."

"It's not the same." Mrs. Marsh shook her head. "Not as good. And it's not the life I want for you."

"Why does that matter if I've found someone I'd be happy to have that kind of life with? Shouldn't I do what makes me happy?"

"Not to your own detriment." Mrs. Marsh crossed her arms. "Tell me who it is, Valerie." Valerie clamped her mouth shut and Mrs. Marsh's eyes narrowed. "...It's Kat, isn't it? She's always been-"

"Stop," Valerie interrupted. "It doesn't matter."

They stood in silence for a moment, and Mrs. Marsh let out a slow exhale, her eyes falling to the countertop. She looked to be deep in thought for a moment, and then her eyes fell shut and the corners of her lips quirked upward, knowingly. She opened her eyes. "Lindsay, then."

"Mom..."

"You went on that date with Lucas, and then she got here, and I haven't seen you on a date since."

"I didn't like Lucas. I don't like-" She cut herself off and licked her lips, realizing how dry they were. It dawned on her how she'd been about to finish her sentence. It had come second-nature to her, despite all of the confusion she'd had about labeling herself in the past. In that moment, she knew how she honestly felt. "I don't like boys."

Her mother seemed to have no response to that, and only reacted by tensing her jaw and straightening up. "Nonsense. We'll see what your father has to say about this when he gets home."

She swept out of the room without another word, and Valerie stood alone in the kitchen, still shaking uncontrollably as the sound of her mother's footsteps faded away.

CHAPTER TWENTY-FOUR

An uncomfortable tension permeated the living room as Valerie rested on the couch, bent over with her head in her hands. She could sense her mother's presence over near the kitchen; could hear the occasional tap of a coffee mug being set back down on the countertop. Valerie wasn't sure how long it'd been since her mother had spoken, but she was beginning to panic. If her father agreed with her mother, then where did that leave things? What would happen to her, and to her relationship with Lindsay? Where could she even go from there?

At some point, the front door clicked, a signal that the lock had been undone. A moment later, it swung open, and footsteps sounded across the hardwood floor. The door slammed shut.

"Hey, Val." She heard her father's voice, friendly and with a slightly surprised tone to it, and she didn't look up. "What're you doing up so l-? Oh, hey, honey. I'm surprised to see you up, too. Is Abby in bed?" There was a pause as he was met with no response, and then, "…What's wrong?"

Valerie heard her mother take another sip of coffee. "I think you should let your daughter tell you. Valerie?"

Valerie grit her teeth and didn't move, her face hidden. She blinked and a tear escaped against her will, sliding down her cheek. Silently, she shook her head.

She heard her mother sigh in response. "Now she doesn't want to speak."

"Val, honey, what's wrong?" The couch sank beside her as her father joined her, and she felt a hand on her back. "Tell me what happened?"

"Nothing happened," she murmured, aware that her voice revealed she was crying.

"Well, it certainly doesn't seem that way. C'mon, talk to me."

Silently, she shook her head again. She heard her father sigh, and assumed he shared a silent look with her mother, because a moment later, Mrs. Marsh did the talking for her. "Valerie has a crush on her friend Lindsay."

"It's not a crush," she couldn't help but counter, and finally lifted her head enough to glare at her mother. "I love her. And she loves me."

"Stop saying that," Mrs. Marsh retorted simply. "You're both too young to know that."

"You *just* told me that you met dad in high school!"

"Valerie," Mr. Marsh warned, but looked to her sympathetically. "I want to hear this from you."

"There's nothing to hear." Valerie wiped her tears away. "I've been dating Lindsay. I'm… I'm gay."

Across the room, Mrs. Marsh shook her head silently, but Valerie's dad's eyes remained trained on her.

"Val… I think that's a very big claim to make at your age."

"But Abby can know she's straight," Valerie shot back sarcastically, wiping at her eyes again.

Mr. Marsh looked thoughtful. "Well… I suppose we wouldn't argue with that, would we? You're right." He paused, watching her carefully. "So you're sure about this?"

"Henry," Mrs. Marsh scoffed, appalled that he'd even entertain the idea.

"I am. I wouldn't say it if I didn't, and I didn't say it until I was sure," Valerie insisted.

"You realize your life will be a lot harder this way," Mr. Marsh told her. "A lot of ignorant people are going to say hurtful things to you. I'll be honest and say I don't feel comfortable with the idea of you going through that…

but I can't stop you from doing what makes you happy."

Even as Valerie felt a wave of relief wash over her, her mother interrupted, indignant. "Of course we can! We agree, Henry: This will make her life much more difficult than it needs to be. She can't handle it. Our job as parents is to protect our child-"

"Our job is to love our children," Mr. Marsh corrected. "And we're going to do that regardless of who she loves in turn. We've both discussed what a good influence Lindsay has been on Valerie since she got here. She's made her more social, gotten her involved with her school, and been a great friend. None of that changes just because she loves her."

Mrs. Marsh shook her head, looking on the verge of tears now. "I just want my daughter to have an easy life. Is that too much to ask?"

"I don't know." Her father shrugged. "But if it's a choice between having an easy life or a happy one, I'd want her to have a happy one."

"Thanks, Dad," Valerie told him quietly. He patted her back reassuringly even as Mrs. Marsh kept shaking her head and then stormed off to the bedroom.

"She'll come around," he insisted. "And I'll get better, too. I'd be lying if I said I saw this coming. I thought you were just a late bloomer."

She shot him a watery smile, and they both turned as they heard footsteps coming down the stairs.

Abby rubbed at her eyes and stared over at them, clearly confused. "What's going on? I heard shouting."

"Your mother's having a rough night, Abby," Mr. Marsh answered before Valerie could. "Go back to bed."

Abby padded back up the stairs with a sigh, and Valerie looked to her father. "How am I supposed to tell her? She knows I'm dating someone but she's convinced my girlfriend's a boyfriend."

"Abby likes Lindsay," Mr. Marsh reminded her. "And she loves you. When you're ready, I think she'll pleasantly surprise you. But until then, I'll talk to your mother about letting you do things at your own pace." He patted her on the back again and then got to his feet, yawning. "And I also think it might be a good idea to have Lindsay over for dinner sometime soon. Once your mother calms down, of course." He leaned down and kissed her on the head. "Goodnight, Val."

"Thank you, Dad."

"Any time." He yawned again and left the room, and a moment later, the bedroom door shut behind him. Valerie eventually made her way up to her room in a daze, trying to take in what had just happened. She was still trembling slightly, and her heart refused to slow down long enough for her to even relax in her own bed. She thought about texting Lindsay, but eventually decided against it. Lindsay was probably already asleep. Her news could wait until tomorrow. In the meantime, getting some sleep after such an eventful night was going to be a struggle.

When she woke up the next morning after getting just a few hours of sleep, the night before didn't feel real.

The reality only hit her when she finally forced herself to go downstairs, and her mother was in the kitchen, silently spreading jam on a piece of toast. Her father was there, too, and he shot her a smile and greeted her, "Good morning, Val."

"Morning," she replied quietly. The room quickly grew tense. "Well... see you tonight."

She left the house before either of her parents could respond, and drove to school in a daze not unlike the one she'd felt when she'd headed up to her room after saying goodnight to her father. Things weren't perfect, but they didn't feel like an ending. They didn't feel resolved, whether in a bad way or in a good way. Just incomplete. She still wasn't out at her school, Abby still didn't know, and she wasn't sure where exactly her mother stood.

She went to her locker and took out a few books, then closed it when she was done and promptly headed for her Drama class. They were casting roles soon, and as one of the lead creators of the play, Valerie had been told by Nathan to expect to have a huge role in choosing who'd play what part. More and more, lately, she'd been looking forward to her first class of the day, and then the sessions after school, as well.

She was early to her class, and only spotted a few of her classmates scattered around the auditorium as she headed past them to go backstage, where Lindsay almost always was.

She pushed one of the curtains aside and found herself just thirty feet away from where Sarah stood face to face with Lindsay, much too close to her for comfort. Lindsay's arms were crossed protectively in front of her and she shook her head at something Sarah had evidently said, murmuring, "No, I don't."

"Don't lie," Sarah replied just as quietly, and Valerie felt her heart stop as Sarah abruptly leaned in and kissed Lindsay.

Valerie stared, unmoving. This wasn't happening. This couldn't be happening. Not after everything she'd done the night before.

Lindsay's arms uncrossed and her hands shot up to Sarah's shoulders, pushing her back and breaking the kiss, but Valerie had already looked away and was hurrying to put as much distance between herself and Lindsay as possible. Her foot clanged against a stray prop, and Lindsay's eyes shot to her even as Valerie vanished behind the curtain and rushed from the backstage area. "Valerie!" she called, hastily moving to follow her. "Valerie, wait!"

It wasn't long before Valerie found herself back in her car, tears streaming silently down her cheeks. She spotted Lindsay heading toward her and quickly locked her car doors. Lindsay tried to open one, and upon finding it locked, sighed and knocked on the window. "Val, please open up."

Valerie wiped her own tears away and didn't respond. Lindsay tried again.

"Let me explain. Please?"

Wordlessly, Valerie fumbled for her keys and slid them into the ignition. Ignoring Lindsay's protests, she started her car up and abruptly reversed, taking care to get out of the parking lot quickly without hitting Lindsay in the process. Within seconds, her phone buzzed repeatedly as Lindsay called her. She didn't pick up. Her vision was so blurry she could hardly see where she was going, and she felt like she'd be sick at any moment.

As her phone continued to buzz, she found an empty parking lot by a gas station and took a break there, trying to calm herself down. She knew, deep down, that it was possible there was a rational explanation for what she'd just seen, but she couldn't suppress a visceral reaction to witnessing Sarah and Lindsay together. Especially not after the emotional roller coaster she'd been on since the basketball game.

She pressed her forehead to the steering wheel and waited for her breathing to slow and her vision to clear. Her phone began buzzing again.

She didn't want to go home in case her parents hadn't left for work yet, and she didn't want to go back to school and face Lindsay. And then there was Sarah, who was certainly smart enough to realize why Lindsay had taken off after Valerie. Valerie felt like her whole life was spiraling out of control before her very eyes. She shut them, swallowing hard.

"She can't handle it."

Was it possible that her mother was right?

CHAPTER TWENTY-FIVE

In the end, she chose home over school, hedging her bets that her parents would both be at work already. She drove home when her crying finally ebbed, and parked out on the street. Her phone buzzed again as she got out of her car, but this time, it didn't continue, which meant she had a text. It was from Lindsay, and she didn't read it.

On a whim, she went to the garage first and peered inside, to check for her parents' cars. It was a good decision; they were both still in the garage.

Sighing, she went to the front door and tried to look through the glass. If her parents weren't in the living room, she could probably sneak up to her room without them knowing. But it was strange that they were even home in the first place.

It didn't take long for her to spot both of her parents on the living room couch together. Her father was talking and gesturing a lot with his hands, and her stomach flopped unpleasantly as she realized her mother was crying. She couldn't remember the last time she'd seen that happen.

She backed away from the door and looked around, unsure of where she could go now and feeling even worse than she already had. Eventually, she went back to her car, got into the front seat, and finally checked her phone.

Lindsay's text message read: *"I'm so so sorry. The thing with Sarah got out of hand and I should've told her I wasn't interested from the very beginning. I also fixed things with Dustin. I love you and whatever decision you make I'll support."*

It only left Valerie more confused. Decision? What decision did she have to make at this point? To be pissed off or not be pissed off? And what had there even been to fix with Dustin? Sure, he was upset, but he was ultimately Lindsay's friend, not Valerie's. If he was upset with Valerie, it wasn't really an urgent problem that needed fixing. Like with his original sadness after Valentine's, Valerie assumed it would soon fade.

She sat in her car for another half-hour until her phone buzzed again. This time it was Amber, to her surprise. *"OMG where r u? R u freaking out right now?"*

Valerie checked the clock. Normally, she'd be in Lit with Kat and Amber right now.

She texted Amber back *"What?"* just as her phone buzzed with a text from Kat.

"Did u know about this?"

Baffled, and beginning to panic, Valerie responded, *"What r u talking about???"*

Kat texted back quicker than Amber did. *"Give me one minute."*

Then came Amber's response. *"U didn't know Lindsay had a thing for u?"*

Valerie stared down at her phone, her heart rate picking up. "Oh, no," she murmured quietly. What had Lindsay done?

Her phone buzzed moments later; Kat was calling her. She picked up instantaneously.

"Kat, what the hell is going on?"

"I'm in the bathroom so I can't stay long," Kat prefaced. "I thought maybe you were in on this because I saw Lindsay follow you out of the auditorium this morning and she was really upset when she came back, and wouldn't tell me what was going on. Then when we got out of class, Dustin came up to her in the hallway and basically called her out, saying he'd figured everything out and that he knew you'd spent Valentine's Day with someone else and knew it was her. She lied for you."

"Why?" Valerie croaked out, hardly able to believe what she was hearing.

"I guess she knew you weren't ready to say something. He put her on the spot, so she had to come up with something, so she told him that she'd spent it with you, but only as friends, and that you genuinely just hadn't been interested in him. He didn't believe her, so she admitted that she liked you but said you were straight and didn't like her back. A ton of people heard, Val. Amber'd already heard about it by the time she got to Lit class."

"I can't believe she did that," Valerie murmured. "That makes her look really bad."

"She covered your ass in a big way," Kat agreed. "Why aren't you at school?"

"I saw Sarah kiss her this morning."

Kat was silent on the other end for a moment. Then she sighed. "Oh, Val. I wish you could've seen how crushed Lindsay was back in the auditorium, after you left. I thought it was because you'd guessed the whole Dustin would happen and told her to say you didn't like her, but I'm guessing she probably thinks it's over between the two of you anyway."

"I got a text from her," Valerie admitted. "She made it seem like Sarah kissed her and she didn't want her to."

"Well, did you see who kissed whom?"

"Yeah. Sarah. I ran away after that, though."

"You should probably hear Lindsay's side of the story," Kat advised. "But the ball's in your court now, you know? If you don't think you can be out at school, now would be the time to end it. And if you can be, well... you can start correcting Lindsay's story and letting everyone know you do like her."

"Why does it have to be one or the other?" Valerie protested. "Why is it come out or break up?"

"Well, I guess you could always just let the rumors go on, but here's the thing, Val." Kat took a deep breath. "Our school is full of assholes. The kind of assholes who wouldn't even tolerate having a gay friend, let alone a gay friend with a crush on them. They're idiots, but they're not stupid. If you and Lindsay stay inseparable after this, and don't have any kind of falling out, it'll be pretty obvious that she lied for you."

Valerie didn't respond to that, but her heart sank as she realized that Kat had a point. She had the option of keeping her public friendship with

Lindsay the same, but it was likely that her closed-minded peers would jump right to the conclusion that she liked her back. Sure, they'd go there because of their closed-mindedness and prejudice, but they'd also be *right*, ultimately.

"Listen, Val, I have to go," Kat told her abruptly. "Please talk to Lindsay, okay? Give her a chance."

"You want me to tell the truth," Valerie countered knowingly.

"I want you to be happy. Lindsay makes you happy," Kat answered shortly, and hung up.

Valerie spent a lot of time texting with Amber after that, mostly to get her mind off of making a decision. Amber didn't know the whole story, and so their conversation mostly consisted of Amber being shocked that Lindsay had a crush on Valerie, and asking Valerie in turn if she'd ever suspected, which then turned into Amber naming all of the "sketchy" things Lindsay had done in the past that suddenly made sense now. Many of those things were statements she'd made about Valerie around Amber when Valerie hadn't been present, so it actually turned out to be quite a flattering experience.

She practiced denying liking Lindsay back with Amber, as well. It didn't feel right, but it did feel safe.

Her parents never ended up leaving their house. Her mother stayed inside the entire time, presumably being comforted by her father. Valerie knew from experience that they'd both be working massive shifts later on to make up for the missed day, and that made her feel terrible.

She drove to school when there were ten minutes left in her last class, solely so that she could give Lucas a ride home. When he finally got outside, he looked surprised to see her waiting.

"I thought you ditched."

"I did. But I came back for you," she told him.

"That's romantic," he countered, and buckled himself into the passenger's seat. "So I'm guessing you left after things blew up with Lindsay and Dustin?"

"Actually, I left before that, when I saw my girlfriend kissing another girl."

The word "girlfriend" sounded strange coming out of her mouth, almost like her decision had already been made. It had only been seven hours since Sarah had kissed Lindsay and only six since Dustin had confronted her, but Valerie already felt as though Lindsay was no longer her girlfriend, and it just hadn't sank in yet.

"Are you serious? Sarah?" Lucas guessed. "There's no way Lindsay was cool with that, c'mon."

"Well, she let it get to that point," Valerie pointed out. "She knew I didn't feel comfortable with Sarah flirting with her so much and she let it go on."

"I guess that's true," Lucas admitted. "But that's no reason to break up or anything." When she didn't reply, he looked to her, surprised. "You're not breaking up with her, are you?"

Valerie shrugged her shoulders and backed out of the parking space, avoiding Lucas's eyes. "I don't know."

"You guys are crazy about each other. It'd be stupid to end it over a misunderstanding."

"And what about Dustin?" Valerie pointed out.

"Dustin's a dumbass; forget about him. So the whole school knows Lindsay has a thing for you. Just play it cool and don't address it, and it's no problem."

"Not at this school, Lucas. Lindsay still admitted we spent Valentine's Day together, and if I don't immediately act freaked out that she likes me, what does that look like? It looks bad enough that I didn't care when the whole school found out she was gay. But to ignore that she likes me, too... someone's bound to figure it out."

"Well, who cares? They're stupid."

"*I* care!" Valerie countered, surprising herself as Lucas flinched. She took a deep breath and lowered her voice. "I do, okay? I care what people think and say about me. You do too. It's easy for you to tell me to just be who I am when who you are is already acceptable. You'll never understand what this is like, okay?"

Lucas shifted in his seat and seemed to consider her words for a moment. Finally, he exhaled, nodding. "Okay. You're right. I don't understand. But I

219

can be there for you, Val. And you have Kat, and Tara, and Lindsay, and your whole Drama class, I'm sure."

"When I have to start counting allies, you know it's bad," Valerie murmured. She shook her head. "Look, I haven't told anyone else this, but I came out to my parents last night. They didn't go to work today because my mom sat at home for eight hours, crying. How do you think that makes me feel?"

Lucas, for once, seemed speechless. "…I don't know, Val."

"Like complete crap," Valerie told him. "And I'm sick of feeling this way. Look, you have no idea how badly I want to be with Lindsay. But I wasn't ever cut out for this. It's like… sometimes I feel like there are people out there who'd be great at being gay. Like Kat. She'd be amazing at the whole coming out thing. She's so strong and she doesn't care what anyone says about her. And then there are the people who'd suck at it. Amber, who'd probably come out at age forty when she's married with two kids. Or Tara; she'd find a way to overthink it and convince herself she's straight, if Kara didn't convince her first. And me."

"C'mon, that's silly. There's no bad way to be gay."

"But there are bad ways to handle coming out, and I've completely botched mine."

"So fix it."

"Why? I can just wait until college."

"But Lindsay may not be around for that. I know she likes it here, but it's a longshot to hope she'll just show up at Cloverdale next year or something with roses and chocolate and a boombox."

"That's the problem," Valerie explained. "What's more important: Being with Lindsay or having a coming out that I feel comfortable with?"

Lucas frowned at her, and then sighed deeply. "Well… I think you and I both know the answer to that."

CHAPTER TWENTY-SIX

Mr. Davis answered the door just after Valerie's third knock, smiling out at her. "Well hi there, Val. Are you looking for Lindsay or Tara?"

"Lindsay," Valerie admitted. "But if she's not here I'd like to hang out with Tara until she gets back."

"They're both here," he told her. "Lindsay's up in her room."

He opened the door and Valerie stepped inside, nodding her thanks to him before ascending the stairs. She walked down the hallway, aiming to go to Lindsay's room, but Tara's door was open and as she passed by, Tara called, "Val?"

Valerie paused, then backpedaled and peeked into Tara's room. "Hey."

"You weren't at school today," Tara observed, eyebrows furrowing in concern as she sat on her bed, several textbooks splayed out around her. "How are you doing?"

Valerie shrugged. "I've been better, I guess."

"Well, what are you doing here? Get in here," Tara demanded. Valerie sighed and obeyed, shutting the bedroom door behind her. She'd planned on getting in and out in a few minutes. She didn't want to drag out what she was about to do. It'd only make things harder.

"I'm just here to see Lindsay."

"I heard about what happened today," Tara admitted. "It's no wonder you left."

Valerie decided to leave out the Sarah part in favor of saving time. "Yeah."

"So what're you gonna do?" Tara asked. "Lindsay lied for you, but... I don't mean to freak you out, but I don't think people are gonna buy it for long. Not as close as you two are."

"I know," Valerie told her, forcing a smile. "Trust me, I've been told multiple times that I have a choice to make."

Tara gave her a sympathetic look. "Val... listen, I know Kat in particular gets a little caught up in all the gay drama, so I'm sure she has a very strong opinion about this, with her dad and all. But I want you to know that even if I can't understand, I am trying, and I think I understand why you'd do what I have a hunch you're doing right now. Sometimes it's too hard to do the right thing for other people. You have to take care of yourself."

Valerie bit her lip, feeling pressure begin to build up behind her eyes. She didn't want to cry. Not now. "I just wish I could do both."

"Everyone does. But I don't think you're the bad guy, okay? And if Kat gives you a hard time, it's because she doesn't understand that things aren't black and white."

"I don't want to lie," Valerie explained. "I don't plan on it. I'm not gonna start dating boys. I just don't want to be honest with everyone right now. And Lindsay and I could... what if we just ignored each other in public and then dated in private, and..."

Tara gave her a sympathetic look even as she trailed off. "If you were Lindsay, would you take that deal? From what I understand, you were doing something similar to that already and she wasn't exactly enjoying it."

"I know," Valerie sighed out, blinking back tears. "I know it's not right to ask her to keep doing it. I was supposed to be making things easier for us as time went on, not harder. I just... this hurts so much."

"It's not your fault." Tara stood up and came over to hug her, and Valerie rested her forehead on Tara's shoulder. "And I'm not going to blame you, okay?"

"Thank you."

After a moment, Tara pulled away and gave her an encouraging smile. "Alright. Good luck."

"Thanks."

Valerie wiped any traces of tears from her face and then left Tara's room, closing the door behind her. She finished her walk to Lindsay's door and hesitated for a moment, raising her fist to knock. She took a deep breath, and then followed through with the action.

The door swung open seconds later, and Lindsay blinked out at her, then raised both eyebrows in surprise. "Val," she murmured, and Valerie abruptly felt herself pulled into a tight hug as Lindsay buried her face in her neck. "God, I was worried you hated me." She pulled back and continued, earnestly, "You have to know that I didn't want to kiss Sarah. She kissed me and I swear I pushed her away. And the whole Dustin thing... I knew you weren't ready to come out and I did everything I could to cover for you, okay?"

She paused, finally, and stared at Valerie, waiting for a response. Valerie opened and closed her mouth, trying to make the words come out. She squeezed her eyes shut, and, at last, forced them out. "Lindsay, we have to break up."

She opened her eyes to see Lindsay staring back at her, stunned. "...What?"

"I... I thought I could handle this, but I can't. I'm not ready. And you deserve better." Valerie swallowed hard, and pushed herself to go on. "I love you, and I know you love me, but... I think we loved each other at the wrong times in our lives. We're in two different places right now, Lindsay, and you should be with someone who's on the same page as you. I'm holding you back. I mean, I came out to my parents last night and-"

"That's good," Lindsay interrupted hastily. "Val, that's a huge step. That's enough for me."

"It's not enough for me," Valerie argued, shaking her head. "My mom spent all day today crying, and I feel *so* guilty even though I know I shouldn't. And this whole thing with Dustin? I want so badly to say that I can just be honest... but I can't. I can hardly handle upsetting my mom, let alone having an entire school against me. You were untouchable, Lindsay. Everyone liked you before you came out, and they still trashed you, so what's gonna happen to me? I'm just the girl who sits in the light booth."

Lindsay blinked back tears and let out a shaky breath. "I really like that girl."

"I know, but I can't do this to you. I can't keep you a secret when I know you don't want to be. I just need to wait until I'm ready and then deal with this on my own."

"So what, we never talk again?" Lindsay argued, voice cracking. "We just ignore each other because you're afraid that if you're nice to me people will think you're gay? Or you don't think I deserve a secret relationship so I'm delegated to secret friendship instead? How could you do this to me? You told me you loved me."

"I do," Valerie insisted. "I just-"

"Then please don't do this." Lindsay was crying fully now, her eyes red-rimmed and tears streaming down her cheeks. "I don't think I can forgive you if you do this."

That hit Valerie hard, and she sucked in a shaky breath as she finally let her own tears fall. "I'm so sorry. I wish I was a better person. Or... braver. But I'm not."

Lindsay bit down hard on her lip. "So that's it, then? Goodbye; have a nice life?"

"I still want to be friends if-"

"If no one is around to measure how closely we're sitting or how often we smile at each other," Lindsay snapped, cutting her off. She shook her head and covered her mouth, smothering a sob, and finally finished, "Screw you, Valerie." With that, she stepped back into her room, and a moment later, the door was slammed in Valerie's face. She stood there in stunned silence, heart aching as she listening to the muffled sobbing on the other side of the door, and immediately wished she could take everything she'd said back. She wished there was some way she could have Lindsay *and* be accepted by everyone in her life, but there wasn't. Not right now.

She wiped away her tears hastily and forced herself to leave Lindsay alone. Without saying goodbye to Tara or either of her parents, she hurried back out to her car and sat alone in the driver's seat, breathing hard as she replayed their conversation over and over in her head. She'd been selfish. She'd done the right thing for herself, and only herself. But maybe Lucas and Tara were right, and it was her decision to make. Kat, however, wasn't going to be happy with her. And Lindsay, undoubtedly, would be even more furious with her when she finished being sad. That would hurt the worst, she knew.

She got home ten minutes later. Her father was in the kitchen, making dinner, and her mother was nowhere to be seen.

"She's sleeping," Mr. Marsh told her in response to her questioning look. "Lots of patients during her shift today. She's exhausted."

"Okay," Valerie replied, her voice sounding hollow even to her own ears. "I'm not really hungry."

"Are you sure? I made your favorite."

"Yeah. I'm sorry, Dad."

His gaze softened as he stared at her. "For what?"

She shrugged, sighing. "Causing so many problems."

"You didn't cause any problems. Your mother's issues are hers and hers alone."

"Okay." She paused. "I think I'm just gonna go to bed." She headed to her room without another word, and fell asleep even more slowly than she had the night before.

The next school day began, as usual, with her Drama class. She arrived one minute before class started and was unsurprised to see Nick give her a warning look the minute she started to head toward him and Kat. Kat didn't even look at her.

She avoided the backstage area for a while, instead spending some time with Nathan going over the play, but, inevitably, he asked her if she minded going and double-checking how many prop swords they had so he could make sure they didn't have fight scenes that required more weapons than they had available to them.

And so, thirty seconds later, she was ducking behind one of the curtains and heading over to the chest where they'd put the swords they'd found during past class periods. Sarah was the only person she saw, thankfully, and they didn't make eye contact as Sarah admired a new dress she'd found. As Valerie counted, she vaguely registered footsteps somewhere behind her, and when she finished and stood up, it was just in time to see Lindsay finish walking over to Sarah and promptly pull her in for a kiss by the front of her shirt, clearly surprising her.

The number in Valerie's head vanished and she couldn't help but stare as her heart thudded painfully in her chest. She forced back tears of anger and turned back to the chest of swords, beginning her recount. Lindsay's message was received loud and clear: "You hurt me, I hurt you."

Eight. Nine. Ten. She could hear Sarah and Lindsay making out across the backstage area, and tried to block it out. Eleven. Twelve. They weren't stopping. Twelve. Thirteen. Fourteen.

She grit her teeth, realizing she'd screwed up somewhere, and abruptly straightened up, glaring at the kissing girls. "Get a room!"

That, to her satisfaction, broke them apart. Sarah stared at Lindsay, still shell-shocked, but Lindsay glared over at Valerie, fuming.

"Maybe we will."

"You do that."

"Fine."

"Fine!" Valerie went back to counting the swords, vaguely aware that Sarah was murmuring something to Lindsay now. Whatever it was, she sounded upset, and a moment later, she'd left Lindsay there alone.

There were sixteen swords. Valerie straightened up again and looked to Lindsay, who seemed stunned by the turn of events, and was still staring at the curtain Sarah had disappeared behind. "You told everyone you liked me yesterday," Valerie recalled. "She knows you were trying to make me jealous."

Lindsay chewed on the inside of the cheek, all of the malice surprisingly gone from her expression. "The funny thing is that I wasn't," she replied, simply. "I mean, it's always an added bonus, sure... but I was trying to move on. Find someone on the same page as me. That's what you said to do, right?" She quirked an eyebrow, glaring at Valerie. "Shockingly, it's not working."

"Maybe it will if you do it right." Valerie let out a slow exhale as Lindsay stared at her. It was hard doing the right thing. Much harder than she'd thought it'd be. "You should ask her out on a date."

"I can see right through you," Lindsay retorted, unblinking. "Stop trying to make yourself feel better. As of last night, I'm no longer yours to fix." She stormed off, disappearing behind the curtain, and Valerie turned away from her, staring down at the chest again even as she took in a deep breath.

She'd forgotten the number of swords again.

CHAPTER TWENTY-SEVEN

Amber scoffed at Kat in Lit an hour later, when she wouldn't sit near or even look at the two of them. Valerie remained quiet, but Amber murmured, "God, she's got such a chip on her shoulder. She takes everything so personally just because her dad's a fag. So you don't wanna hang out with a girl who has a thing for you. Big deal; it's your choice."

"Amber, I don't really wanna talk about it," Valerie replied. "And can you not call her dad that? He's actually really nice."

"What, a fag? That's what he is."

Valerie shot her a tired look. "Amber…"

Amber rolled her eyes and raised her hands defensively, turning away. "Whatever."

At lunch, Tara found Valerie while she was still in line to get her food and warned her, "We're gonna be sitting with Amber from now on, I think."

"We?" Valerie repeated, raising an eyebrow. "What did you do?"

"Kat wasn't very happy with what you did, so she decided to vent to me this morning. When I told her that I let you know I'd support you regardless, she didn't take it too well. So I don't think either of us is welcome over there." She gestured to their usual table, which was now only occupied by Lindsay and Kat. They were both eating in silence.

Valerie couldn't take her eyes off of them. "Tara, this is so much harder than I thought it'd be," she admitted quietly.

228

"You can always change your mind, if you want," Tara reminded her. "It's not too late, is it?"

"I think it might be."

They got their food and went to Amber's table, where the cheerleaders typically sat. Amber introduced them needlessly.

"Hey, girls, you remember my best friends Tara and Valerie, right?"

"Oh my God," one of the girls laughed out, looking directly at Valerie, "You're the one that dyke's crushing on, aren't you? You can sit here for as long as you want. We'll protect you."

Valerie felt Tara shift uncomfortably beside her as the other girls laughed along. She barely managed to force a dry laugh of her own. "Thanks." She sat down.

Over the course of the next few weeks, the color seemed to quickly drain from Valerie's life. Her mother rarely spoke to her, and Lindsay changed seats in their shared Cooking class so that they were on opposite sides of the room. Kat ignored her, and Nick didn't dare speak to her either, for fear of upsetting Kat. Lindsay hardly looked at her, but she did look at Sarah quite a bit, and it wasn't long before Sarah started looking back. And every day, Valerie sat at Amber's lunch table and said a silent prayer that Lindsay wouldn't be one of the topics of conversation for the day. Most days she wasn't, but some days she was.

Lucas and Tara remained her only support systems, with the exception of her father. Lucas helped her cool down in Chemistry if Amber said anything to set her off in Lit, and Tara comforted her in Calculus if something went wrong during their Lunch period. In Drama, she worked with Nathan more than anyone else, and although she considered him somewhat of a close acquaintance, it wasn't like she could confide in him. Tony knew she was gay, but Nathan didn't, and she wasn't eager to tell anyone else. Not even her own sister, and especially not anyone who went to her school.

She was safe from teasing while in the closet, but it wasn't a comfortable kind of safety. Unexpectedly, she felt more uncomfortable with herself than she'd ever been. Far more comforting was the idea of having Lindsay around to hold her and tell her that everything was okay; that she'd get through it. But Lindsay was busy trying to move on with Sarah, someone who was actually proud to be with her once Lindsay convinced her she was over what had only been a tiny crush on Valerie. Valerie still wasn't sure how Lindsay had explained away Valerie's reaction to their first kiss, but whatever she had said, it'd worked.

She knew this because on a Friday night, she went to the ice cream place down the street with the intention of meeting Nathan to discuss the play together. She was the first to arrive between the two of them, but Sarah and Lindsay were there, having ice cream together. Valerie pretended not to see them, and Lindsay pretended not to see her, and she sat as far away from them as she could get while she waited for Nathan.

It was Tony who met her instead, greeting her with a tight-lipped smile. "Hey. Sorry, Nathan couldn't make it so he asked me to come in his place. I know I'm not much of a writer, but he told me what you guys were supposed to talk about. That is... if you still want to."

"That's okay, Tony," Valerie insisted. "I was kind of eager to leave anyway."

"You were?" He looked confused until she glanced across the room and he followed her gaze. "Oh. I... I don't think Nathan knew they'd be here. Not that he'd know about the whole... you know. Um." Tony scratched at his head awkwardly. "You can go if you want. My ride's picking me up in half an hour."

"Oh. I won't make you wait alone," Valerie insisted. "We can stay for half an hour. I'm kind of craving ice cream anyway."

Tony nodded, and they ordered together before retaking their seats. Soon, Tony cleared his throat. "I don't mean to pry... and you don't have to tell me if you don't want to, obviously. But you two seemed really into each other."

"So did you and Nathan," Valerie pointed out. "But I don't see you talking as much lately."

Tony was quiet for a moment. Finally, he sighed. "Well, I guess it's only fair if we both share. Nathan and I never even got off the ground."

"Really? I thought you two were dating for sure at one point. What happened?"

"He wanted to hold hands," Tony replied simply, setting his ice cream down. Valerie stared at him, eyebrows furrowed.

"Oh."

"Nathan's very proud of who he is. I couldn't keep up. He's stronger than me, and I wouldn't have been able to handle being with him in public the way he wanted. So it never happened." He shrugged his shoulders. "What happened to you and Lindsay?"

"I think that Lindsay and I are probably what you and Nathan would've become if you'd ever dated," Valerie told him matter-of-factly. "Almost to a T, I think."

"You wouldn't come out for her," Tony acknowledged. "I guessed as much."

"It's not what it looks like, though. She didn't ditch me for some out-and-proud girl because I wouldn't make out with her in the hallway. I broke up with her and told her to move on."

"Why?"

"Because I wasn't moving at her pace, and I knew it. And I kept telling her that I would, but I was lying to her and to myself. I've always wanted to wait until college to come out. I feel comfortable with that decision. And she didn't really rush me, but I knew she wanted to... well, be able to hold my hand."

"You did the right thing for yourself," Tony decided. "But why aren't you two talking anymore? She'd mad at you?"

"I think she understands. She hated me for it at first, and maybe she still does... but she understands. I don't know if we'd be as close as we were regardless, but it was either stop hanging out or get accused of dating each other anyway. I can't lie my way out of a paper bag, so."

"I get it," was his short response. Valerie eyed him curiously.

"You know, I think you may be the only person I've ever spoken to that totally and completely *does*."

He let out a short laugh, and took a bite of his ice cream. It struck Valerie how little he seemed to desire being open about his sexuality, despite the fact that he *was* open.

"Tony, how did you come out?"

He raised an eyebrow at her. "You don't remember hearing about it?"

She shook her head. "Honestly, I was pretty oblivious to all things gay until this year."

"Well, it was a couple years ago. Someone I thought was my friend outed me."

"That's terrible."

"Yeah, it was. But the worst part was that I lost the chance to do it myself. It even got to my *parents* before I could say something. That's probably the worst thing that's ever happened to me. You're lucky you have friends you can actually trust."

Valerie let out a bitter laugh. "Hardly. Kat's done with me and Amber'd hate me if she knew I was a lesbian. Most of the time it feels like I have no one."

"Their love's conditional," Tony echoed. "They're not real friends, then, you know."

"Kat means well," she told him. "She just knows I was a bitch and hasn't forgiven me for it yet."

"Looking out for yourself doesn't make you a bitch," he countered. "You love Lindsay and you were caught in a tough situation. I'm not an asshole for refusing to do something I was uncomfortable with when it came to Nathan, and you aren't a bitch for breaking it off when you realized the alternative was coming out before you were ready."

"I'm starting to wonder if I'll ever be ready," Valerie admitted. "What happens if I get to college and I still can't say it?"

"You can cross that bridge when you come to it. I'm out and I'm still not ready to be. Everyone's different. Maybe you'll take longer than you thought you would, but maybe you won't take as long."

She mulled that over for a few minutes as they finished their ice cream. Valerie heard a loud bout of laughter from across the room, and was unsurprised to see it coming from Lindsay and Sarah. Tony, to her surprise, smirked at her.

"A few weeks is a short time to move on completely from someone she claimed to love. You have to know this is all about you, right?"

"She said it wasn't," Valerie told him, shaking her head.

"Well, she's not gonna tell you she's waiting for you to change your mind, now is she? I mean, *I* wouldn't. I'd make it so that you have to make the first move. But that doesn't mean your window of time isn't closing, either."

"I can't do that," Valerie murmured, her eyes finding the table. "Make the first move, that is."

"Neither could I," he pointed out, smiling at her. "And so here we are."

Tony's ride picked him up just a few minutes later, and Valerie drove home and went straight to her room. She laid awake in bed for a while, staring at her ceiling, and eventually murmured, "I'm going to end up exactly like Tony."

It wasn't a pleasant prospect, and the idea plagued her until she finally went to sleep.

CHAPTER TWENTY-EIGHT

"You ready for this?"

"What on Earth are you doing?" Valerie couldn't help but laugh out, wide-eyed as Lucas slammed his locker shut and turned away from her, as though he was hiding something. She heard the brief squeak of a sharpie, and her eyes only widened further. "Seriously, Lucas, what the hell? Are you writing on your face?"

"Don't ruin this," he insisted. Valerie noticed a few people watching nearby. Some of the girls were giggling, and one or two looked jealous. Valerie realized what was going on a moment before Lucas spun around.

"No! I don't want another public one!"

"Too late!" He looked down at her, grinning, and she saw he'd drawn a giant box on his forehead, with the word "yes" sloppily written next to it. He handed her the sharpie calmly, then reached down and unbuttoned his shirt, revealing the writing on his chest: "Prom?"

"Where's the 'no' box?" she asked, raising an eyebrow. Lucas grinned and reached for his belt buckle. "Okay! Okay. Jeez." She stood on her tiptoes and checked the 'yes' box, and he took the sharpie back from her and then wrapped his arms around her waist, lifting her up into the air and then kissing her on the cheek as she smacked at him in an effort to make him put her down.

"Sweet! Senior prom is a go!"

Prom was scheduled for April 20th, which gave Valerie just under 3 weeks to get with a Prom group, buy a dress, and find the perfect hairstyle. The first task was easily completed, as Amber had already pulled Tara and Oliver into her group and so Tara convinced her to let Valerie join as well. Amber wasn't very excited to include Lucas, but even she had the common sense to realize Lucas and Valerie were only going as friends.

Through Nick, who'd taken to talking to her occasionally when Kat wasn't around, Valerie learned that he and Kat were in a group with Lindsay and Sarah, as well as some of their other Drama classmates, two of which included Nathan and a boy who wasn't Tony.

Tony, who wasn't going to Prom at all, was certainly worse off than Valerie, but she found herself talking to him much more frequently as the date drew nearer. She found out that he actually planned to attend Cloverdale the following year, and surprised herself when she realized she was relieved to know she'd have a friend there. She wasn't sure why she considered Tony a friend so quickly, but she knew that she did, and she knew that the more time she spent with him, the more their mutual affection for each other grew. Tony could relate to her, was understanding and kind, and he was also gay, which eliminated the whole awkward "we're friends but do you like me?" situation she'd run into with Dustin and Lucas.

She invited Tony to help her and Tara get their dresses for Prom, and he agreed to go, but turned out to absolutely no help, apparently not a carrier of whatever gene typically gave gay men good fashion sense. It turned out that having Tony around was about as affective as having Lucas around, which made Valerie glad that she'd invited Tara along, too.

Tara picked out a dark purple gown with matching earrings that looked great with her skin but wasn't too revealing. Tony, to his credit, *did* help a little bit with Valerie's dress in that he encouraged her to pick the one that showed a decent amount of skin without going overboard.

Despite the fact that Lindsay seemed relatively happy with Sarah and hadn't mentioned Valerie to Tara at all, Tony remained convinced that Valerie still needed to try and get her attention. Valerie, for her part, wasn't nearly as convinced that there was anything salvageable between herself and Lindsay. She treated her memories of being with Lindsay as just that: memories. Fond ones, sure, but not anything that'd ever happen again.

When she got home after the shopping trip, both of her parents looked surprised to see her walk in with a dress on her arm.

"I didn't know you were planning on going to Prom," her mother observed, and then continued, awkwardly, "Lindsay must be happy."

"I'm going with Lucas," Valerie responded shortly. Her father asked after Lindsay every now and then, but she knew her parents had both attributed the lack of Lindsay's presence to her mother's homophobia. Valerie hadn't told them about the break-up. She didn't want to give her mother the satisfaction.

"Why aren't you going with Lindsay?" her father questioned curiously.

"She has someone else to go with."

She left them to put the dress away in her room, but Abby caught her hanging it up, and was immediately eager to question her about it.

"Are you going with Dustin?"

"Dustin and I broke up. I'm going with Lucas as friends."

"Why'd you break up?"

"Because we were never dating in the first place," Valerie retorted, brushing by her without further explanation. Abby followed her, much to her annoyance.

"What? Why'd you say that you were?"

"Because you were being annoying and wouldn't stop asking me questions. Kind of like now. What a coincidence."

"Who pissed in your Fruit Loops?" Abby snapped, just as they reached the living room her parents were still resting in.

"Language, Abby," her father chided.

"Valerie lied to me about who she was dating," Abby told them, as though she expected Valerie to be punished for the offense. When her parents said nothing, she scoffed, and continued, "How come I have to tell you everything about me and Ben but she can go on dates and no one cares?"

"Shut up, Abby," Valerie retorted with a roll of her eyes, heading to the kitchen to retrieve an apple from the refrigerator. As she ran it under the water, she added, "You're thirteen. I'm almost an adult."

"Valerie," her father cut in abruptly. "Perhaps you should be more honest with your sister."

She looked over at him, and he raised an eyebrow at her, the hidden meaning in his message clear. She turned off the water and washed off the apple, then took a bite of it. "I'm not in the mood for this."

Then she took the stairs to her room two at a time and slammed her door shut, intending on spending the rest of her night the same way she always did: On her computer, trying to forget how lonely she felt.

Abby ruined those plans just minutes later, barging into her room without warning. "If you weren't with Dustin and Lucas is just your friend, who were you with?"

Valerie sighed deeply, glaring at her sister. "None of your business."

"Why won't you just tell me?"

"Honestly? Because I don't feel like having you freak out on me right now, and I don't want to deal with your shit. Go text Ben about the scandalous peck on the cheek he gave you after your last date."

"Screw you," Abby retorted, and stormed out of the room. The door slammed shut behind her, and Valerie immediately put her head in her hands, groaning. Living like this was absolutely miserable.

She sat up and took a deep breath, running a few choice sentences through her brain to see how they sounded. She heard Abby slamming things shut through the wall, and rubbed at her temples momentarily before sucking in a deep breath and hopping off of her bed. "Might as well get it over with," she mumbled, and went next door to her sister's room, knocking on the door.

It swung open and Abby glared out at her. "What."

"I'm only gonna say this once, okay?" Valerie prefaced. Abby crossed her arms and waited. "I'm gay. I dated Lindsay for three and a half months. When I told mom and dad, mom didn't take it well. I broke up with Lindsay and now she's going to Prom with another girl, and I'm going to Prom with Lucas as a friend. Mom and Dad don't know Lindsay and I broke up. I was never involved with anyone else. The end, okay? Are you happy?"

Abby blinked at her, dumbfounded. Valerie stared back as Abby tried a couple of times to speak, slowly taking in everything she'd been told. Finally, she swallowed hard, looking a bit uncertain. "...Okay?"

Now it was Valerie's turn to look confused. "Okay? That's it?"

"I mean... yeah." Abby shrugged. "You could've just said that. Lindsay's kind of pretty, I guess." She shrugged again. "I don't hate you or anything. I *do* have a gay friend, you know."

"I didn't know that. But even if I had, it's still different when it's your sister."

"Hardly. What crawled up mom's butt and died? How long has she known?"

"Just a few weeks. Dad's helping her get over it."

"Cool. Well, I'm sure she will eventually." Abby stared at her for a second, then cleared her throat and moved to shut the door. "Have fun in your room."

"You too."

The door shut and Valerie let out a quick breath, blinking in surprise. "That was weird," she mumbled, and then went back into her room to finally get some peace and quiet.

Telling Abby, unfortunately, *did* mean that it wasn't long before her parents found out that she and Lindsay had broken up. More specifically, they knew by the next morning. Valerie wiped the small smile off of her mother's face by informing her, "Before you throw a party, I'm still gay. Maybe my next girlfriend won't be some charming British girl with good manners and a pretty smile. I feel like every lesbian's gotta date a tatted-up biker chick at least once in her life."

To her pleasure, her father seemed to find that amusing, at least. "I'm glad to see you making jokes," he told her. "I understand now why you've seemed so down lately, between your mother and what happened with Lindsay."

"Oh, I wasn't joking," Valerie insisted, even as her mother frowned at her father's words. That earned another laugh from him.

Her phone buzzed suddenly in her pocket, and her eyebrows furrowed when she saw she had a text from Lindsay. She hesitated briefly before opening it.

"Sorry, I know this is awkward... do u have my blue scarf? I think I left it in ur room a month or so ago."

"Be right back," she told her parents, barely registering her mother chiding her father for his comment as she went to her room and searched through her dresser drawers. Finding nothing, she looked around, only to spot the scarf in question hanging off of the edge of her desk. She texted Lindsay back, *"Found it. I'll give it to u in Drama."*

She received a response seconds later. *"Thx."*

When she got back downstairs, her father was nowhere to be found, but her mother intercepted her on her way out, looking concerned. "Valerie, I want you to know that in no way do I want you to be miserable."

"Yeah, I know, Mom. Can I go?"

"I want you to have a happy life. I'm just... a little bit pickier than your father regarding what that entails, as all."

"Well, a girl will be involved," Valerie told her shortly. "Sorry." She pulled away from her mother and left, Lindsay's scarf gripped in her hand.

She entered her Drama class early, hoping to avoid running into Sarah and Lindsay together, and got her wish: Lindsay was standing near the stage, texting someone, and Sarah had yet to arrive. Valerie fidgeted with the scarf as she approached her.

"Hey."

Lindsay looked up, and then smiled when she saw the scarf. "Thanks. I've missed that for a while."

"Why'd you only just now ask me for it?"

Lindsay shrugged, but then seemed to change her mind, and admitted, "I wanted to wait until some time had passed."

"Oh."

They stood there in silence for a moment, staring at each other, until Valerie finally cleared her throat and collected herself.

"Well anyway, have a good day."

"You too," Lindsay told her quickly, and they hurried to go their separate ways: Lindsay to backstage, and Valerie to find Nathan.

Today was the first day of casting, and the class had taken a vote and agreed to do it during their class period in the morning as opposed to after school. Ms. Merriweather joined Nathan, Valerie, and the other students in their class who had primarily worked on the script in sitting on one side of the auditorium, while the rest of the students ran over their lines one last time on the other side of the auditorium.

There weren't many parts, and so the auditions went quickly. Valerie huddled together with her group to discuss casting for the last fifteen minutes of class, but ultimately, everyone agreed to let her and Nathan make the final decisions.

She met up with him in the parking lot after school together, and they sat in her car, running through the notes they'd made during auditions.

"Lindsay told me she doesn't want the lead, and she auditioned for the witch," Nathan pointed out. "So she seems pretty solid for that, which means Kat and Nick for the leads. Remember, it's the senior play, so we have to remember to give the seniors the most important roles."

"Tony's a senior," Valerie reminded him.

"Yeah. I was thinking maybe he could play the expert fighter who escorts Nick. He'll need to learn how stage-fight, though."

"I could practice with him," Valerie suggested. "I mean, if you're taking control of blocking, I've already gotten the lights stuff down for this, so I'll have a lot of free time."

Nathan eyed her critically. "You and Tony have gotten pretty close all of a sudden, you know that? For someone who ditched one of her closest female friends for having a crush on her, you sure are gay-friendly."

"I'm one of those vapid straight girls who love gay men because they're good shopping partners but can't stand lesbians because ew, they might like me," Valerie informed him calmly.

Nathan grinned at her knowingly. "So why'd you two break up?" When Valerie raised both eyebrows at him, he laughed. "C'mon, I'm family. When we know, we know, and it also helps that I've spent enough time with you to know what kind of person you are... which is not the kind that'd give up a friend for the reason everyone thinks you gave up Lindsay. I won't tell."

"It feels like everyone knows at this point," Valerie sighed out.

"I'm sure it does. But I like that feeling." Nathan's eyes lit up, like he was recalling a fond memory. "Coming out is so... *freeing*. I know it's cliché, but it really is. I felt like I could finally be myself. And I feel really bad for you and Tony. I'm sorry you guys just aren't comfortable with it."

"Why didn't you give Tony a chance?" Valerie suggested without warning. "I mean, I know it's too late now, and you're going to Prom with someone else... but he was out. He just didn't want to show affection in public. You would've had it so much better than Lindsay had it with me, and we dated for over three months."

Nathan looked serious now. "Because I'm worth more than that." He took a breath and went back to his notes, and Valerie's gaze lowered to her lap. "Anyway, I was thinking Sarah for at least a minor role, even though she was only gonna do costumes. She *is* a senior, after all..."

Valerie nodded, but she was already halfway to tuning him out, his words swirling around in her head until all she could think about was *"I'm worth more than that"*.

She swallowed hard and waited for Nathan to finish, anxious to go home and sleep.

CHAPTER TWENTY-NINE

It rained on the weekend before Prom.

The entire Marsh family, stuck inside for the full two days, spent most of their time watching movies together. They took turns both days: one movie per person on Saturday, and one on Sunday. On Saturday, Valerie's movie was a chick flick she'd seen one-hundred times, but on Sunday, she gathered enough courage to show her family one of the lesbian movies Lindsay had shown her during her self-discovery period, back before they'd ever started dating.

Her mother, to her credit, sat through it without comment, and she snuggled with her father throughout its duration. Abby just asked a lot of inappropriate questions, most likely to purposely rattle her mother.

They followed up that movie with Abby's choice, an action flick, and halfway through it, their doorbell rang.

When no one else moved to answer, Valerie sighed and got to her feet, padding over to the door and pulling it open. Her eyes widened. "Lindsay?"

Lindsay was huddled under the small area by the front door that was shielded from the rain by their roof, but she was still damp due to her trip from the car in the driveway to the front door. Valerie recognized the car in question as Mrs. Davis's. It was empty, but the engine was still running, and so were the windshield wipers.

Valerie glanced back inside to see that Abby had paused the movie and her entire family was subtly trying to get a good look at what was going on from their respective spots on the living room furniture. She sighed and moved to close the front door, huddling under the small dry area with Lindsay as they faced each other. "What are you doing here?" she asked.

"Mrs. Davis let me borrow her car," Lindsay explained. "I told her it was important."

"If you forgot something else, I could've brought it Monday," Valerie pointed out.

"I didn't forget anything," Lindsay told her. She took a deep breath. "I came here because..." she hesitated for a moment, rubbing at her biceps. Valerie was suddenly aware of how cold she was.

"Should we go inside?"

"This won't take long," Lindsay insisted, and pressed on, "I don't know... if I..." She swallowed hard. "Prom's in a week and I'm going with Sarah. And I know you're going with Lucas. And I know that's probably not changing, but... I just wanted to give you another chance. One last chance."

Valerie stared at her, confused. "What do you mean?"

Lindsay huffed at her, shivering. "What it sounds like. God, Val. Sometimes you're so..." She trailed off, watching Valerie hopefully. "Jesus Christ, it's freezing," she finally huffed out, and then abruptly leaned forward and closed the distance between them.

If Valerie's brain was like a lightbulb, it would've flickered and then died in that moment, because she felt completely caught off-guard and on autopilot as Lindsay's lips warmed her from the inside out. She'd never even fathomed they'd be here again. Not in a million years.

Lindsay's arms wound around her and pulled her closer, and they kissed so fervently that on more than one occasion they almost ended up out in the rain. Valerie vaguely registered that Lindsay's lips still tasted like vanilla lip gloss.

Lindsay finally ended the kiss first, resting their foreheads together and murmuring, eyes shut tightly, "Please just be brave, Val. Come out for me. I know you can do it. I'll do everything I can to make sure everyone leaves you alone. Just say the word and I'll tell Sarah to go."

Valerie licked her lips, panting hard. She squeezed her own eyes shut tightly, trying to make sense of what exactly had just happened. "Isn't Sarah good for you?" she asked, confused.

"I honestly don't care. At all." Lindsay pulled away and looked to her pleadingly. "Val, I don't want to keep coming back and begging you to take me back, so this is the one time I'm doing this. I'm begging you to just come out and be with me. You'll be in college in four months, and done with high school in one. That's all you'll have to get through, and we can be together."

Valerie pulled away abruptly. "Until when? Until you go back to England?"

Lindsay opened and closed her mouth, at a loss for words. "No, I-"

"Because we never talked about that, did we?" Valerie pointed out. "You want me to do this for you so that you can have a month of me and then leave."

"That's not it," Lindsay insisted. "Valerie, I love you."

"I'm worth more than that. More than a month. And so are you," Valerie told her, shaking her head. "So... spend your time here with someone who wants you enough to do it openly. And I'll come out in September and find someone I can date for longer than a month before we have to never see each other again. It's better that way."

Lindsay barely reined her tears in long enough to tell her, "I'm not coming back if I leave, Val. I'm not saying that to be mean. I'm just being honest."

"I know." Valerie nodded. "Maybe if... the timing had been different, or... I don't know; *we'd* been different." She fought back her own tears even as she wiped away one of Lindsay's. "You did so much for me, okay? You were the first person I ever loved, and that's always gonna mean something. No one else will ever be that for me. You helped me find what I loved, and who I loved, and you helped me accept that. The only reason I'm not kissing you with everything I have right now is because there are people out there who would tear me apart for it, and I'm not ready to face that."

Lindsay nodded her understanding, tears streaking down her cheeks now, and Valerie lost her own battle with her tears, hastily wiping them off with her sleeve. But they kept coming, even worse than they'd been when she'd broken up with Lindsay.

"How am I gonna even look at you?" Lindsay murmured, shaking her head and pressing her hands to her eyes, as though willing herself to stop crying. "Every day."

"It's just for a month," Valerie insisted, trying to reassure herself even as she reassured Lindsay. "We don't have to ignore each other. We don't have to be angry, like before. This is just... how things turned out. If we had met at a different time in our lives, things could've been... not like this. But we met now and this is how it is. Lindsay, I will always have a special place in my heart for you."

She stopped speaking, her voice choking up, and Lindsay pulled her into a tight hug, crying quietly into her neck. "I'm sorry that I tried to make you jealous," she admitted, her voice muffled by Valerie's skin. "Sarah doesn't deserve that and neither do you."

"It's okay. You guys will have a great time at Prom."

Lindsay pulled away from her at last, nodding and wiping the last of her tears away. "I'll see you in class, okay?"

"Okay."

They stepped back, and Valerie reached for the knob of her front door even as her eyes stayed trained on Lindsay. She could still taste Lindsay's lip gloss on her lips and in her mouth, and seared it into her mind so she wouldn't forget it. She tried several times to get her next words out, but couldn't.

Lindsay said them for her, still trembling. "Bye, Val."

She bit her lip so hard she thought for a second it might bleed. "Goodbye."

Lindsay turned away from her and dashed back out to the car, and Valerie felt a fresh wave of tears hit her as she opened the front door and headed back inside, her family forgotten until suddenly a hand was on her shoulder, helping her back into the living room.

"Henry, I've got her," she heard her mother demand. "Take Abby."

Mrs. Marsh led Valerie to the couch even as Valerie's vision blurred and she struggled to wipe the tears from her cheeks. Abby and her father left the room at some point, and Valerie found herself burying her face in her mother's shoulder as her body was wracked with sobs. Mrs. Marsh shushed her gently, rubbing at her back, and neither of them said anything for a while.

When Valerie's tears finally managed to subside, and she quieted, Mrs. Marsh finally spoke. "I may not understand being attracted to other girls, but I understand heartbreak. Do you want me to make you some hot chocolate, and then maybe in a little bit we can call your father and sister back in here and you can pick another movie?"

"I'll watch Abby's movie," Valerie told her, aware her voice still sounded a little tearful. "But yes to the hot chocolate, please."

"Okay." Mrs. Marsh got to her feet, and Valerie spent the next few minutes watching her bustle around the kitchen. Soon enough, she was bringing a mug back to Valerie and warning her, "Be careful. It's hot."

She took a sip and it burned her tongue, but not enough for her to not keep drinking it. Eventually, her mother sighed beside her.

"You know what I don't understand. I thought you'd already broken up a while back?" Valerie nodded, and she continued, "Then what happened outside to make you so upset? Not a second break-up?"

"Not a break-up," Valerie confirmed hoarsely, taking another sip of her hot chocolate. "That was goodbye."

Mrs. Marsh sighed, and then rubbed at her back again. "Oh, honey. When you love someone, it's never truly goodbye."

Valerie stared down at her hot chocolate for a moment, and then glanced to her mother. "Thanks, Mom."

For the first time in a while, she began to wonder if people really could change for the better.

CHAPTER THIRTY

"Shots! Shots! Shots! Shots! Shots!"

The chanting in the limousine picked up as Amber's Prom date, Jimmy, downed his fourth, and cheers erupted amongst their group as he sat the shot glass down proudly and stuck a fist in the air. Oliver, Tara, Valerie, and Lucas each clapped politely, clearly out of place in the group of predominantly cheerleaders and their football-playing dates.

Their limo slowed down and one of the boys stood up and stuck his head out through the sunroof, letting out an obnoxious yell before declaring, "We're here!"

Finally, the limo stopped, and they all piled out of the vehicle. Lucas offered Valerie his arm, and together, they headed inside, Tara and Oliver just behind them.

The Prom, held in their school gym and the surrounding outside area, was already packed with students and teachers alike. The center of the gym served as a makeshift dance floor, and that was where Amber and her cheerleader friends immediately headed with their dates, with the exception of a few of the boys, who murmured something to each other about spiking the punch.

"Are you guys gonna dance?" Lucas asked Tara and Oliver, who simply looked at each other and then shrugged simultaneously.

"We might wait for the slow-dancing," Oliver suggested.

Lucas nodded his understanding. "I think we probably will, too," he agreed seriously, and then nudged Valerie and grinned when Oliver wasn't paying attention.

Lucas and Oliver went to get drinks a few minutes later, and Tara and Valerie stood together, watching the various couples on the dance floor. Tara gasped suddenly at something and started to point, but seemed to think better of it and put her hand down, embarrassed. Valerie looked to her curiously. "What?"

"Nothing!"

"C'mon, seriously."

With a sigh, Tara pointed, and Valerie followed her finger to where Sarah, Lindsay, Kat, and Nick were all goofing off and dancing together in the center of the dance floor.

"They look like they're having fun," Valerie observed.

Tara let out a soft sigh. "I miss Kat."

"I do, too."

They both stared for a good minute or so, until Lucas and Oliver arrived with their drinks. "What are we staring at?" Lucas asked. "Did someone get into trouble for grinding?"

"Not yet," Tara told him, and pointed again to Kat's group.

"Aw, c'mon," Lucas chided. "It's Prom night. Can we forget about the grudges for two seconds and have some fun?"

"We weren't grudging," Valerie protested. "We were saying it looks like they're having fun."

"Exactly," Lucas set his drink down and snatched Valerie away from her, then set it down, too. "So let's go! C'mon, Olly. Tara." He gestured toward the dance floor with his head and then yanked Valerie forward before she could protest.

"Lucas, no! It's awkward!" Valerie insisted, but Lucas pressed forward, catching Kat by the shoulder when they reached her.

"Hey!" he shouted over the music once he had her attention. "Can we wave the white flag for at least tonight? From what I understand, Val's life kind of sucks without you!"

Kat looked past Lucas to Valerie, who stood stock still, staring back at her as her hands fidgeted in front of her. Then Kat glanced to Lindsay, who seemed unaware that Sarah was still dancing beside her, and offered a small nod, despite avoiding Valerie's eyes. Kat looked back to Valerie and sighed, then reached out and took her hand, pulling her closer until her mouth was right by Valerie's ear.

"I didn't want to ignore you, okay? But I couldn't leave Lindsay and I did kind of think that what you did to her was mean. But if she can move on then I can, too."

Valerie nodded at her, grateful, and Kat pulled her into a brief hug.

Lucas clapped happily on Valerie's other side, and then immediately went into dance mode, shimmying over to Sarah, who looked completely unamused by his antics until Lindsay hastily saved her from him. Kat laughed loudly and grabbed for Nick, and Lucas shrugged at Valerie as if to say, "Guess we're stuck with each other."

It wasn't long before Tara and Oliver joined them, and it was an hour before any of them parted. The slow dances started up, and Valerie and Lucas were the first to bail on those, heading back to get more punch. Valerie determined that it had indeed been spiked, which led Lucas to get two more cups of it before the first few dances were over.

Valerie, meanwhile, scanned the dance floor. Amber looked happy with Jimmy, to her credit, and Kat and Nick and Tara and Oliver looked as obsessed with each other as usual. She considered stopping her search there, but curiosity got the better of her, and she looked around until she found Sarah and Lindsay swaying together on the edge of the dance floor, their faces just inches apart. She couldn't see Lindsay's face, but she could see Sarah's, and it was the face of someone who'd fallen completely head over heels in a matter of weeks. Valerie knew that look.

Her staring was interrupted by Ms. Merriweather, who turned out to be that token teacher that was doing the rounds telling everyone how cute they looked and insisting they dance with each other. Lucas did most of the talking, trying his best to shake her off, but he was ultimately unsuccessful, and so that was how Valerie ended up pressed up against him with her arms hooked around his neck while his hands rested on her hips.

"You do look really pretty," he admitted, eyeing her dress with approval. "I'm glad you made such an effort to impress me."

"It was all for you. You got me," she countered, winking at him.

He offered her a small smile. "So what happens after this? You finish out the month, graduate... and then?"

"Well... go to Cloverdale, first," Valerie admitted. "Then get a girlfriend, and major in Journalism. That's about all I've got at the moment. What about you?"

"Ah... I'm gonna go to community college, I think," he told her. "My GPA isn't all that great. So I'll be around if you need me. I'm definitely moving out of my parents' house, though. I've been saving up. I think I can afford a $350 rent if I find a job in the next four months."

"Good. You need to get out of there," she told him.

"That's the goal."

They danced for all of two songs, and then only stayed at the dance for few minutes more before eventually deciding to leave early to go back to Valerie's and play video games. They could now say they'd gone to Prom, which was satisfying enough for the both of them, as neither of them was a huge fan of their Prom group and hadn't really wanted to go to dinner with them, anyway. Valerie felt bad about leaving Tara and Oliver, but she had a sneaking suspicion that they had alternative plans of their own, too.

It was, all in all, a good night.

The last month of high school blew by after that. For the seniors, it meant easy busy work, maybe a few semi-difficult tests amidst constantly watching movies in class, and frequent house parties. With Tara and Lucas by her side, and the occasional addition of several different combinations of Kat, Nick, Tony, Nathan, Amber, and Oliver, Valerie enjoyed it all.

She and Lindsay rarely talked, if at all, although she often saw Lindsay sneak glances at her during the couple of classes and the lunch period they shared. Deep down, she knew they still had feelings for each other, but she also knew that Lindsay liked Sarah and that Sarah liked her back.

With two weeks of school left, the senior play ran for three nights in a row, and then had to put on a fourth performance a couple of days later that hadn't been planned, because the word had been spread by those had already attended that it was actually very good, leading to a higher demand for tickets. Nathan and Valerie went on record as the primary writers of the play, and received a standing ovation along with the rest of the cast at the end of the final show.

Graduation crept up on the class of 2013, and before Valerie knew it, she and all of her friends were donning caps and gowns and being driven to their school on a Saturday morning by tearful parents accompanied by annoyed siblings who'd wanted to sleep in. Valerie cheered the loudest for Lucas, Tara, and Kat. Lindsay didn't participate in graduation; she'd told Valerie long ago that she'd have to go back to her old school for that, as Valerie's school's policy was to not issue diplomas to foreign exchange students.

And then, just like that, Valerie's high school career was over.

She went to dinner with her family afterward, and spent the subsequent week planning a graduation party of sorts. She didn't want to throw an actual party, but she did want to get everyone together at least one last time. That meant finding a time and place convenient for everyone she'd become friends with and remained close to, as well as for their various significant others. She made a list, and determined that she'd invite Tara, Oliver, Kat, Nick, Lucas, Tony, and Nathan. She wanted to invite Amber and Lindsay, as well, but she wasn't really sure where she stood with Lindsay any longer, and she had a feeling inviting Amber to hang out with Lucas, Kat, and two gay guys wasn't the best idea.

She finally managed to plan something that worked for everyone: dinner at, ironically, Mackie's, at eight o'clock on a night Amber wasn't working.

Valerie and Lucas rode together, and everyone had arrived by around ten after. They grabbed a massive table together and Valerie found herself in between Tony and Lucas, the former of which looked nervous to be there. She had a feeling that had a lot to do with Nathan's presence, but luckily, he sat on the other end of the table from Tony. "Thank you for coming," she murmured to him, and he offered her a smile and a nod.

"Alright, guys!" Kat announced excitedly, dominating the conversation once they'd gotten their drinks. She tapped her knife against her glass to get everyone's attention, and then raised her cup of ginger ale. "Can I just take a moment to toast to being fucking done with high school!"

Their table cheered and clapped, and beside her, Nick suggested, "How about we all go around and say where we're off to next?" There were some murmurs of agreement, and Nick cleared his throat. "Alright, I'll go first. I'll be headed to Burnell, and so will my lovely lady here."

He gestured for Nathan to go, who announced, "Cloverdale U it is!"

"Me too!" Valerie cut in, leaning across the table to high-five Nathan. "And Tony!"

"You better take some creative writing classes with me," Nathan threatened playfully, grinning at her.

"I will!"

"Let's get Tara over with," Kat decided, smirking.

There were some chuckles around the table before the majority of the group chorused, "Brown!", and clapped happily for her as she blushed.

"Girl, if you don't get a MRS degree while you're there, you are wasting a fantastic opportunity," Nathan told her.

"Hey!" Oliver cut in, feigning mock-offense and earning more laughter from the group.

"Oliver, where are you going?" Valerie asked, realizing she genuinely didn't know.

"Oh, I'm going to Hudson. It's a few hours south of here, but I think I'll like it." He turned his attention to Lucas. "What about you?"

Lucas took a long sip of his drink, milking the suspense, and then cleared his throat. "Drumroll, please." Nick, taking the initiative, patted rapidly on the table. "I, Lucas McConnell... slayer of Chemistry assignments... flirter of girls who aren't interested in me... serial dater... experienced salesman of certain desirables..."

"Lucas!" Kat cut him off, aggravated, and his grin widened.

"...have chosen to attend..." He raised a fist victoriously. "Community college!" The group gave him the loudest applause of all, distracting many of the other patrons at the restaurant, and Lucas stood up and took a few dramatic bows, before collapsing back in his seat with a satisfied sigh.

"God, I'm gonna miss you guys and that special way in which you all consistently humor me."

Tara shot Valerie a thankful look. "I'm glad we all took the time to see each other. I know I don't know Nathan or Tony that well, but you guys seem really nice. I wish I'd taken Drama!"

"Told you!" Kat cut in victoriously, crossing her arms. "Lindsay and I had a bet that you'd cave eventually. Too bad it wasn't until after graduation; she would've owed me ten bucks."

"She can still pay you," Valerie pointed out, causing Kat and Tara to exchange awkward looks. There was a moment of silence, and apparently Kat won whatever silent argument she and Tara had, because Tara was the one who turned to Valerie and spoke next.

"She left yesterday, Val."

Valerie's eyebrows furrowed and she forced a laugh. "What? You're kidding?"

Kat shook her head. "Kara's flying back in tomorrow morning. They're officially switched back."

The entire table was silent now, the mood abruptly intensified as Valerie argued, "But... I didn't even get to say goodbye."

"I asked her about that," Tara insisted. "I swear. She said you two already did." She hesitated, and then added, "She told me to give you something, but I think I should wait until later. I have it with me."

"I'll take it now," Valerie retorted, feeling a bit emptier than she had just sixty seconds ago.

"Are you sure?" Tara asked. When Valerie nodded, Tara leaned down to dig through her purse, and then sat up a moment later and extended her hand across the table to Valerie. Resting in her palm was a tiny silver charm: a small circle with rainbow-colored stripes running across it. Valerie knew immediately it was meant to go on the charm bracelet she'd gotten from Lindsay for Christmas. She never took it off.

Valerie took the charm from Tara with a fond smile. "It's really pretty," she admitted. "...And kind of gay."

Several of her friends raised their eyebrows in surprise at her openness, and Nick and Oliver looked most shocked of all.

"I've graduated," Valerie reminded them, and then looked to Oliver and Nick. "Sorry to leave you guys out all year."

"I knew it," Nick hissed, nudging Kat. "You lied to me!"

"Had to protect a friend," Kat told him, watching Valerie fondly as Lucas helped her put the charm on.

"Are you gonna try and get in touch with her over the summer?" Tara questioned, referring to Lindsay. "I know she said she wanted to try the long distance thing with Sarah... but I don't think she'd hate to hear from you, too."

Valerie shrugged. "I don't know. We kind of stopped talking after we broke up. And she's right... we said goodbye. Maybe this is all I should have." She gestured to the bracelet on her wrist. "Every time we talk it just makes things hurt more, I think."

"Clean breaks are way easier," Lucas agreed. "And it's rough being friends with someone you were in love with."

"Or are," Kat corrected, eyeing the look on Valerie's face knowingly. Then she cleared her throat. "We should get dessert."

They did, and sat at the table for another hour, none of them very eager to be the first one to leave. At last, Tara broke the spell, pointing out that Kara would be home the next morning and she had to wake up early to drive with her parents to the airport.

After Tara and Oliver left, it wasn't long before the rest of them split up, vowing to meet up again sometime. Valerie wasn't so sure it'd ever actually happen, but the idea was nice.

She took Lucas home and then went inside her own house, relieved that her parents were asleep already. There was something she was anxious to do.

She went to her room and got on her computer, then logged on to Facebook and searched her friends list for Lindsay's name. She found her and went to her page, and couldn't help but see her more recent posts. There were a couple of pictures of her with her friends, presumably at some kind of coming home party. Kara was in a few of those, too, evidently not having left yet.

Resolutely, Valerie accessed her settings from Lindsay's page and checked the box marked "hide all posts from this user". She saved the setting and then promptly logged out before she could think about undoing it. Now, she was still friends with Lindsay on the site, but wouldn't be getting constant updates on her life. She wanted a clean break, especially now with Lindsay back across the Atlantic. She wanted to be able to move on.

The next part was harder. She dug her cell phone out of her purse and opened her contact list, then scrolled down to Lindsay's name. She pressed another button that pulled up a menu of options, and scrolled down to "block this number". And then she stared, her thumb hovering over the "select" button. She bit her lip and hesitated, staring for at least another sixty seconds. Then she groaned at herself. "Come on. Do it." She let out a huff and glared down at the phone, then counted down. "Three... two... one." She pressed the button to block the number, and then, before she could rethink her actions, scrolled back to the menu and deleted it from her phone completely. There was no going back now.

Maybe at another time and place, she and Lindsay could've worked. But as it was... it was time to move on.

CHAPTER THIRTY-ONE

"Two-hundred fifteen, two-hundred sixteen... two-hundred seventeen!"

Mr. Marsh grinned at the door in question, then looked to the trail of people behind him. First was Mrs. Marsh, who, like her husband, had several bags and suitcases in her hands, as did Abby just behind her, followed by Valerie. Lucas brought up the rear. "Ready to see where you'll be living for the next year?" her father asked excitedly.

Valerie rolled her eyes. "Just unlock it, Dad."

"You got it." He fumbled for the set of keys they'd been given at the front desk, and a moment later, the door was unlocked and Mr. Marsh was leading the group of five into a empty room save for two beds, two desks, and two chairs. "Well, this is nice," he observed.

The room was tiny, and Valerie sighed as she put the stuff in her arms on the nearest bed, unofficially claiming it. "I guess."

"Have you contacted your roommate yet?" her mother asked her. Valerie shook her head, and received a disapproving look in response. "You found out her name back in *July!* You've had at least a few weeks to get that done."

"I was hoping she'd say something first," Valerie insisted.

"Well, maybe it means she's shy," Lucas pointed out.

"Or she's just unfriendly and doesn't care," Abby input. Her father pinched her side playfully.

"Don't listen to your sister. She's just trying to make you miserable because she's nervous about her *own* big day on Monday."

"Ooh, high school. Scary," Valerie retorted, moving to leave the room. "Can we just finish carrying up the rest of my stuff?"

"Hey, as I recall, high school was plenty terrifying for you," Lucas murmured to her, catching up with her in the hallway.

"Shhh," was her quiet response. He laughed and followed her back down to the car.

They passed Abby and her parents on their way back up, and when they arrived back at the room, it was just as another girl did the same from the opposite direction. She was tall and blonde, and when she smiled at Valerie, her teeth were almost *too* white. "Oh, hi! Do you live here?"

"I will soon," Valerie told her. "Are you Amy?"

"I am," the girl confirmed. "What was it...? Valerie?"

"The one and only," Lucas answered for her, moving forward and blatantly eying the girl up and down. He gestured toward the doorway a moment later. "Ladies first."

"Thank you," Amy replied, flashing him a smile and heading inside. Valerie and Lucas followed her in.

"Where are your parents?" Valerie asked her.

"Oh, I'm moving myself in," she replied. "They don't think I can be independent, so I'm proving them wrong."

"I'm sure my family'd be glad to help," Valerie insisted. "And this is Lucas, by the way."

"Nice to meet you."

"You too," Lucas replied, grinning a little too widely. Valerie elbowed him subtly in a silent attempt to tell him to cool down.

Seconds later, her parents and Abby returned, and they introduced themselves to Amy, as well. They spent the next hour or so getting moved in and organized, and then, after a lengthy speech from her mother about staying safe and going to class, it was finally their time to go. "If you need anything tonight, call me," her mother insisted as she hugged her goodbye. "We're only a couple of hours away."

"Get some sleep tonight, Mom," was her amused response. "I'll be fine." She hugged her father and sister goodbye, next, and then it was Lucas's turn. "Thank you for helping me move in. You know you didn't have to."

"Well, you know me. Anything to get out of the house."

"Are you moving into your new apartment soon? I'll totally return the favor."

"Just two more weeks," he reminded her, grinning. "I'm pretty much forever indebted to Amber for getting me that hookup at Mackie's, but now I can afford the rent, too."

"How's she doing?" Valerie couldn't help but ask. She hadn't talked to Amber since around mid-June. After graduation, she hadn't cared nearly as much about keeping a lid on her sexuality, and it had only taken a couple weeks for it to get back to Amber. They hadn't really spoken since.

"Fine, I guess. Still dating Jimmy. She finally figured out how to do the whole steady relationship thing, I think."

"That makes one of you," Valerie teased. He grinned at her even as he moved to wrap her up in a hug.

"I'll miss you, Val."

"I'll be home all the time," she promised him. "It's not too long of a drive. And you can come visit, too."

"I will." He kissed her on the top of the head and glanced up to Amy, who offered him a polite wave. "I *definitely* will."

She sighed at him even as he moved to leave the room. "Dick."

"The only one you like!" he called back, and disappeared around the corner without further warning. Valerie, chuckling, closed the door behind him, and then faced her new roommate.

"So…" Amy questioned, raising an eyebrow. "Brother or boyfriend?"

"Neither," Valerie replied. "I don't have a brother, and…" She shrugged her shoulders, only briefly hesitating, and finished, "I'm actually a lesbian."

Amy, to her surprise, looked amused at first, and then curious. "Really? What's that like?"

"Um... okay so far, I guess?"

"But, like, you've hooked up with girls?"

Valerie laughed uncertainly, not exactly anticipating this kind of reaction. She was more used to either blatant acceptance or blatant homophobia. "Yes."

"Well, how do you feel about straight hookups? Like, if I brought a guy back?"

"Um, I don't really care, honestly. You can do whatever you want."

Amy grinned. "Awesome. And it's totally cool with me if you bring girls over. Just text me if you need the room to yourself for the night, and I'll do the same. We should exchange numbers, by the way."

Relieved, Valerie moved to get her phone. She and Amy hung out for an hour or so, mostly talking about their major and their classes, when Amy wasn't grilling her about lesbianism. She quickly learned that Amy was a Fashion Merchandising major, that she aimed to join a sorority as soon as she could, and that, in her words, she'd always wanted to meet a lesbian before but had never known any back in high school. She reminded Valerie of Amber a little bit, only vaguely more bi-curious. She could tell they'd get along, but wouldn't exactly be best friends.

Later that night, she used her computer to video chat with Tara and Kat. Kat had moved into her dorm over a week ago, but Tara wasn't leaving for Brown for another two weeks.

"Let us see the room!" Kat demanded, and Valerie laughed, turning her computer around 360 degrees so they could see everything. When Amy was onscreen, she looked up briefly from where she was painting her toenails to offer them a wave. "Congrats on moving in! It looks awesome!"

"We're totally getting you a housewarming gift," Tara added. "A rainbow flag to match your rainbow charm. It can go right up on your wall." She grinned to let Valerie know she was kidding, and Kat cut in there.

"You wouldn't be able to blame us, you know. You never take that thing off. What would Lindsay say?"

"Uh, she would say 'who is Valerie again' because it's now been longer *since* we dated than how long we actually dated for," Valerie pointed out.

"Ooh, you have exes?" Amy called out, raising a curious eyebrow. "Me too. I know what we're doing tonight…"

Both Kat and Tara laughed. "Make her tell you everything!" Kat shouted loudly enough for Amy to hear.

"Don't encourage her," Valerie warned Tara before she could add anything to Kat's yell.

Instead, Tara asked, "When are you coming home, Val? We miss you already!"

"Totally," Kat agreed. "We're missing our third Stooge here."

"We've decided to take in Lucas if you don't come visit," Tara explained. "And that could get awkward because knowing him, he'd probably end up crushing on one of us. Or Kara."

"What about me?" Valerie heard a distant voice ask. Tara turned away from her computer.

"I'm talking to Kat and Val. Val just moved into her new dorm at Cloverdale today."

"Oh, really?" A moment later, Kara's face appeared on the monitor beside Tara's. They sported matching grins as Kara greeted, "Hey, Valerie! You're welcome!"

"Yes, thank you," Valerie told her for what felt like the hundredth time. Kara was very proud of being indirectly responsible for bringing Lindsay and Valerie together, however briefly. "Anyway, guys, I think I'm gonna go to bed soon. Amy and I decided to go walk around campus tomorrow and figure out our class schedules ahead of time."

"Alright," Kat replied. "Goodnight!"

"Goodnight!" Tara and Kara chorused. Valerie waved goodbye to all of them, and then disconnected from the call and prepared to go to sleep.

The next morning, she and Amy ventured out onto the rest of campus to try and find their classes. Valerie had Spanish, Political Science, and History on Monday, Wednesday, and Friday, and Biology on Tuesdays and

Thursdays, with a lab every Thursday. It wasn't the schedule she'd hoped for, but she'd been told she wouldn't get into many of her major-related classes until at least her sophomore year.

Once she and Amy found all of their classes, they went back to their dorm, and Amy tried to find a few girls to go to one of the dining halls for dinner with them. It turned out there were a lot of girls on their hall that were anxious to make friends, and so they ended up as two of a group of ten. While Amy was much more social than she was, Valerie did get the chance to talk to a few of their companions, and was confident she'd find at least a few friends amongst them.

Aware that classes were due to start the next day, Valerie laid down in bed that night with her mind buzzing and tension in every muscle of her body. College didn't seem hard so far, as long as she stuck to the everyday living part. Eating meals with friends, living on her own with one roommate... that seemed easy. Being a lesbian in college wasn't hard, either. One of the girls had noticed her bracelet at dinner, and when she'd told them what the rainbow charm was for, they'd just accepted it and moved on. No one cared in college... at least not at Cloverdale.

She woke up early the next morning and got dressed, taking care not to wake Amy, who didn't have classes until later in the afternoon. She double-checked to make sure she had everything she'd need for the day, and then took the five-minute walk from her room to the building where her Spanish class would be held.

As it turned out, it was in a classroom that reminded her of the ones back at Riverbank, with two-dozen desks in neat rows and a teacher with a dry erase board at the front. Senora Rose was kind, though, and the syllabus she gave out made the class seem easy.

After that was Political Science. That one, Valerie knew, was in a lecture hall. It was a ten-minute walk from her Spanish class, and so with only fifteen minutes between classes, she got there with just under five minutes to spare, entering the giant hall and peering out at the students who were already seated, trying to find a spot for herself.

She glanced to the less-populated, higher-up rows, and then froze. She blinked, and then blinked again, but the blonde girl sitting in the center of the row didn't change; just examined her fingernails briefly, tucked a strand of hair behind her ear, and then began to flip through the notebook in her lap while frequently glancing at the syllabus being projected to the class on a screen at the front of the room.

Valerie wasn't sure whether to confront her or ignore her, but she knew this wasn't an opportunity she could just pass up without at least asking a couple of questions. She ascended the stairs and excused herself a few times as she wiggled past several students already in their seats, all so that she could eventually reach an empty seat in the middle of the row and sit herself down next to Lindsay Walker.

Lindsay, to her credit, hid her emotions well, only glancing over at Valerie briefly before biting her lip to hide a smile and then turning and facing the front again. Valerie cleared her throat and leaned down to retrieve a pencil and notebook from her backpack. They both eventually relaxed in their seats, side by side, and Valerie finally spoke first. "Sooo…" she trailed off, then glanced to Lindsay, quirking an eyebrow and finishing calmly, "What the hell?"

Lindsay tried hard to hide another grin. "This is not what it looks like."

"Really? Because it looks like you go here, and it looks like you find this *really* funny."

"You have to admit that it's kind of hilarious."

"Why didn't you tell me you applied here?"

"Maybe because you *dumped* me?" Lindsay countered quietly. Class was starting. Valerie lowered her voice to a whisper as well.

"Before that."

"Well, I only applied just in case I decided I liked it here in America. As it turns out, I did. But I still wasn't going to go here because I knew you were going here and I know we talked about moving on… until I made the mistake of telling Sarah that I applied here. She insisted I commit so that we could see each other, and I was pretty neutral to the whole college thing, so I listened to her. Which is really ironic, because the entire reason I kept it from everyone else was so that none of you would influence my decision. And, also, it's kind of ironic considering we broke up a month later."

"Long distance claims another couple, huh?" Valerie acknowledged.

Lindsay laughed shortly. "Uh, more like cheating claims another couple."

"You or her?"

"Her. But I wasn't that into it anyway." She shrugged and looked to the front of the room, then proceeded to copy down notes. Valerie was still trying to take her explanation in.

"So… long story short, you go here. Like, you live in a dorm and you're planning on going to school here?"

"Yes. For my freshman year, at least. But I'll have to see what happens after that. I might go back to England if I don't find a reason to stay here." She glanced to Valerie, and then her eyes dropped to her wrist, where the bracelet Lindsay'd given her still rested. For the first time since their conversation started, Lindsay turned serious. "Oh my God. You still wear that?"

Valerie laughed nervously. "Yeah. I pretty much never take it off. It's kind of useful now. A couple girls at my dorm have already asked about the rainbow charm."

"Wait." Lindsay paused, a slow smile spreading across her face. She looked almost… proud. "Your dorm mates know you're gay?"

"Dorm mates, roommate… yeah. And I'm actually meeting Tony and Nathan for lunch today. I'm on a mission to make them realize they're perfect for each other," Valerie explained. "I'm up to my ears in gay."

"Wow. Things have changed so much in just three months. I mean… I don't think you've changed, but-"

"The environment changed," Valerie explained. "That's all I needed to have happen." She let out a small laugh, shaking her head in disbelief. "God, I can't believe you're here."

"Trust me, me either. I can't believe I let a girl I'd been dating for two months talk me into going to a college in a different country."

"Well, you liked living here for six months," Valerie reminded her. "Maybe you'll like a year of it."

"Maybe," Lindsay agreed. "I bet you'll like college a lot more than I will, though. You're totally gonna blossom."

Valerie chuckled. "You sound like my mom."

Lindsay shot her a quick grin, and then faced the front again. Valerie watched her as she furrowed her eyebrows in concentration and began scribbling notes onto the pad of paper beneath her, her tongue sticking out of her mouth just slightly. She considered the circumstances.

Lindsay was single. *Valerie* was single. They were now both willing to be open about their sexuality, and that meant they were both officially baggage-free. Perhaps college qualified as "a different time in their lives"?

Valerie leaned over until her lips brushed Lindsay's ear, and she held back a smile at the barely noticeable shudder it induced in the other girl. "Do you wanna come with me to meet Tony and Nathan for lunch today?" she asked, her voice a whisper.

Lindsay's answer was instantaneous.

"Absolutely."

ABOUT THE AUTHOR

Siera Maley was born and raised in the Southern Bible Belt. After coming out as a lesbian as a teen, she relocated to a more suburban area and is now living with her girlfriend and very adorable dogs. Time It Right was her first book, originally published in 2013. Since then, she has published three more books: Dating Sarah Cooper, Taking Flight, and On the Outside. You can visit her online at sieramaley.weebly.com or follow her at https://twitter.com/SieraMaley.

26510035R00166

Made in the USA
San Bernardino, CA
29 November 2015